Strife

Strife

Shimmer Chinodya

WEAVER PRESS

Published by Weaver Press, Box A1922, Avondale, Harare, 2006
Reprinted, 2007
Second edition 2014

© Shimmer Chinodya, 2006
© Introduction: Taurai Chinyanganya, 2014
Typeset by Weaver Press
© Photograph of Shimmer Chinodya: Weaver Press
Cover Design: Design Duo
Printed by Directory Publishers, Bulawayo

The author would like to express his gratitude to the Kunstlerhaus
Schloss, Wiepersdorf, Germany for awarding him a fellowship that
enabled him to write the first half of this book.

ISBN 978-1-77922-267-1

'Passion and strife bow down the mind.'

Virgil
70-19 BC

Introduction

Taurai Chinyanganya[*]

The novel *Strife* opens ominously with a mysterious moon huntress: Hilda Tsvangira, wife to Dunge Gwanangara and the mother of the family about which the novel is written. She's an unusual character and the reader's curiosity is immediately aroused by her anxious temperament. She sleeps 'fretfully' and dreams of 'impromptu journeys' for which she has always packed her clothes in a state of nervous anticipation. One asks who she is and why she is so neurotic. Her actions and internal struggles immediately introduce the reader to her problems and the dark forces that are at play in her family.

Slowly, we learn that the main object of her worry is her eldest son and his epileptic condition, which makes its debut on the night of his wedding. The reader, like Hilda, may wonder at the possible provenance of the disease and the significance of the fateful coincidence of its initial attack on the first night of Rindai's married life. In many African societies a cultural stigma is attached to epilepsy. In consequence, the moon huntress dreams of the whole world laugh-

---

* Taurai L. Chinyanganya has taught English Language and Literature at a number of schools in Zimbabwe. Currently he is a lecturer in the Languages and Literature Department of the Zimbabwe Open University based at the Mashonaland Central Campus (Bindura).

ing at her and of both God and her ancestors mocking her. Notice the juxtaposition, God *and* her ancestors: Christianity *and* tradition. Contemporary Zimbabwean society has not yet fully accepted that epilepsy is a medical condition, and it associates the affliction with evil, often blaming the victim (and their family) rather than seeking appropriate medication. The moon huntress thus cuts a desolate figure, especially with the implied nonchalance of 'the man sleeping beside her ... ... He, the man of the house, he, the father of her ailing son'. (p.1-2) In other words, her husband. This tension between husband and wife raises several issues that the discerning reader may want to consider. Does Hilda, the mother, represent tradition, with its possible negative, superstition; does she try to retain the old ways and seek to challenge the new? Does she represent faith-based belief against rational education? Does the father, Dunge, a quiet pragmatist who works to give his children an education and hopefully a better life, represent the antithesis to his wife? Where does the narrator sit? Does he idolise his mother and diminish his father? As you read the novel these are questions you must ask yourself and try to find the evidence to support or deny.

Hilda's life is one of strife (as is aptly captured by the title as well as the language, imagery and symbolism of the book). Her world appears to be constantly afflicted by disease, madness and calamity. The moon huntress has to contend not only with epilepsy in her eldest son, but schizophrenia in Kelvin, her third son; and, later, she herself suffers cancer, delirium and bouts of schizophrenia. Death is also a frequent visitor to the family: her husband, Kelvin and Tapera all die before the story draws to a close. However, arguably, in spite of all these tribulations, the narrator depicts her as an emotionally strong, very determined woman. Would you agree? The 'moon huntress' is an emotive metaphor with symbolic overtones possibly of love, change and quest. (There are many cultures and traditions around the world, which have worshipped the goddess of the moon.) How is this metaphor or symbol used in the book? Is there a tension or a consistency between Hilda, a mother, portrayed as very concerned about the welfare of her children, and the 'moon huntress'.

Examine also Hilda's beliefs, do they or her concern for her children bear positive results? Or does her intervention often make matters worse? Is the father's low-key, pragmatic, sensible approach to each crisis not more potentially effective than the high drama volunteered by the mother? Indeed, she finally challenges fate by offering herself as a sacrificial host to the disease so that her children may be cleansed. One must ask, does her challenge to mbuya Matope (to cleanse her children by migrating their diseases into her) actually materialise in her own illness, cancer, which culminates in an untimely, painful death? And is illness the result of fate, or one's angry ancestors? Today, for example, we know that cancer has many medical causes, and can be triggered by stress, but, diagnosed early can be treated. The novel, *Strife*, constantly requires that you compare and contrast belief systems, consistency and inconsistency as revealed in the characters' actions and words.

The moon huntress tries to assert control, yet instinctively she acknowledges that one cannot be completely in control of one's life, especially when one believes, as she does, that what happens to an individual may be influenced by one's ancestors, the moon, and other mystic powers. Her dreams of 'pythons, of fires consuming her house, of beheaded creatures running amok, of still births' (p.1) point to such connections. The moon huntress is therefore amenable to seeking solace from traditional rituals and we see her consulting with different diviners and herbalists in an effort to purge the family of the curse that she believes has been cast on them. How do her various interpretations of the cause of this or that disaster help, or do they? Notice also her reliance on dreams, and the role that they are said to play on the decisions that people make.

Dunge Gwanangara (Hilda's husband), on the other hand, is Christian and sceptical about traditional beliefs and what they entail. He sees no redemption in believing in things past. 'The dead are best left alone,' he declares. To him problems are better solved through Christian faith and modern medicine. He educates his children to extricate them from this 'primitive' belief in the *vadzimu* and departed spirits. The movement away from kwaChivi, to Gokwe, then Gweru and later to the plot is symbolic of the journey from the clutches of the primordial forces to modernity and the provision of a modern Christian upbringing for his children. Their plot near Gweru becomes a symbol of the Gwanangara dream of 'cocooning' his family from the extended family and severing the link with traditional family customs. Not surprisingly, his visits to Chivi are rare and undertaken only when they are unavoidable. Communing with the people from his rural past is quite tenuous. For example, no one from Chivi is present at Rindai's wedding or at the *bira* in Gokwe and/or on a number of other traditional, familial occasions.

Perhaps it is within this disconnection between traditional and modern beliefs and customs that the genesis of strife in the Gwanangara family lies. The story opens with the authorial comment 'this is the story of a woman who sought to defy the odds... This is the story of her, her husband and children and what became of them when they tried to cut the umbilical cords of their ancestors, to challenge fate...' Think this statement through very carefully. What does it tell us about the narrator's position? How, subsequently, do we expect the story to unfold?

Ironically, Gwanangara's Christian beliefs and the flight from kwaChivi bring no joy as his wife, then he, Kelvin and later Tapera and Bramson, all die at the plot. They are never at peace despite the relative comforts they build around themselves. The questions that arise are: Is their suffering a form of reprisal from the ancestors? Do their deaths have a rational cause? Is their suffering individually or collectively sheer coincidence, or is the family ill-starred and marked by fate to suffer at the mercy of the gods who 'kill them for their sport'? Or are the illnesses and break-downs a consequence of the constant tension in world view between husband and wife? What does the ominous description of the way that Dunge points out the ox, Blantyre, for slaughter at the *bira* in Gokwe tell us about the narrator? Is he suggesting that fate has a crucial role to play in the lives of the Gwangura family: 'He [Dunge] points out to the ox to be slaughtered. Its name is Blantyre... [He thinks] Is this how God singles us out in the shuffling crowds, knee-deep in our own dung, prodding us in the belly... marching us to accidents or asylums, or condemning us to urine-soaked, soiled deathbeds?' (p.103)

Strife plays itself out in the children's lives. The gloomy mood that permeates the text attests to their misery. Godfrey initially takes a rational, scientific approach to their plight, but with the preponderance of bad omens (that come as a presage to graver situations), mysteries, diseases and death it becomes necessary for him to re-visit his belief systems. As the novel draws to a close, his confusion is dramatised in a play within the text. The dramatis personae of the piece are TRADITION, PATRIARCHY, FATALISM, SHAME, MODERNITY and MEDICINE, which are the conflicting ideologies and beliefs that are at play as the Gwanangara children ponder their plight. Central to these different ideologies or belief systems is the idea about whether one can take responsibility for one's own actions, one's own life? When we do not do so, causes can be attributed to almost any belief system. Within *Strife*, the arguments presented by each of these facets/ideologies of life (to an extent) help Godfrey to resolve his own personal struggle, the tension between tradition and modernity: 'Science, bones or Bibles' (p.210). Even though he is a modern, educated person, he seems to be prepared to re-establish his link with the past: 'I'm not very keen on hunting for these spirits... But I am their product...and I can't just ignore their existence.' (p. 218)

The ancestral link is demonstrated in the plots of the story. The main plot (that involves Dunge Gwanangara's family) is firmly anchored on another, ancestral subplot, which holds on tenaciously to the main one, giving it energy and tincture. The Gwanangaras cannot prosper without venerating the departed forebears who it is suggested seem to have a stake in the genesis of the troubles that torment their family. The complexities wrought by the fragile relationship with the ancestors are reflected in the plot of the novel, which is intricate, moving backwards and forwards spatially and chronologically and spanning different centuries. Within the whole matrix, Godfrey envisages a reconnection with tradition, after all the Gwanangara children continue the line left by the likes of Mhokoshi, Njiki, Zevezeve, etc. (Notice the likenesses shared among them and their ancestors). He is the first-person narrator and is also vested with omniscient powers that enable him to articulate the metaphysics of Africa, that the dead have something to do with the living and that one ignores this connection at their own peril.

i

She searches the sky for a slice of moon. Sometimes she is too early by a day or two and the darkness yields nothing to her anxious eyes. She knows nothing of lunar calendars, but her instincts are alive to the power of the moon. It knows the secrets of wombs, the ebb and flow of the human tide. The moon knows everything, regulates everything. Once or twice she is late and she stumbles upon the startling, razor-thin fingernail in the west. She gasps. Her heart heaves and she hurries back into her house. She does not sleep. Her bag is already half packed. It dreams of impromptu journeys. She waits for the phone to ring. Waiting is a form of death.

She sleeps fretfully.

She dreams of him – her son – always, in his wedding suit, smiling his handsome white smile and signing his vows at the pulpit. She dreams of him kicking and yelling on his wedding night, thrashing against the arms of his weeping wife. She dreams of the long night drive to the hospital, the bouncing truck, her son limp on the front seat, the wheelchairs, the doubting orderlies, the night he spent in the hospital, the inappropriately cheerful doctor. The young nurses' casual laughter cackles crisply in her ears. She dreams of pythons, of fires consuming her house. She dreams of the whole world laughing at her, of God, her ancestors, mocking her.

She sleeps fretfully.

The phone does not ring. Sometimes she thinks she hears it ring in her sleep and she jumps out of bed. He – the man sleeping beside her – her husband, gently grabs her and pulls her back. He, the man of the house, pleads with her to go back to sleep. He, the father of her ailing son, snores gently through the night. After all, he has to go to work in the morning – six days a week.

Men have no wombs, know little about moons. But the worry smoulders in his eyes.

***

His name was Mhokoshi. He was a hunter; he had no wife and hunting was everything to him. He lived in a cave alone in the forest, away from relatives. He hunted buck, ostrich, buffalo, eland, kudu. He crossed paths with lions, hyenas and elephants. Sometimes when the dried meat became too much to store he delivered it to his people down in the village, but he never stayed long. Often he hid in the shadows of the trees at the edge of a homestead and called out to a child. Thus he got to know if anybody was sick, or if a woman had given birth, or if there was to be a bira *– a traditional beer party – of sorts; he hurried away when he saw any elders coming, hurried away leaving his sudden gifts of meat, back to his cave, his spears and knobkerries, to the forest where he belonged.*

He was lucky he never fell ill; nature knows how to look after animals and outcasts – creatures without roots or religion. Madmen walk barefoot and half naked in forests, without catching fevers or diseases of the chest. He must have been in his late teens when he started living this way, a dreadlocked outcast drenched with the smell of the outdoors. Nobody was sure when he began slipping off into the bush. Some nights when the moon was young, or full, he slept fitfully, and woke up with a whimper – but that was nothing because he did not drink alcohol and his constitution was strong. His people left grain – for his sadza – on the edge of the village for him to collect – which he did shyly and rarely.

His people worried about him – he had a handful of brothers and sisters and was one of the last born in the family. His parents were dead – but he had dozens of uncles and aunts and many cousins, nephews and nieces. His people thought he was insane and they prepared a brew, slaughtered an ox and poured libation on the doorsteps of cooking huts, pleading with the ancestors to restore his sanity. They found a young wife for him, a belle from the neighbourhood,

2

and sent word for him to come, marry her and settle down, but he never did.

The hunter lived in this way into his mid-thirties, perhaps early forties – back then the sharp sickle of death spared few and forty was a ripe age. Nobody knew when he died, where, or why. They only noticed that his visits ceased; no one came to collect the grain any more. They dared not go looking for him; the forest was infested with lions, hyenas and snakes; they were scared of his spirit; they thought he was a curse on the family, on the clan. They consulted diviners to inquire about his fate. One said that he had been torn apart by lions, another that he was swallowed by a python, a third blamed it on a wicked spirit hounding the family.

All three diviners advised atonement, urging that his bones and weapons be found, brought back from the forest, buried and cleansed.

***

Fretfully, she sleeps, waiting for the phone to ring. He, her husband, grunts longingly and puts an arm over her shoulders. She shudders. Since the wedding of their son on the last new year's eve, they haven't made love, they haven't really talked. When she goes out to look for the moon, he watches her quietly. He knows she knows there is something he knows – but he does not really know.

He does not know.

He does not really know what happened and why; why this misfortune has chosen him and his son, singled out his family. For forty years he has placed his complete faith in the Bible, and throughout his life God has shielded him from trouble, but the incident on his son's wedding night has shocked him; rent him like old cloth. But he carries the bad news like a man, smiling to colleagues and customers at work, respecting his Indian bosses, hiding his fatigue behind the mountains of shirt boxes and trousers, the backbone of his job for three decades. Forty years of faith have not dulled his fear; like a true black man he listens to the words of his neighbours.

After his son returned from hospital with a card and a bottle of pills, he brought a herbalist home. A big fire was made in the yard, a drum full of fresh roots and leaves boiled on the embers, secret ablutions were conducted at night in the bathroom; steaming blankets, scented grass and coals smouldering like incense, bitter por-

3

ridge that had to be swallowed, spoon by spoon; signs and symbols invaded his home.

He did all that, but she – his wife – instinctively feels they should do more.

***

The phone rings at last, a sharp cruel stab.

She stumbles to the living room. He – her husband – sits up in bed to listen. She is breathless on the phone, her voice trembling prophetically. She is on the phone a good fifteen minutes, struggling with her fear. When she returns she says, 'It's happened again. In the bedroom, while he was sleeping.' He does not probe her with questions. She goes to the bathroom, takes a quick bath, dresses hastily and rummages through her bag. He knows he cannot stop or reason with her.

Sunrise sees her at the market place, waiting for the bus. It's a ninety-minute ride to her son's home and when she arrives he – her son – the one that fell sick on his wedding night, is just finishing his breakfast, getting ready to go to work. His wife – her daughter-in-law – makes tea for her and they chat casually for a while. She – the mother – notices that the young woman has a fresh scar on her finger.

'He bit you,' the mother says.

'He bit himself, too,' says the young woman.

'Open your mouth,' the mother tells her son. He swallows his tea jerkily so it almost burns him and obediently slides out his tongue. He is like a six-year-old boy who has hurt himself. The light falls from his face and she notices how deep his eyes are, how tired he really is. There is a raw pinkish mark on his tongue.

'Did you rinse it with salt water?' she asks. He looks at his wife and shakes his head. He goes to the kitchen to gargle with salt.

'Next time it happens put a spoon between his teeth,' says the older woman.

'I'm off to work,' he announces with boyish zeal, adjusting his khaki trousers and tying the laces of his farmer's shoes.

'Have you taken your pills?'

'Yes, Mother. I'm all right. Really, I am.'

'We'll see you at lunch, then.'

'I'll be back for tea at ten. I have to go. I have a meeting in five minutes.'

He lopes off to his office, which is just behind the trees, bordering his house. He is a busy young man with no fuss about appearances, a graduate plant breeder who will not be held back by anything, not even this unpredictable misfortune, this mysterious ailment that shook him up on his wedding night.

His wife is six months pregnant and when her husband has left, the mother turns to her and asks how she is feeling.

She's a deep, quiet girl with a beautiful, rather sad face, one of those people destined for silence, for unhappiness, one of those who will never start a conversation. She answers that the pregnancy has been going well – going well the way of first pregnancies because problems are unanticipated, unknown. She shows the older woman her clinic cards.

When her son – the plant breeder – returns for tea there is a bowl of bitter porridge waiting for him. She – the mother – the woman who is always searching for the moon, makes sure he spoons it all up and busies herself showing additional herbs to his wife. She spends the night with them, lying awake on the bed in the spare bedroom, listening. She thinks she hears him yell and she sits up, her heart in her mouth, the word, *'Mwanangu!'* leaping to her tongue. Embarrassed, she lies back and tries to sleep.

She leaves, reluctantly, the next morning, knowing that there is nothing else she can do. Staying on with them is good for company, but only heightens her concern.

***

His three brothers went to the forest to search for him. They scoured the caves but could not find him, not his bones, nor his knobkerries and spears.

They were not happy with the way things had turned out, and they blamed their brother for the way he had lived his life, away from his people. They let their thoughts of him wither like the flowers of winter, yet their memories remained and they trembled like dry elephant grass in June – grass awaiting a veld fire – at the thought of him – his bones lying naked to the rain, his weapons unfound, his spirit unatoned.

He had several living brothers and sisters. Their mother was dead, bitten by a puff-adder on her way from the fields. After that their father had become a surly craftsman, carving objects out of stone and wood, who would sit staring at the fat moon, talking little and eating less. He never re-married. They called him Zevezeve, the whisperer. Mhokoshi's brothers and sisters were all married, and there were plenty of children, and goats in the pens. One brother was a renowned farmer, growing millet, groundnuts and sweet potatoes and the other was a famous dancer – a broad-faced man with strong hips that made other men's wives ogle and giggle at the harvest parties. The dancer was an adventurer who had amassed four wives and several concubines by the time he turned forty. One of the sisters was a potter and the other a basket-maker and they lived with their husbands in the hills.

The family, the clan, was scattered over the broad hills near the Save River. That was before the scorching cycle of drought descended like a bitter curse on the land, when the forest still abounded with fruit and the river was generous with fish. Hippos stumbled starkly out of the floods and crocodiles slithered in the mud. Life was easy – or seemed easy enough – progeny was a subtle gift of soul, seed and blood from the ancestors and death was something that had to be expected. In between those two states there were lean years and fat years, mean hunts and good hunts, unappeasable spirits and resolute witches, evil and laughter, good relatives and bad relatives and rules about good neighbourliness. If your neighbour stole your wife you took an axe and settled the score with him. The chief and his council of elders picked up the pieces at a village court and you were fined or let go. No act, no crime was too great for a fine and the hangman and his noose was unheard of. If somebody pointed a finger at you and said you were a witch you hauled him to the court to be fined a beast. Illness and death were to be expected but nobody died from illness alone – your ancestors played a hand. They cleared the path for wicked spirits to molest you either because they were weak or because they had allowed themselves to be bought off to settle a grudge with their peers or with you. Or because you had offended them. Your ancestors blessed you or they cursed you.

***

She, the moon huntress, has seven children, and he, the determined plant breeder, aged twenty-four, is her first born. The second-born, male too, aged twenty-two, is completing his university studies and is in love with languages. The third, a taciturn twenty-year-old, is a first-year political science student at the same university. The fourth-born is a girl – a student teacher. The fifth and sixth children are girls at secondary school, and the last and youngest is a boy at primary school.

The country is masquerading under the oddly double-barrelled surname of Zimbabwe-Rhodesia. A fierce civil war is raging through the country; the air is saturated with an insipid pessimism. Sell-outs and betrayals are the order of the day. Roads are mined; schools, shops and clinics closed, the economy reeling under sanctions and the call-up of all able-bodied whites. Thousands of black children have run off across the borders, in thirst of freedom and respect; to train as guerrillas, to chant slogans in forests; to fire guns and throw grenades, to act as fodder for Ian Douglas Smith's bombs. But this is not a story about that war. The story of that bitter conflict has been told elsewhere, many times before.

Her children are safe from the turmoil. They go to safe schools. They come home to their little house in the township, secure from the savage fighting. They are 'brilliant', and in these colonial seventies when education for blacks is regarded as the be-all and end-all, hers is considered a glorious household. Her children are the envy of the town, but there is a steep price to pay for it. Silence. Uncommunicativeness. Seriousness. No father drawls rudely, drunkenly, excitingly, in the sitting room, ordering his children to bring him another beer from the small but efficient fridge. No woman swings buxomly, fatly, pleasantly; chidingly shaking a sausage pan in her husband's face.

She has defied poverty and tradition and carved a niche for herself in the town. For fifteen years she has lived another life, almost single-handedly building a home in a new land among strangers – a woman braving the morning dew in her gumboots.

Her story has been told elsewhere. But this is her tale again, a new version, the story of a woman who sought to defy the odds, the capable, sad woman who gave all for her children, the woman called my

7

mother. This is the story of her, her husband and children and what became of them when they tried to cut the umbilical cords of their ancestries, to challenge fate.

***

What year was it – 1850? 1860? How does one transport oneself a century and a half to capture one's ancestry? Revisit faces, smells, clothes, food, music, stories and dances? Talk to people, seek out griots and historians, peruse books, hunt out photographs, registration and baptism certificates, ransack museums and the documents of teachers, priests and district commissioners – those surly agents of the colonial past? Your relatives, your parents'people, shake their heads laconically as if to say, 'Young man, leave history alone; what use does your empty little head want to make of time?' Or should you drink seven-days brew at the family bira *and wait to dream up the past? What if your story, your real story, is about the lack of it, your ignorance, your inability to penetrate events, your bemoaning of the fact that there are no griots in your clan? What if you can only salvage the bare bones of your history? Are you then allowed to invent, to imagine, to fill up the vacuum and flesh out bygones?*

My great-grandfather – the sullen craftsman who would not speak when his wife was bitten by a puff-adder, father to the hunter who died in the mountains – was soft spoken and people nicknamed him Zevezeve, the whisperer.

Beyond him is a void – the swirling dust of the savannahs, muddled memories of the great wild-hoofed trek from the north. Or did our clan come from the south-east, from that little country now known as Swaziland? Or did we come from the north and go south to Swaziland and back north again to the domain where the umbilical cords of our grandfathers and grandmothers were buried? And where were our great-great-great-grandparents buried? What marked their graves? Or were their bones scattered over the vleis of Africa, only to be trashed out of anthills by ploughs, tractors and Caterpillars? Do their ghosts shine at night? Are their spirits at rest?

Oh, Zevezeve my forebear

Help me tell this story.

Now, what year was Zevezeve born? 1830? 1835? Come Chigs, my dear history teacher, help me reconstruct the past. Let's dress

Zevezeve up. Give him a loincloth and maybe a leopard-skin hat and a cow-hide in winter. Offer him snuff and a pot of millet beer, though he won't drink much. Give him millet sadza and derere, *though he won't eat much. Make him a fire, plenty of wood; the night is young, winter is weeks away and the young moon has not set, but already his wives and children are asleep. Don't talk to him too much, don't ask him too many questions. He is a silent man, given to listening to the noises of the night, to the noises of other men; a philosopher embroiled in his own thoughts. The clearing is small, the forest looms darkly over the grass enclosure and the huts; owls hoot in the trees; a hyena coughs in the night; across the river a lion roars insistently but he, Zevezeve, has no need of a spear or an axe; lions – inveterate cowards – are afraid of fires; his goats, chickens and precious hoes,* mapadza, *and his grain are locked up in the huts with the children; a lamb bleats foolishly from one of the huts.*

Crouch, kneel, sit in the dust, reader; Zevezeve is forty-five or fifty, not very old – people die young, death harvests richly here; but already he has married off three or four of his daughters and paid off his last remaining oxen as lobola *for two sons. His head is white as maize-meal. Clap your hands softly and speak of your mission; he is not a sage or* n'anga *or diviner or rainmaker, just an eccentric whisperer. He is a man given to giving advice to others, a pacifist, a rationalist, a counsellor of sorts – a man who knows that if problems cannot be solved, they can't be solved and life has to go on despite* Mwari *and* midzimu. *Of course, he respects God and ancestral spirits, but he knows that the true way of solving problems is not through herbs or* biras *or axe fights, but through soft talk, through whispering. He is a man far ahead of his time.*

Why have you come here in the night anyway, reader, braving the ghosts and the snakes of the night paths? To seek his advice? To pay your respects? To offer your condolences? His wife died a month ago, bitten by a puff-adder on her way from the fields, and she is fresh in her grave, but he – the whisperer – will not weep.

But we are only describing his person, his personality and his household. Like old-fashioned anthropologists. What about the times in which he lived? The times, the place in history? Come Chigs, my dear teacher, you are good at this. 1835, 1840; the Pioneer Column is half a century away; great Great Zimbabwe is in decline – the Rozvi architects have at last given up mounting ladders into the sky to try and retrieve the moon which they believe is their king's rightful necklace; the bellicose Ndebeles under Mzilikazi have begun their infamous raids into Mashonaland. The Munhumutapa Empire is in decline – the Shonas are scattered over the land and ruled by many chiefs; there are no real wars yet; the Shonas are busy planting and gathering and hunting and fishing and weaving and carving and dancing to shangara *and* ngororombe *and drinking and mounting their wives and laughing and crying and raising their children; sickness and drought and death are the only real tragedies.*

This, then, is the world which Zevezeve inhabited, the land in which he breathed and whispered. Ah, but Teacher Chigs, this is not a history textbook and we have to move on. We have a long way to go and we have to be brisk.

2

She waits for the phone to ring. The moon is full, but because of the township lights its fluorescence is a dullish yellow. The moon knows everything: the chemistry of destabilised minds, the plight of mothers in distress.

She sleeps fretfully.

He, her husband, the man who has worked for Indian business-men selling shirts and trousers for thirty years, gently puts an arm around her but she does not respond.

The phone does not ring.

She sleeps fretfully.

She dreams of pythons, of beheaded creatures running amok, of fires consuming her house, of still-births.

Her daughter-in-law, the young woman with the sad face, the one destined for unhappiness, lies in the same spare bedroom where it happened on her wedding night. She is ten months pregnant – four weeks overdue. Her son, the plant breeder, brought her here two weeks ago and returned to his greenhouses. She should really have gone to her own mother to deliver, but traditions change. And isn't that the tragedy for all aspirant middle-class blacks, that none of them can find their way back?

He, the plant breeder, calls once every three days. His voice is shaky on the phone, thinly masked by his usual bravado; always brusque, clearly eager to get back to his seedlings. His mother, the moon huntress, suspects it has occurred again, as it has happened four or five times since his wedding night. He has lost weight – his

11

clothes hang off him like a scarecrow. She pleads with him not to drink – even the herbalists have advised this and his medication requires total abstinence – but even had she not heard from his sad young wife, she knows that he drinks. He drinks to drown his anxiety, to kill the minute-by-minute fear that it might happen anytime, that he might collapse in the fields, in the office, on the street, in the church and disgrace himself and his family publicly.

She, the young woman, feels the onset of her labour pains. The baby is coming. The plant breeder is called and comes over at once. Together with his mother, the moon huntress, they take her to the hospital. She delivers a beautiful, hairy baby girl after a protracted, ten-hour struggle, a beautiful baby girl, and is detained two nights at the hospital.

Even when her son is at home with her and she cannot expect the phone to ring, she does not sleep.

It happens that night again in the little spare bedroom which he shared with his brothers when he was young. He begins with an ox-like bellow, followed by the wild thrashing of feet. The moon huntress runs out of her bedroom in her petticoat, calling his name. The moon is full. She was expecting this, expecting it on the night of his child's birth. She switches on the light and dives towards him. His hands are balled into fists, his arms stiff at his sides, his eyes glazed in an incomprehensible stare. She tries to hold down his feet but his compulsive kick is so strong that it sends her stumbling to the floor. His sheets are twisted into a perplexed knot around his chest. She keeps calling out his name, kneeling at the side of the bed, her bosom heaving, slapping the sides of his face. She pushes her fingers into his mouth to stop him biting his tongue and he snaps at her thumb instead. She flinches with pain. She wants to wake him up, to snatch him back from this magnet of torture which has contorted his frame. Her husband, the man of the house, the man who has sold clothes in an Indian shop for three decades, the man who has put his arm around her and grunted longingly for months now, looms bare-shouldered and hairy-chested in the doorway, watching helplessly.

Men do not understand the riddles of the moon, of wombs, but the worry smoulders in his eyes.

The plant breeder lies still, whimpering softly, his eyes fluttering.

He slowly regains consciousness and stares around, his eyes sorry, guilty, perplexed. He slides his tongue out of his mouth to check if he has bitten himself. There are no cuts but he tastes blood – his mother's blood. She covers her bitten thumb with her fingers. He swallows, wondering where the taste of blood came from if he did not bite himself, but there is too much else to worry about.

'*Chiiko mwanangu?* What is it, my child?' The moon huntress asks.

He turns over, away from her face and eases into a gentle snore. The man of the house who has spent the last thirty years living in this little four-roomed house steps forward, covers his son with the blankets and pats him gently on the shoulder. The plant breeder is facing away from them, staring blindly at the wall and when his father touches him he wriggles away, almost instinctively. Hurt, the shirt-seller steps back and puts his arm around the moon huntress to guide her from the room.

When they go to the hospital in the morning they don't tell his wife, the new mother blessed with a beautiful baby girl, about this latest mishap. There is a small crowd at the side of the bed and the young nurses threaten to turn away any further visitors.

That afternoon the moon huntress consults, against her husband's advice, a traditional healer who lives in the same township. She is given some herbs and told, 'When your *mroora* is discharged from hospital, she must not bring the baby to your house. It must not enter the room where her father fell ill. That baby must be taken straight to its parents' house.'

And so when the young mother is discharged from hospital with her baby, she is taken straight to the bus terminus by her mother-in-law and husband.

The mother-in-law, the moon huntress, stays with them for a week. She cooks, washes up, and minds the baby while the young woman recuperates. Before she leaves, the moon huntress pleads with her son, 'Please don't drink, *mwanangu*. There will be plenty of time to do that once your doctor says it's OK. And remember to use the herbs that ambuya gave us.'

'Yes, Ma,' says the plant breeder, nervously, chewing a fingernail, 'Yes, Mhama.'

When Zevezeve died he left several children. Mhokoshi, the hunter, was barely twenty. For ten to fifteen years nothing unusual happened. But two years after Mhokoshi died – or rather, disappeared into the mountains – strange things began to happen and all within a space of two months. A huge python was discovered coiled up in a chicken coop after swallowing eight hens; lightning split a muchakata tree into two equal halves in the middle of a yard; a woman gave birth to a one-armed baby after a pregnancy of only six months; an unoccupied hut burst inexplicably into flames in broad daylight, and a babbling two-year-old child woke up in the middle of the night and announced in flawless Shona: 'I am Mhokoshi. I want my weapons back.'

Mhokoshi's brothers and sisters consulted n'angas *and were told to brew more beer and kill an ox and to buy substitute weapons – a spear, an axe, a knobkerrie – and offer them to their departed brother. This they did, but they quarrelled with themselves; some argued that it was wrong to atone to somebody they were not absolutely sure was dead, somebody whose corpse no one had seen; others argued that Mhokoshi had spurned the woman they had found for him to marry in the first place, the beautiful young belle from across the river; still others asserted that atonement must be enacted at all costs. The* n'angas *warned them not to quarrel, saying that this would not augur well for the future. In the end they brewed beer and offered the weapons and a young woman – of course with the assistance of* n'angas *– to their departed brother and for two nights the drums thumped and barked in that household, and people ate and drank and sang and danced.*

There were no further visitations in that household, and people soon forgot, as people must forget when there is a lull in the storm of their lives, and so they returned to their spears, hoes, axes, grinding stones, mortars and pestles, the tools which constituted their daily survival and once more there was laughter at their hearths.

***

Rindai, the plant breeder, buys a car. It is an old Peugot 404 sedan, a sturdy automobile, and he gets it at a bargain price. Typically, he makes it a surprise and drives it home at the weekend with his wife Mazvita and their young baby Nda. His mother, Mai Rindai, the moon huntress, is washing clothes on the lawn when a white car suddenly turns out of the road and ploughs up the narrow dust path, aiming straight at her. And there he is, her son, grinning at the wheel, as she scuttles her washing out of the way. He bumps to a stop right beside her and hoots loud and long before stepping triumphantly out of his car. His mother laughs and pumps his hand with her wet, soapy one. Her doek falls to her feet, exposing her prematurely greying locks as she emits a short, sharp ululation and sketches an impromptu dance. Meanwhile Mazvita, his wife, is gathering up baby Nda and a bagful of shawls from the back seat. Swiftly, the moon huntress moves to help her and struggles to open the back door.

'This way,' Rindai says proudly, as he grabs the door handle from her, but the door does not snap open – there is a slight problem with the handle which he has not quite mastered; he gets it right at the third attempt and the moon huntress plunges to her knees at the open door to receive the baby.

'Oh, Nda, my sweet grand-daughter! How you have grown!'

And who should then arrive but Dunge Gwanangara, Rindai's father, the man of the house, dismounting from his old Humber bicycle with empty shirt boxes, a squashed loaf of bread and half a pound of tripe, grinning handsomely, incredulously. He stands his bicycle against the wall near the lavatory of that little four-roomed house, and puts a cautious hand on the bonnet of the car.

'So, isn't it nice?' Rindai demands.

Next come the neighbours, the people from the street, cackling, cooing and chirping, pumping hands and strutting about in their torn *mariposa* and farmer's shoes and patched jackets: 'Oh what a nice car! Oh what a nice, nice car! Oh what a good, good son to marry only six months after leaving college, and buy a car after only working for a year and a half. Oh what a clever, clever son! Please give us a ride down the street where you grew up.'

And so neighbours and relatives by totem, fat dames and wizened, bad-toothed old men, butchers, builders, part-time preachers and *madzimai esungano*, pack themselves into the seats so that Rindai barely has room to squeeze into the driver's seat while outside on the dry lawn his mother and father stand back. He reaches for the gear stick from under a woman's skirts, the engine shudders and coughs as he backs up slowly into the road and they're off, down the street lined with bemused spectators, round the bend, past the primary school where he came first every year for eight years, past the green grass where he munched shallots, pilfered carrots and played paper football with his friends, on past the row of churches and the grocer's where every morning during the sixties he bought a half a loaf of bread and a half a pound of tripe, and round back into Hoffman Street.

And when he turns back into the narrow dust path and rolls onto the lawn, and the car disgorges its exuberant passengers, his father throws aside his empty boxes and puts a cautious hand on the bonnet. His mother is busy already, fixing her doek with one hand, and rocking the now wailing little Nda with the other. Mazvita, the beautiful young mother, fumbles with the boot to remove their bags while Mai Fanwell, one of the women who did not go on the trip, a neighbour from two doors down, spits into her handkerchief and mutters loudly to no one in particular, *'Zvipiko imi?* You have guts to be driven by an epileptic!'

Next day, a Sunday morning, before returning to work Rindai drives his parents and his wife to church. Mai Rindai shows her grand-daughter off to the other women, while Dunge Gwanangara invites his peers – too many of them – for a ride in the car to their various homes.

Two or three weeks later, Dunge is busy at work when his Indian boss passes by and hands him a letter. He carefully puts down an empty shirt-box and tears open the envelope. The letter is from his in-law, the father of his *mroora*, Mai Nda.

> We received the good news that Baba Nda has bought a car. We are very happy for him and our daughter. But please, our in-law, don't you think it's a little early for that? Don't you think he should get well first, be treated for this thing which is bothering him before he can drive? We are worried about what could happen to him while he is on the wheel and for

the safety of those who might be with him. Please urge him to reconsider.

Dunge Gwanangara re-reads the letter, folds it up slowly and puts it into his breast-pocket before he returns to re-ordering his shirts.

3

So who are Rindai the plant breeder's siblings? Where are they when it happens? Where are they when it begins on that ill-fated wedding night? Where are they during the wedding? Where are they when their brother bellows and thrashes in the little spare bedroom on New Year's eve, when Baba Tariro's truck races and bounces to the hospital, when the orderlies load his limp body into a wheelchair and pretty smiling nurses take down his details on khaki hospital cards; when the young doctor casually dismisses him with a bottle of pills and a prescription? Where are they when the stern-faced herbalist makes a blazing fire in the yard, then holds a steaming blanket over him, over the huge pot of boiling roots in the little bathroom till the sweat pours out of their brother? Where are they when the herbalist cuts *nyora* on their sibling's chest, arms and legs with a blunt old razor-blade and rubs sooty medicine into his bloodstream? Where are they when he burns oily scented grass in the little Christian four-roomed house to drive out the bad spirits? Where are they when the church people come to sing and pray in that little house or when Rindai returns to work, or when his mother can't sleep, or when the phone doesn't ring or when it does and she hurries away to catch the bus with her pre-packed bag full of herbs? Where are they when her son bellows and thrashes on the night of his daughter's birth, or when he buys the sturdy Peugot sedan and bounces to a halt on the lawn and the neighbours gather to ululate? Where are they when he gives the neighbours a ride, and Mai Fanwell spits bitterly into a tattered handkerchief saying, *'Zvipiko imi?* Who would drive with an epileptic?' Where are they when he comes home for Christmas and collapses in a supermarket, and white women run to help him? Or when he regains consciousness, climbs straight into his Peugot and drives home to slump in a battered sofa, playing sad blues music?

Who are Rindai's siblings? Why have they been kept out of the story so far?

***

OK, OK. There are many ways to tell a story. Let me introduce myself. My name is Godi, short for Godfrey. Godfrey Gwanangara. Alias Wamambo. I don't know why I was given my first name, but it definitely has no allusions to God or to freedom. Oh no! Perhaps you have met me before, in different settings, other stories, as Godfrey Wamambo. Anyway, I'm Rindai's brother. I come straight after him. I'm younger by two years. I'm much older now, but when this story begins on his wedding night in 1979, I was barely twenty-two and just finishing my first degree. I'm the one who loves words – a scribbler – the one destined for the chalkboard and the pen. I'm the one telling this story. I'm a reserved guy, perhaps the worrier in the family, but I enjoy people. I'm sometimes precocious and hypocritical, but I like a good laugh if I can have one. What else is there to say?

Kelvin, will you stop combing your hair and step out please? Yes, this here is my young brother, the one who comes after me. He's nearly twenty and has just finished his A-levels and is as smart as a trooper on parade. When we were young we used to call him washer-boy because you couldn't trust him with a bar of soap, a tube of toothpaste or a bottle of Dettol. Once he brushed his teeth so hard the toothbrush broke in two. Don't expect him to say much, but he's the sort that knows all about our culture, our relatives and how we're all related. He's the brooding type, given to supporting righteous causes – he says he wants to do political science. His is an odd intelligence – often insightful, but sometimes unpredictable.

Come, Shuvai, don't be shy. Folks, this young lady is eighteen and she is our oldest sister. She was born after Kelvin. She looks like me, doesn't she? At least that's what people say. She had a boil or something on her leg when she was young and had to have an operation and now one leg is very slightly shorter than the other and she walks with a stoop. She has a pleasant, diplomatic character just like our mother. Ah yes, when she started school she was a reluctant beginner, and our older cousin Bhudhi Dzenga often had to bind her down to the bicycle-carrier with old inner-tubes and cycle her off, kicking and screaming, to the very door of her classroom. Yes, Shuvai, you used to do that.

Ah, Vimbai, put down those dishes and meet these people. They want to know about us. You don't have to work so hard all the time, cooking, washing, clearing up, cleaning and checking whose shoes have soiled the floor. You don't have to live for our parents all the time. Yes, father caught you with your boyfriend Marko smooching on the green grass and marched you home to a four-hour lecture which put you off boyfriends forever, but now you can relax a bit. Don't blame yourself too much. Introduce yourself. Tell them you are a worrier like me and that when you were twelve you could look after this house and we called you *menija* – the manager of 33 Hoffman Street; that you had only two skirts, one of which we called the curtain, much to your disapproval; that one day while we were warming ourselves at a *mbaura* the curtain caught fire and you leapt screaming to douse yourself in the shower while we laughed like drains. During our dew-in-the-morning days in the country when you were barely four, you would go back and forth to the water pump with a tea-pot, singing *'Senkaya, senkaya, Senkaya senkaya,* I'm home, I'm home,' till you'd filled two buckets with water. Tell them how Ian Douglas Smith's Rhodesia cheated you out of a place in a boarding school, and how you're now doing Grade 11 instead of Form 1V.

And this is Tendai *tada tovi* – huger than her eleven years. They call her giant at school and she is awkward like many young adolescents. They say she's the spitting image of Mbuya VaChivi, my father's mother. There's a gap of five years between her and Vimbai. She was born when mother thought she'd done with babies. What is there to say about you, Tendai? That you could speak by the time you were one? That you could count up to hundred at two? That I used to teach you the names of insects, birds, animals, trees and flowers and hoist your little wet bum onto my shoulders and race with our dog Simba to the vlei to hunt for *maroro* during our blissful dew-in-the-morning days? That you kept visitors laughing with your antics? That when I was a fresh Form 1 boarder, I sent you a packet of ginger biscuits for your birthday, but when the postman delivered them, they'd been crushed to dust? That I loved you, dear sister?

Tapera, will you stop knocking about with that ball, shouting and running, chasing nothing, but flying like a Boeing 747? Come and greet these people, you silly boy! You broke a window last week and Dad wasn't amused. But he didn't beat you because his arm has grown limp from beating the five of us over the years, and besides, he's grown lenient with time. At eight you ought to know better. When I was your age I was picking *madora, mazhanje* and mushrooms in the forest, swimming in deep rivers with Lulu and weeding ten-acre fields of groundnuts. But you still sleep coiled up in your cot in the bedroom with *mhamha nababa*, squirming and banging at the wooden panels so we can't sleep. At school you giggle and make faces when the teacher tells you to sit under the table for disturbing the class, you restless, intelligent boy. When anybody brings you sweets you say, 'Don't give anything to Sisi Vimbai, she's beating me up these days.' And on the school open-day you paint your mouth up like a clown and recite the lines – *'Iwe muromo wangu unondiparira.* You, my mouth, you get me into trouble...' Oh Tapera, you naughty boy, you mindless child, you lucky little bastard, and my mother's last-born, do you have any idea what is happening to us, what we are going through?

So that's us in a nutshell. We were there in church for the wedding – we formed the bridal troupe with Maiguru Mazvita's pretty young sisters, and I was a witness. We were there when it happened on that New Year's eve, we boys sleeping on the floor in the sitting room, the girls in the kitchen with Maiguru Mazvita's sisters, and we thronged the doorway, agape, behind father while he, Rindai, bellowed, whimpered and shook. Yes, I went to the hospital with him in Muzukuru Baba Tariro's car and held him in the front seat, his head on my shoulder. After we came back from the hospital we sat in the sitting room with our in-laws, who'd been summoned from a nearby house where they'd been bedding with their relatives; we sang a hymn and father said a prayer. Maiguru Mazvita's father, a quiet man, a priest, also prayed elaborately and when Maiguru Mazvita's mother started speaking, rather peremptorily declaring that all necessary rituals had been performed before their daughter was handed to the Gwanangaras, that a blanket had been offered to the elders and their blessings secured, father trembled and guiltily asked her to be quiet. As the neighbours dispersed we heard whisperings in the night:

'*Mamhepo!* Evil spirits.'

'The young woman is a witch.'

'They didn't consult their elders.'

'*Kubatira church pamusoro!*'

'Put too much belief in the church!'

'Some wedding, without real relatives!'

And in the morning it was I who had the sorry task of going round informing the priest and other elders in the township about what had happened. Yes, we celebrated the birth of Nda and proudly rode in the Peugot, though we worried when he drove jerkily and struggled with the gears. Yes, we saw Mai Fanwell spit and say '*Zvipiko imi?*'

Yes, we were there all the time.

***

One fine blue May morning when the air was crisp, the elephant grass yellow-green, and the millet ripe and ready for harvesting, my father's grandfather Kapadza woke up to find his totemic animal, the porcupine, at the centre of his yard. Now porcupines are rare creatures that seldom venture into human settlements but here it was bristling, in the middle of the yard, without a trail on the ground to show where it had come from. It was as if it had landed gently from the sky, or someone had found it in the forest, carried it in a basket and plonked it in the midst of the huts tottering with age.

At first Kapadza thought the creature was dead, but when his children impudently prodded it with a stick, it moved its quills very slightly and he urged them to stop. He called his neighbours, sent for his sister Magwei and his uncle Gweme, his father Zevezeve's younger brother, who in turn brought three peers, including the n'anga of the village, and the men sat with their chins on their knobkerries at the dare, *consulting.*

'*It's Mhokoshi,*' *said one.*

'*It's your family's spirits paying you a visit,*' *said another.*

'Mashura. *It's a warning that something evil will happen soon.'*

The n'anga *among them, as lean as a hound in a drought-stricken household, with a face like a knife, shot arrows of phlegm into the heart of the fire, as he cleared his throat. 'Such things don't just happen. You, Kapadza, as Zevezeve's favourite son, have been singled out to receive the blessings and the curses of your spirits. There is a lot to be done. You have not been brewing* doro rechikaranga *regularly. Your spirits are thirsty. They have chosen to appear directly to you, in the form of your totem, to alert you of this. Suppose they had chosen another way? Suppose they had picked on a beast in the kraal, or stricken a person, a woman, a child, even a man? It could have been worse than this. Your father Zevezeve was a good man, but he left many things undone, things you have to do. Think of this.'*

And so the party crouched in the dust round the porcupine and sprinkled snuff round it, clapping their hands, ululating, pleading and singing their praises to it: 'Wamambo! Ngara! Zimuto! Chikandamina! Chinungu! Chinjenje! Masvingo aGovero!' *They placed it carefully on a rack of poles and carried it back to the forest, where it belonged.*

***

He drinks.

He drinks to drown his anxiety, to kill the fear that it might happen at any time, that he might collapse on his desk, fall off his stool at this very bar, or that the Peugot 404 might at some distracted moment plunge over a bridge and cause him to be a disgrace to himself and his family.

He buys beers for his friends, cracks jokes, laughs nervously, and belches. Sometimes, while telling a story with his customary bravado, the laughter is cut from his face in mid-sentence; he stops talking mid-word – round-eyed and tight-lipped – the glass of beer frozen in his hand, mid-air, like a figure in a film that has suddenly jammed, and he feels himself go, go, go, but his body fights it off and his hands loosen and relax and he comes to but the drink falls from his hand before he can get a grip on it and the sound of glass crashing on the floor causes a sudden hush in the bar and all eyes leap at him and he swallows hard, as if a fishbone had stuck in his throat, and stares straight ahead of him, and he feels himself come back and the barwoman smiles reassuringly and rushes with a broom to clear up the mess and a friend steps out to hold his hand and lower it and lead him out of the smoke-filled maze, out to the fresh air on the veranda, where he half struggles to reach for the pills in his back pocket and pop two tablets into his mouth, there, on the spot. Then, himself again, he might insist on going back to the bar, to his seat and his drink; or perhaps the friend, after persuading him to leave, might take the car keys from him and drive him home to his sleeping wife.

'It happened again, didn't it?' Mazvita, still in her night-dress, demands with exasperation, and he shakes his head and mutters inaudibly.

'You've been drinking again.'

He grunts feebly, curled up beside his wife and his baby, drifting off already into a deep sleep.

Every time he drinks, it happens, Mazvita phones mother. Now mother, Hilda Dolly, Mai Rindai, Masiziva, the moon huntress, no longer comes every time it occurs. For the fits usually happen with amazing regularity, at midnight on Thursdays, every fourth week of the month when there's a new moon, and it is just after pay day. I wonder now whether the coincidence was not just psychological, pressures of work on an early marriage. Or perhaps the demands of a wedding on a light pocket. He takes his pills and his herbs as he should. Mother consults widely. Once she brings a man who treats people by making them sick, vomit out the bug lodged deep in the bowels and clean the bloodstream. The man gives Rindai a small chip of wood to chew and Rindai immediately throws up, throws up a dishful of yellow slimy liquid, shits and wets his pants, groans and swoons till mother panics, wiping him, desperate to call an ambulance, but the man calmly packs his bags and leaves, refusing to take any payment until his patient is well, and advises him not to eat fish or eggs and to stay off drink for the time being.

For three and a half months Rindai religiously keeps away from the hard stuff – he goes to the bar and resolutely drinks orange-juice, shrugging off offers of his favourite lager, playing snooker with his friends, and it doesn't happen.

But some weeks later, when the moon is full, when we are beginning to nurse hope – it happens again, with a new ferocity.

24

***

Now what year is it?

1980.

Zimbabwe is newly independent; the war of liberation is over and a black government is in power; there is celebration in the air but we're already beginning to harvest thorns, blah, blah, blah....

We have left our little four-roomed house in the township. We have left our three-hut home in our dew-in-the-morning village to Mukoma Tavengwa Gwanangara (whom you will meet later). He and his wife have taken over the ten-acre field, five cattle, plough, scotch-cart, twenty-something chickens and a sagging double bed. We have moved, without ceremony or goodbyes – which embittered forever some of our dear neighbours – to a five-acre plot just outside town with a three-bedroomed house and a cottage. My father's Indian boss, the one-time Mr B.V., has given Dunge Gwanangara – the man who has worked for him for thirty years, the man who regularly carried half a pound of tripe on his Humber bicycle, the deacon of the Dutch Reformed Church – a loan to buy a house and a little land.

These are the days of *Farai's Girls*. During vacation I work in the department store beside my father, selling shirts and trousers, and banging at the grocery tills on Saturdays; feasting my roving, late-adolescent eyes on the girls. They are buoyant days of deodorant and braid-straightened hair and flared trousers. One Monday afternoon Mai Fanwell walks into the store and locks her eyes with mine from forty metres away. I feel something sharp stabbing my heart, my head reels, the empty shirt-boxes fall from my hands, I feel faint. The bright fluorescent lights are burning, my knees turn to water, I clutch onto the edge of a stand till the shock slowly dissolves. I come back to myself but my ears roar like a bus engine and I can hardly hear the noise around me, the swirl of voices, the tinkling of tills, and the dry laughter of Mai Fanwell chatting with my father, and greeting me. That day my heart races at different speeds and my hands swell. Next morning I lie in bed and tell father that I'm not well and cannot go to work and he tells me that Kelvin and I were tossing, turning and yelling in our sleep on the squeaky three-quarter bed. Later that morning I go to the clinic. I'm told that

25

my blood pressure is high for one so young but there is nothing else wrong with me; but the thought of Mai Fanwell in the doorway of the store sends shivers down my spine and I cannot go back to those blinding fluorescent lights and the crowds and the noise. And so I resign from my part-time job and everybody says, 'Oh, what a pity you're going,' because they like me, but it's only a week to the start of the new university semester.

Oh, the follies of superstition!

Now, what else do you need to know? Am I not weighting you with too much detail?

Sure. You might have told this story differently. But this you have to know – that in May or June that year my cousin sister Ratidzo (whom you will definitely meet later), second daughter of Tachiona Gwanangara, my father's only brother and sibling, *buda ndibudewo,** visits from our original rural area, ostensibly to see our new home, the plot, bringing with her a short but stern letter from Uncle Tachi – Tachiona Gwanangara, Vamutazviona – urging caution:

> My dear brother Dunge
> Now that you have taken Babamukuru Chari's son Tavengwa under your wing and let him live under the roofs of your homestead, beware that the evil winds may follow him into the walls of your household. You know that we never got along with Mukoma Chari. Beware that Tavengwa may bring curses into your family. Be warned.
> Your brother
> Tachi

Ah, yes, reader, and you need to know that on the night of the day Ratidzo came, my sister Vimbai, Vimbai the *menija*, manager of 33 Hoffman Street, wearer of burning curtains, starts hiccuping, nose-bleeds all night, and has to be hospitalised for two days.

***

Once upon a time there was a whisperer called Zevezeve who gave birth to many children, one of whom was called Mhokoshi, who died hunting in the mountains, and another called Kapadza, who gave

---

* Come out sibling, so that I can come out too!

26

birth to eight children, one of whom was called Gwanangara, his fourth-born.

Gwanangara was my grandfather. Now some people say he was a good man who honoured his parents and his ancestors and preached tolerance – a true porcupine; others say he was just an average man who drank moderately and quarrelled occasionally with his neighbours; still others say he was a secretive man who gathered roots, herbs, wild flowers and snake-skins and dabbled amateurishly in magic, temporarily at least. It's amazing how opinions can vary so much. Or how quickly people can forget within the short space of a hundred years, or choose to tamper with or disguise the truth about a man, to protect his reputation or their own. The wicked, the outrageous and the brave, the Mhokoshis of the world, earn themselves ready places in the mythology of their clans, while the Gwanangaras must plod under the yoke of ambivalence and mediocrity.

Anyway, the facts that can be ascertained are that Gwanangara had two wives and three children, all sons; one by his first wife Maribha and two by his second wife Njiki; that he drank moderately and even urged abstinence from alcohol; that he had two ferocious dogs called Svibe and Ndoga and that he loved eating dried mice stewed in peanut-butter sauce.

***

The moon huntress cannot stop inquiring what it is that bit her son, what creature sank a fang into his naked heel, at some unguarded moment on his wedding night, and shot its venom into his veins; what restless worm is burrowing in his brain and making him stiffen or fall, bellow or thrash about in his sleep. She believes in the Holy Ghost and in medicines, but she is convinced that some cases are best left to the traditional healer's bones. Her instincts tell her that black people can never escape from themselves, from their customs. If this had been a problem he was born with, or something that had begun in childhood, or indeed at any other time rather than on his wedding night, she would have been happy to leave matters with Jesus and the hospital doctors, but this is something else. On his wedding night!

The moon huntress consults far and wide and her husband the shirt-seller goes with her, reluctantly at first, then dutifully. My father believes that *n'anga's* bones cause nothing but trouble. He wants to be supportive, but tries to maintain a detachment. Our parents don't tell us, their children, about the verdict of the bones; Rindai thinks they're doing nothing about it. At one point he writes them a strongly worded letter accusing them of dragging their feet. He's a scientist, a rationalist, but he feels there must be spirits who need appeasing. Mother talks little but I, always a fence-sitter, begin to suspect that in these conflicting, confusing and sometimes dangerously arbitrary diagnoses, patterns are emerging.

My suspicions are confirmed when, towards the end of the second university term, father writes an urgent but cryptic letter summoning Kelvin and I home, so that we can travel with the rest of the family to the home of my father's brother, Uncle Tachiona Gwanangara, in Masvingo. Every member of the Gwanangara family is required to be there for 'an important function'. I go to Kelvin's room to discuss the letter with him and we agree to meet after supper in order to catch the overnight train.

After supper I go to my brother's room to look for him. His roommate Sabastin tells me there has been a demonstration on campus and a group of students has been arrested by the police. He thinks Kelvin is in this group.

The train leaves in an hour and there is no Kelvin. The minutes tick by and I know we will not catch the train.

Idiot Kelvin, going off and getting arrested when we have a journey to make. Stupid Kelvin, messing himself up with varsity politics when he's only in his first year. Fool Kelvin, joining his vague, righteous causes when there are urgent family matters to attend to.

At midnight, when I have given up all hope of seeing him, Kelvin turns up to say he has been released after paying a fine and that he is cent-less. I am too angry to question him or complain. First thing in the morning we go to the marketplace to catch a bus home and, of course, I pay his fare.

We arrive home and find the house locked, everybody out. I go to the orchard and eat an orange and an apple, contemplating the situation. I haven't been to Uncle Tachiona's home in seventeen years – the last time I was there I was barely five, and I can barely remember the trip, or the people I met. I have the name of the bus stop and the

28

directions all right, but will we find a bus? Will we get there on time? Oh, the time, the time.

Thanks to Kelvin and his politically conscientised views, we are stuck here at the deserted plot, munching fruit.

We catch the evening bus to Masvingo and arrive there at one in the morning. We sleep in the waiting room, fidgeting in the cold, waiting for dawn. At nine in the morning we board another bus for the last leg of the trip to Chivi. We are fortunate to sit with a woman who knows where we're going and before we disembark she points out the way. After an hour we alight. The bus stop is flanked on one side of the open gravel road by blue mountains and on the other by a dry, rolling landscape of thin, harvested millet fields, *muunga* trees and a line of huts. Yes, this is the land of my ancestors all right, the land where my father grew up; the smell in the air is of dust, cow dung, goats and the sun-muted stink of human refuse. We take the only path there is, away from the huts, towards the west. We cross a parched riverbed, and pass a school of mud walls and grass roofs; because it is Sunday there are no children in sight. We meet a bare-footed, grey-haired old man in a torn vest and patched shorts carrying a spear, knobkerrie and axe – I wonder strangely if I have seen him before, and if so where, and when. We greet him and again ask for directions. He coughs, spits in the grass and points out the way.

'You are going to Tachiona's place?' he says, slowly, and we nod eagerly. 'Keep along this path till you reach a clump of rocks and big *mutamba* tree, where the path will fork out like the fang of a snake. Take the left turn and go straight. Don't turn till you cross a small, dry stream and a little forest. Walk through the trees, and beyond them you will cross more fields, and then you will see a row of huts. Ask and the villagers will point you out Tachiona's home. You are not far away, in fact, you're nearly there.'

The man coughs again and I wonder if he has TB. He asks, 'Who is Tachiona to you?' I explain, and the man says, 'You are Dunge's children? Dunge? Your father's brother, Tachiona, had a naming ceremony for his late mother, your grandmother VaChivi, last night. I passed through their place yesterday morning, on the way to see my *mukwasha* Timoti who broke his leg falling from a tree. Tachi was killing a young bull for the ceremony. The beer was ready for your grandmother's rituals and your father was expected.'

Now it's too awkward, too complicated – I can't explain that father and the rest of the family are already here and that Kelvin and I missed the train, so we thank the man and leave him; I look back and see him leaning on his spear, staring after us.

'You are not far, you are nearly there,' turns out to be another eight to ten exhausting kilometres but we don't need anybody to point out Uncle Tachiona's homestead. We hear people singing and the drums thrumming and we see Muzukuru Baba Tariro's green Mazda truck parked incongruously in a yard, between two huts. We hurry on.

The drums, the singing and the stamping of feet come from one of the huts, and figures are milling around it. We enter the yard and are soon noticed by the guests. The music peters out and people, strangers to us, pour out of the hut to shake our hands with their work-chiselled palms. There is father, barefoot and grinning sheepishly in his overalls among other men; mother hesitant between two small women, one of them Maiguru Mai Ratidzo, our severe-looking aunt, Uncle Tachiona's wife; Vimbai is there, solemn as usual, in her new curtains, and Rindai stumbling, tall, careless and inebriated leans over the stoep of the hut; my brother, Baba Nda, holding a Christmas-size mug of seven-days brew and saying, half-accusingly, half-exuberantly to Kelvin and me, 'So where were you, you two? Getting here today! We're about to go. You're late – the naming ceremony for grandmother is over. We killed a bull and offered a brew. VaChivi's name was given to our cousin Shuwiso. It's over!' Maiguru Mazvita, Rindai's wife, baby Nda on her back, holding him back reproachfully and saying, *'Baba Nda, ndo zvaita sei?'**; our cousin Jonah, Ratidzo's brother, Tachiona's second son, withdrawn as ever, smiling his slow, sad ex-combatant smile; and that big charcoal-skinned man over there, Babamukuru Tachiona, my father's one and only brother, Tachiona Gwanangara, emptying his urine bags behind the hut, Babamukuru Tachiona who had a prostrate bypass operation years ago and was fixed up with plastic tubes and urine bags, Babamukuru Tachiona ducking his bags into his dangling greyish khaki shorts and flashing me a white smile with his white Gwanangara teeth, Babamukuru Tachiona hugging me with

---

* 'Baba Nda, what is it now?'

his urine-wet hands and bursting into tears, 'Godifiri, is it you?', and his wife, Maiguru Mai Ratidzo cutting in, *'Imi Vamutazviona, musaite somunopenga imwi*[†]; no, but is that Sisi Ratidzo, my cousin sister Ratidzo, Uncle Tachiona's second daughter, Ratidzo with a black dress and a black headband marching like a man through the crowd, taking out her man's *chipako* and offering me snuff and me lamely holding up my right palm, Ratidzo thrusting her face aside at the crowd and saying in her strange commanding man's voice, 'Show him the correct hand', and Kelvin holding up his left palm, Kelvin always correct, receiving the snuff and saying, *'Maita Sekuru.'*

We pile into the back of Baba Tariro's car after a lunch of millet sadza and beef. Our cousin Ratidzo is Ratidzo again and our cousin Shuwiso, Babamukuru's youngest daughter and the new Njiki, VaChivi, our grandmother, offers father a mug of water. It's crowded in the car; the skinned leg of the bull stinks in the narrow space at our feet. Babamukuru Tachiona says to no one in particular, sprinkling snuff round the car, 'They're running away from the dirt,' and he says to my father, as Baba Tariro starts the car, 'You hear, Dunge? Now that you have started brewing beer and killing a beast for your ancestors you will have to do it every year. Every year, you hear!' And then, blowing his nose and wiping his fingers on his aged grey-khaki shorts and hitching his urine bags as the car heaves forward, out of the yard, between the two walls of the awed, waving, rag-bag crowd, he says, 'I am Tachiona and no Gwanangara is going to die as long as I live.'

I think, 'Is life a mere fact of bathtubs and urine bags, or something larger and more precious?'

***

They say Gwanangara was a good man who honoured his father and mother and his ancestors and preached tolerance. Some have it that he was an average man who occasionally drank heavily and quarrelled with his neighbours; and that one morning after a long harvest drink, he was found lying unconscious but unhurt on the edge of his yard. They thought he was merely drunk, but when they

---

† 'You, Vamutazviona, don't behave like a madman!'

31

touched him his body was cold and there was no pulse. His wife, Maribha, Mai Chari, raised the cry and the neighbours came. They made a big fire next to him, covered him with goat skins and sent for help. The village n'anga came and administered various potions. After a while Gwanangara blinked, sneezed and slowly sat up, staring vacantly around him. They helped him onto his feet and walked him into the bush to pass water.

'The things of the night got him and nearly finished him off,' the n'anga said, 'but his mudzimu said to the things of the night, "No, you cannot have him. He cannot go like this. He cannot go because he has work to do."'

After a day or two Gwanangara became well, but they say he was never truly himself again. For a year he stopped drinking altogether, and afterwards he took only very little. He became reserved and secretive, sometimes mumbling to himself in the night. He stopped hunting with the other men, choosing instead to tend his fish-traps, mouse-traps, millet field and goats. He took to gathering roots, herbs and wild flowers and some say whenever he found the skin of a snake he picked it up – but he had no real use of these things. Perhaps he had delusions of himself as a n'anga, but nobody taught him divining or medicine and his dreams were clear – he did not take himself seriously. Nature was a mere hobby; he was an amateurish magician, tearing flowers open and sticking locusts onto bits of wood, because he had nothing better to do, nothing to engage his mind.

Gwanangara had a wife, Maribha, and with her he had one son, Chari, who was five or six, old enough to look after the goats. Already people were talking, that he should have another wife, more children. During a year of drought, a man from two streams away had offered him his eight-year-old daughter as a betrothed wife, in exchange for bags of millet. But Gwanangara had a mind and an eye of his own and he declined. After all, he loved his wife Maribha.

Now one evening when the sun was sitting on the crowns of trees, Gwanangara came out of the forest with a large goat-skin bag full of nhedzi, aloes and wild fruit. As he was going down to the stream to have a drink of water he saw a girl kneeling on the bank, filling her gourd.

'Good evening, girl,' he said, looking out for crocodiles, and she replied, 'Manheru Sekuru.'

'May I have a drink of water?'

She dipped her gourd in the stream, and, kneeling, offered him the gourd. He drank deeply, and thanked her before enquiring of her name.

'But I don't know you,' she answered. 'My mother told me not to talk to strangers.'

'My name is Gwanangara. And I am not a stranger. I know your father, Shuro the hunter.'

'My father told me not to talk to strangers.'

She put her gourd on her head and hurried away home, her young hips swishing through the leaves.

The next day he came again at sunset and found her filling her gourd and singing to herself.

'You sing beautifully,' he said, 'like a bird.'

'You startled me.'

'May I have a drink of water?'

'My mother told me not to give water to strangers.'

'I am not a stranger. You know me.'

'No, I don't.'

'May I have a drink of water, please?'

'But you can kneel down and drink with your hands, from the stream.'

'Yesterday I drank from your sweet gourd.'

She dipped her gourd in the stream, came over, knelt before him and offered him the gourd. He drank long and deeply, handed her back the gourd, and said, 'But I don't know your name, little bird.'

'I'm not a bird. And I am not little. My father warned me not to give my name to strangers.'

'I brought you some mice.'

'My mother warned me not to accept gifts from strangers.'

She put her gourd on her head and hurried away home.

Several times more he met her at the stream and they went through the same routine: he asking for water and she giving him her gourd; he offering her gifts of mushrooms, fruit, bangles woven out of reeds and grass but she steadfastly declining to tell him her name. He knew it already, of course, and he was aware that her father was a *famous hunter in the parts, but etiquette required him to feign igno-rance. One day when he asked for her name she finally said, 'My name is Njiki.'*

'Njiki. That's a nice name. You are as beautiful as loquat fruit. I want to be drinking from your sweet gourd always, Njiki. I want to be licking the soup from your pots always, Njiki.'

'I am a bad cook.'

'I don't believe that.'

'And besides, I don't cook for a married man.'

'I have already told my wife about you.'

That night Gwanangara said to his wife, 'Mai Chari, I like this girl Njiki. May I have your permission to marry her? Do you think you could live together with her?'

Mai Chari kept quiet for some moments, then said, 'What is it I don't have that this woman has? Don't I have a hearth? Or is my hearth too cold for you, already?'

Gwanangara pushed the blocks of wood into the fire and shifted his stool. In the hut nearby, little Chari's robust snoring could be heard among the grunting and shuffling of goats.

'Just because I have only given you one child you want me to share you with another woman?' said Mai Chari, bitterly.

Gwanangara threw chips of wood into the fire and shifted his stool again. 'She'll be your helper, Mai Chari,' he said as gently as he could.

'Am I an old woman to need help from this child woman, from anyone? Am I not a woman? Look, Baba Chari, I have nothing against her and you can do as you wish. But don't think things will ever be the same. You men never learn.'

4

Kelvin's problem begins slowly, so slowly that we hardly notice it happening. We are pre-occupied with Rindai, fretting every minute over him, so that everything else is squeezed into the margins of consciousness.

God, this present tense is becoming a nuisance, and I'm swearing too, taking that great creator's name in vain. This present is already the past – twenty-something years ago as I write this. The present is always the past. The present is already the past, but it's immediate. The present continuous tense is no better – it gives a false sense of the drama, authenticity and continuity of life. The past is, or only seems, straightforward – finished, accomplished, ordered. How I wish now I could simply say: It began like this ... this is what happened ... But I am foundering over beginnings and I mustn't confuse you or myself. I have to be consistent and stick with the recalcitrant present.

Let me begin again.

Kelvin's problem begins slowly, so slowly that we hardly notice it happening.

We are pre-occupied with Rindai, fretting over him, so that in our unschooled fear of dis-ease, in our superstitious ignorance of the complications of epilepsy, we switch off the world around us – well, almost.

It began – begins, like this.

August 1980. It is a few weeks after we've returned from the ceremony in Chivi. We're settling in to our new plot, enjoying our three-bedroomed house, the cottage, the orchard, the garden, the generous electric water-pump, the sprinklers, the more than ample water-tanks and fields; enjoying the space, the fresh air, the vegetation, the shift from the stifling little township house and its jealous, gossiping neighbours; the shift from the smell of death in our once fresh but now putrefying dew-in-the-morning village.

It's vacation time at the university where I'm doing my final year and Kelvin is doing his first. With youthful ardour, he and I are harvesting a very successful crop of ox-heart tomatoes and carting them on the carrier of father's old Humber bicycle to supermarkets and grocer's shops. One morning Kelvin lies late in bed saying he has a headache. I go alone to town to deliver a large box of tomatoes and when I return in the afternoon he is not planting early maize as he should be, but still lying lethargically in bed.

'You're just lazy,' I suggest in my cruel, bossy tone. He does not reply. At supper he eats very little, and that night and subsequent nights he does not sleep; I wake up several times to find him awake, lying on his back in the bed we share, his eyes gleaming in the dark, staring at the ceiling. At the clinic he is given painkillers, but for the rest of the vacation he talks very little and mostly stays in bed.

When we return to the university I don't see him sitting with his friends in the dining hall so I go to his room to check on him. I knock and there is no reply; I open the door and step in. He is lying on his back on the bed, fully dressed, his arms neatly folded on his chest. I sit on his roommate's bed.

'Have you eaten?' I ask him, superfluously. He does not reply, look at me or move.

I go to the dining hall and return with sandwiches, a salad and some coffee but he does not touch the food.

'You have to eat,' I say.

'I have to go now,' I say, again, awkwardly, standing up and reaching for the door.

'There were drops of blood on my pillow this morning,' he says, without looking at me – the first full sentence I have heard him utter in a week. I yank the pillow from under his head to check. There is nothing, and I turn the pillow over. Nothing there either.

'The cleaners changed the pillowcases this morning,' he says soberly, and I realise he's not making it up.

I sit again on the unoccupied bed.

'Where is Sabastin?' I ask. His room-mate is a lean, reserved fellow with pimples and slouching shoulders, but a porcupine, like us. It hadn't taken Kelvin, our resident traditionalist, two nights to find this out. They have been bedding together since the beginning of the year but whenever I come to the room Sabastin smiles awkwardly at me, hastily packs his books and leaves, ostensibly to give Kelvin and I the chance to talk.

'He left yesterday. Went home.'

'Why?'

'He's not well. He talks to himself at night. He's on medication.'

'Is he coming back?'

'Probably not. He's dropped out.'

I fling Sabastin's wardrobe open. Empty, except for a half-full bottle of white pills.

'So what's unusual about blood on a pillow?' I grumble, against my better judgement. 'Maybe you have bleeding gums, or a pimple on your neck, or maybe you just had a nosebleed.'

'It's not the first time it has happened.'

'Don't think too much about it. You must get some sleep. Do you want me to buy you sleeping tablets?'

'I think Sabastin's spirit is doing things to me.'

'Oh, come on.'

'He took my jeans with him.'

'So? Maybe he did so by mistake.'

I return to my room to work on my assignments. I try not to think about Kelvin too much. I have exams in a few days' time. Next day at four in the afternoon when I'm dressing to play tennis with my girlfriend, Vongai, Kelvin knocks and enters. Being in final year, I have the room to myself, so he sits on the edge of my bed, holding his face in his hands.

'Did you sleep?' I ask him, tapping on the bed with my racket. Damn it! I have forgotten to buy him sleeping pills.

He holds his face in his hands and stares at the floor.

'Well, I'm going off to play tennis,' I tell him. 'Vongai is waiting for me. Just close the door when you leave.'

As I'm going down the stairs from my room I see a group of

first-year students – Kelvin's mates, sitting in a group on the lawn, talking. When they see me they lower their voices. I play badly and lose a set to Vongai for the first time. When I return at a quarter to six, Kelvin is still in my room, still sitting on the bed clasping his face in his hands and staring at the floor. I take a quick shower, go to the dining room to eat and bring him back some food. He picks up a sandwich, nibbles at it and puts it back in the plate.

'Sabastin's spirit is doing things to me,' he repeats. I sit at the head of the bed watching him, my back against the wall, wondering how a living person can have a spirit outside of the self. Silence falls for a good three minutes.

'But why didn't you tell me?' I say, again pointlessly. 'You could have found a new roommate.'

'I've been having bad dreams.'

'What kind of dreams?'

He does not reply. Silence falls again, then he says, 'I'm the black sheep of the family.'

'Why?'

'I failed my Form 2 examinations and had to repeat the class. I never told you, but when father accompanied me to look for a new place he lectured me and then beat me up. I failed him completely. I am the *dhandahead* in the family. I passed by pure chance. I'm totally useless. I'm not going to finish my degree, just like Sabastin.'

'Kelvin …'

'I let you down at the plot with the tomatoes and the maize. You thought I was lazy. You thought I was pretending. My head and my eyes were giving me trouble.'

'Maybe you need to see an optician.'

'You're older than me but there are things you don't know.'

I know I should let him speak.

'You are the big brain in the family – you, with your fourteen A-level points and your scholarships. Dad's blue-eyed boy. *Dhandaheads* like us had to scratch for six points. You think you know everything. But you know absolutely nothing.'

'I'm taking you to the doctor tomorrow,' I announce resolutely.

'Tell me, Mr Fourteen Points, what happened to our brother Rindai on his wedding night? Tell me about the trip to Chivi. Why did I get arrested on the day we were supposed to go to Gweru? Why did we miss the ride in Baba Tariro's car? Why did we have a hard time getting to Chivi and why was the ceremony over when we arrived?'

'What do you think, Kelvin?'

'You don't know a thing. Something – somebody – some force, didn't want you and I there at that ceremony. You think it's over – one trip to Chivi and it's over, isn't it? Sisi Ratidzo strutting about like a man, dishing out snuff and pretending to be Sekuru Mhokoshi. And Shuwiso being given Mbuya VaChivi's name. That ceremony was a lie, a big hoax. How can our ancestors choose only Tachiona's children when Dunge has offspring too?'

'What do you know about these things?'

'See, you don't know a thing. You are only good at twisting other people's questions into your own. You don't have any answers. And your father is even worse. Your Standard Six father, thinking he can whip everybody up into being a genius. Thinking that education is everything. Your father, staging Rindai's wedding without consulting his elder brother Uncle Tachiona. Your Dutch-reformed, English-washed, Indian-starched father, fooling himself that he can run away from his blood relatives and his past and solve everything with propriety and prayer.'

I am struck by the truth of Kelvin's words, by the eloquence of his anger. Nobody has ever described father like that, so aptly. But I remain defensive. I say lamely, 'OK, OK, Kelvin, don't go to your room. Sleep here tonight; maybe a change of place will give you some rest. I'll come back first thing in the morning and we'll go and see the doctor.'

'And you?'

'I'll find somewhere to sleep – with a friend maybe.'

'You're going to sleep with Vongai, aren't you?' he says, sighing wearily. 'You think I don't know? I came here several nights and couldn't find you. Just be sure not to mess her up.'

He stretches out on my bed and I rise to give him more space and stand in the middle of the room, hovering over him. He lies on his back facing the ceiling, his hands beneath his chest, eyes for once bunched shut.

And so I leave him there and close the door softly behind me and run down the stairs, straight past the dining hall, round the hedge and up the hill to the women's residence. It is five minutes after the visiting hour but there is no matron at the entrance and I sneak in, down the passage and up the stairway to Vongai's room.

God, I do want to sleep with Vongai. Yes, I want to hold her firm young flesh to my soul so that I can feel her heartbeat. I want to clutch at something warm and real, so that she can love me and exhaust me and blot out this confusion in my brain and make me sleep.

***

At a quarter to six in the morning I come back to my room and find it deserted and the food uneaten. I run to Kelvin's room and find it empty too, the door unlocked. I walk back slowly to my room and sit guiltily on my bed, wondering what to do next. There is a knock and I open the door to find Temba, Kelvin's best friend, standing in the corridor in his pyjamas. I let him in and he sits on my bed, next to me.

'Is everything OK with you, Mkoma Godi?' he begins ominously, and my mind races in several directions at once. He tells me Kelvin is in his room, Temba's room, lying in his bed, Temba's bed. He tells me Kelvin came to his room at three in the morning, stark naked, complaining that he could not eat or sleep, and that he wanted to talk. He tells me that he fetched Kelvin's clothes from my room and gave him his bed. He tells me Kelvin had talked all night, some things which he, Temba, could not understand, and that I, as his brother, should talk to him please. He tells me that Kelvin has come to his room in the middle of the night on several occasions, but never before naked, saying that he wants to talk, that there is no one to talk to and that if he tries to talk to me, his brother, I dismiss his utterings as nonsense. He tells me that Kelvin seriously believes the spirit of Sabastin is affecting him; that Sabastin took his jeans with him to do something evil to him, to put a spell on him.

I go at once with Temba to his room and find Kelvin lying on the bed staring at the ceiling, his clothes flung onto the sofa. When I talk to him he does not answer or move, but when Temba offers him a towel he takes it, gets up and the two of them go to take a shower. I go to the dining hall to eat and while I'm preparing some food to take back to him I see people looking at me and whispering in one another's ears and even the waiters nodding slyly at each other and there is a hollow feeling inside me and I think, God, everybody knows everything except me, Oh God, how could I be so blind and so insensitive! When I return to Temba's room with the food Kelvin, now bathed and dressed and combed, refuses to look at it, but Temba persuades him to eat two slices of bread and drink a cup of coffee.

At eight o'clock, Kelvin and I are sitting in the university clinic waiting for the doctor. I leaf blindly through the magazines; Kelvin sits with his head in his hands, staring at the wall and the nurse shuffles her paperwork behind the glass panel. The doctor arrives after what feels like an eternity, but it is only an hour later, and the nurse shows us into the consulting room. The doctor, a bald-headed young fellow, thirty-five at most and casually dressed in a T-shirt and jeans under his white dust coat, skims over the nurse's notes and asks, 'So which one of you having problems?'

I shrug suggestively and the doctor asks me to leave so that he can be alone with Kelvin. After fifteen minutes he sends Kelvin out and calls me in to hear my side of the story.

I tell him everything I know, that Kelvin has not slept for over a week, that he is eating erratically and visiting his friends in the middle of the night, wanting to talk but not talking much to me; I tell him about the alleged blood on the pillow and his queer roommate Sabastin and the missing jeans. The doctor suggests examination stress as the cause and I tell him that Kelvin has always been reserved and that, ever since he failed Form 2 and had to transfer to another school and father whipped him all the way up to his new dormitory, he has suffered from feelings of inferiority, worthlessness and self-denunciation. The doctor asks me about our family and I tell him about father and mother and us, about Rindai and that wedding night and how now I'm struggling alone to contain this new case in order to protect our mother, and he leans back in his chair and says, 'This might also be a mental condition – a genetic problem,' and when I stare back at him in disbelief he continues bluntly: 'Mental problems manifest themselves in various ways and this might be an early case of schizophrenia. Have you heard of it?' I nod my head slowly and he asks, 'Has he exhibited any signs of violence?' I shake my head vehemently and he says, 'You have to go and see a psychi-

41

atrist.' I ask him if this is a problem that can be cured and he says, 'There are drugs to control it and in some cases cure it altogether.' He writes us a referral letter and dismisses us. I thank him and go out to the waiting room where Kelvin is sitting with several people. A schoolmate of mine who is now studying engineering inquires if I am sick but I hardly hear him.

At two that afternoon Kelvin and I join the queue on the benches outside the psychiatric ward at the hospital annexe. I try not to look at the people in the queue, most of them look OK, anyway. But there is a young man with a shaved head that keeps bobbing up and down, saliva trickles steadily out of his open mouth onto the wet chest of his shirt. The temperature is sizzling hot but a once attractive woman is wrapped up in a black fur jacket, woollen hat and thick, knee-high stockings, and she goes up and down the queue offering aces, spades and jokers to us all and repeating, in sweet English, 'Please come to my wedding. Please do come to my wedding.' A fat orderly in a faded white uniform carting a tray of khaki files stops her and asks, matter-of-factly, 'So, Cynthia, where is your wedding this month? Liverpool? Chicago?'

There is only one doctor and the queue moves slowly, oh, so very slowly and Kelvin removes a handkerchief from his jacket and wipes his forehead; Kelvin, the washer-boy, suddenly fishes for a comb like a cowboy reaching for his gun, and ploughs it through his hair and dabs some lip-ice on his mouth. Just before five we are admitted. The doctor is a young man, obviously English and so-o polite but clearly fatigued – I wonder if he doesn't need help; I wonder why people think medicine a glorious profession, especially psychiatry, but he is very thorough and listens patiently, oh so very patiently, assiduously taking notes in neat upright handwriting and saying very little. We leave with a khaki card and two bottles of pills – large ones almost half the size of peppermints and little yellow ones, and instructions to return at the end of the month.

That night I take Kelvin back to my room and bring him something to eat – he nibbles a little and falls into a deep sleep two or three hours after taking his medication. I stretch out on the sofa with a blanket over my body and as soon as he starts snoring I sneak out to the reception to make a phone call home: the doctors, Temba, and my friend Wilbert have all advised this, and I feel I can't contain the anxiety any more – the situation is now beyond me; father and mother have to know, whatever the consequences.

The phone rings for a while and I'm expecting mother's moon huntress voice but father answers from far away. He is quiet, cautious as I explain everything in my calmest tones. I tell him that I am bringing Kelvin home the next day, a Saturday, that I have examinations on Monday and there is no alternative. Father readily agrees, as if this is something that was to be expected, but I know it's his style, to appear calm and unruffled, and not to panic those around him even when everything is going wrong, even when worry is smouldering in his eyes.

Next morning at nine Kelvin and I catch a lift home; he agrees to come without question or argument and here we are, squashed on the front seat of a rattling old pick-up truck, next to the driver. We're quiet for most of the three-hour trip, the driver and I occasionally conversing in monosyllables, but when we are fifteen minutes away from our destination Kelvin suddenly shudders, and tears stream down his face. I put a reluctant hand on his shoulder, shake my head and say, 'No, Kelvin,' and the driver glances sideways at us, his hands trembling at the wheel so the truck rolls off the shoulder of the road, onto the grass.

'Are things all right where you're going?' the driver asks, hitting the brakes and swerving the car back onto the road. I offer no explanation and he says again, glancing at Kelvin, who is sitting sandwiched between us, 'Are you going to a funeral, perhaps?'

I offer Kelvin a clean handkerchief but he rejects it and wipes his eyes with the back of his hands. I wonder if he is acting. When the pick-up truck drops us off at the garage he marches homeward, faster and faster, gathering speed as if something is drawing him to the plot. I trot after him.

When we reach the house Kelvin bursts into the lounge and mother staggers out of the bedroom in her *zambia*, adjusting her doek. Kelvin says, 'Where is he?'

'Chiiko mwanangu?' Mother gasps. 'What is it?'

Our dog Shumba welcomes us with yelps and a thrashing tail but Kelvin kicks it aside.

He marches past her and throws open the door of the main bedroom, thrusts in his head, searches the other bedrooms and the kitchen, bangs the door after him and stomps out to the garden. Father is crouching in his overalls in the garden, picking ox-heart tomatoes. Mother and I run out to the garden, after Kelvin.

'You there!' Kelvin barks, in a strange, angry voice, wagging a finger in father's face, 'Do you know who I am?'

Father rises to his feet and steps back.

'Throw down that tomato!' Kelvin shouts, shaking a fist in father's face. 'Do you know who I am?'

The tomato falls from father's hand, bursts on the ground and bleeds at his feet and he takes another step backwards.

'I am Mhokoshi! I want my weapons back!'

Our young brother Tapera flies happily round the hedge with his ball, towards me, yelling, 'Bhudhi Godi, Bhudhi Godi, have you brought me chocolates?' but draws abruptly to a puzzled halt when he sees Kelvin confronting father.

'I am Njiki!' Kelvin snarls, in an old woman's voice. 'My spirit is roaming in the forest.'

'I am Sabastin.' Now a strange young man's thin breaking voice. 'I need rest!'

Then again, whispering in an old man's voice, 'I am Zevezeve the porcupine. You shat and spat on me when I visited you.'

'I am Edgar Tekere. I'm back from the war. I see blood everywhere.'

Father kneels in the dust facing Kelvin, his eyes beseeching.

'Get up!' says Kelvin, kicking him hard in the belly.

I jump at Kelvin and pull him back. Mother grabs him by the other arm and we march him back to the house. Tendai awkwardly steps out of our way and clasps her exercise books into her oversized uniform.

We enter the lounge and Kelvin shakes his head, sighs heavily and looks around him, like someone waking up from sleep. We plant him in the nearest chair, the chair next to the main bedroom, dad's chair. I rummage in my bag for his pills and Tendai brings some water. He tosses the pills into his mouth and takes a gulp from the mug. Tendai brings orange juice and biscuits.

Father slowly enters the lounge and cautiously sits on a chair at the other end of the room, opposite him. Kelvin looks quickly away from father, picks up a biscuit and nibbles at it, takes a sip of orange juice. He sighs again and stretches out on the sofa, his face softening a little.

***

For weeks the rain had poured down incessantly and the Save River was full. Njiki was more than eight months' pregnant and she should have gone home to her mother to deliver, as tradition required, but as the river could not be crossed she was confined in Gwanangara's household. One night her labour pains began.

Maribha, Mai Chari, Gwanangara's first wife, made her rupiza, a thin bean porridge, and fed her with a wooden spoon.

'I'm ill, Maiguru,' the young woman groaned, struggling to sit up and swallow a few mouthfuls. Maribha hurried out to the dare where Gwanangara was sitting in the spitting drizzle, sharpening his axe.

'Njiki is not well today,' she said, 'I think her time has come.'

It had been an easy pregnancy so far, easy in that heedless way of first pregnancies. It had only happened to Maribha once, but her instincts told her that something was amiss. Gwanangara stopped sharpening his axe and listened to his first wife. He had the wisdom to realise that women know better in such emergencies; that at some point men became impotent in the drama they had themselves invented. The rains had come without warning and he had left things too late – Njiki should have gone back to her mother while there was time, but now the river, the raging river rippling with crocodiles, could not be crossed. Gwanangara sent his son Chari to call the village midwife and she came immediately. Maribha made a fire in Njiki's hut and the midwife prepared her tools.

Gwanangara heard the unbearable noises coming from Njiki's hut and sought escape. He took his axe, knobkerrie and spear, slung his goatskin bag over his shoulder, called his dogs and disappeared into the forest. When he came back in the afternoon with his dogs panting dutifully at his heels, bag brimming with mushrooms, flowers and a dead rabbit dangling from his shoulder, there was no noise from Njiki's hut. He heard a familiar whimper and the midwife came out with a pot under her arm and said to him, smiling, 'It's a boy.'

'Is the boy all right? Is Njiki all right?'

'They're both all right,' said the midwife, 'but you can't come in yet.'

Gwanangara leaped in the air like a warrior, spun half-way round and back again on one foot, spilling mushrooms and flowers and dead mice on the sand and said, grinning, 'Where is Maribha?'

'She's in there with Njiki and the baby. I'll get her for you.'

Maribha came out beaming. 'He's a big dark boy, bigger than his eight moons. Njiki was very strong. Are you happy, Baba Chari? Are you happy now, my husband?'

Gwanangara said, 'Oh, Maribha!' and he handed her the rabbit. 'Make her a soup. Make us all your good, strong soup.'

He unslung the goatskin bag from his back and, bending down to pick the fallen treasures, announced, thoughtfully, ' His name is Tachiona.'

Maribha fetched water, swept, cooked and looked after the household until Njiki recovered from childbirth.

Little Tachiona was no problem. He fed robustly at his mother's breast and at first woke up frequently at night, but soon settled down to a more tolerable rhythm.

The two women, Maribha and Njiki, got along well, initially anyway. Njiki had a young, sometimes sarcastic nonchalance which Maribha found amusing, and the latter tolerated her because her cheekiness was short-lived and she did not mind being ordered about. The Gwanangara household had no hard and fast rules. Each woman had a separate hut, but they went to the stream, to the field, to fetch firewood and pick mushrooms or gather wild spinach together, laughing and chattering like sisters. Together they attended weddings, funerals, biras and humwes. Gwanangara scrupulously tried to be fair, sharing everything equally and honouring his respective in-laws alike. He insisted on eating every dish together with his two wives – never letting on that he had gathered at some beer talk that enlightened polygamists did this to rule out the possibility of love potions or poisoning. When Njiki was busy or unwell, the other woman gladly took the baby on her back and did the chores. The baby knew whose breast to feed from, of course, but did not mind whose back offered him sleep. In turn, Njiki bathed and cooked for Chari. And when his two mothers were away, or busy, Chari took *his brother Tachiona and held him on his lap and sang to him and taught him to talk .*

The two women became known as 'Mapatya aGwanangara' – *Gwanangara's twins.*

But nature has many ways of driving wedges between people, especially trios. Perhaps there isn't, has never been, in human history, any true formula for successful polygamy. Barely a year after the birth of Tachiona, Njiki fell pregnant again but delivered a stillborn girl. Another year later, she delivered another stillborn – again a girl. Meantime, Maribha's womb refused to yield another child. The atmosphere grew tense. The older woman became anxious, the younger one bitter and suspicious. The inevitable happened – word went around that Maribha was eating Njiki's children.

Wicked tongues wagged with glee. Jealousy cackled through the thin reed walls of pretence. At first, Gwanangara refused to listen to the buzzing in the air. He followed the example of his grandfather Zevezeve and refused to seek out the tricky verdict of n'angas' *bones. Some people say he secretly sought out* n'angas *in the middle of the night, as time passed; after all he had dabbled in magic once – or so people said – and that at the bottom of his goatskin bags, under the seemingly innocent flourish of flowers, fruit, mushrooms and mice lurked roots, herbs, snake skins and crocodile teeth. He could have even won Njiki's love by a charm, and this charm was now vengefully drinking the blood of his children and killing them off, one by one.*

It's amazing how opinions about one person can vary so much, how fact can blend so perfectly with fiction. Anyway, the facts of the matter are that Maribha got disconcerted with the gossip, and accused Njiki of fomenting these unkind rumours; a fight between the two women followed, and when Gwanangara tried to intervene, Maribha, seeing his intervention as her condemnation, packed her bags and left, despite his pleas, never to return, taking her son Chari with her.

Njiki stayed on, looking after Gwanangara and Tachiona. Shortly after Maribha's sad departure, Njiki fell pregnant and gave birth to a healthy son who, because he crawled about chasing ants with a stick and lisping, 'Du-nge-du-nge-du-nge', they named Dunge.

Dunge Gwanangara.

5

You were there, you are there, Mai Tariro, you our urban *muzuku-ru*. Baba Tariro's wife, you, our family's long-time friend, you our Hoffman Street relative, when they take him on the direct bus to Chivi.

Yes, you were there, you are there, at the back of the bus, sitting on one seat with him, holding his hands and pleading with him in whispers, you on one side and mother on the other, he in the middle, staring ahead.

'Sekuru Kelvin, please!'

Father is sitting at the front of the bus, near the door, ready to bolt. The passengers, the conductor and the driver suspect nothing at first and you are all praying, praying that nothing goes amiss on this journey.

I wasn't, I'm not, there – all this you tell me later, *'Sekuru Godifiri zvenyu, zvatakaona imi! Mashura chaiwo.'** You should have been there, Sekuru.'

I wasn't, am not, there, with him, with you, with them, on the bus to Chivi – no, I'm returning to university that morning, this morning, back to my examinations and to Vongai, oh sweet Vongai, with no pills to administer, no insomniac to watch over.

Yes, you are there, Mai Tariro, when Kelvin breaks out of your grip and mother's, marches right up to the front of the bus and gives father a terrific blow on the jaw with his fist and the whole bus goes 'Haaaa!' and the driver stops, engine revving and throbbing, and you

---

* 'What we saw Sekuru Godifiri is simply unbelievable!'

48

desperately explain and plead with the conductor not to be thrown out.

'Sekuru Kelvin, please!'

Yes, Mai Tariro, you get off the bus with them and plod the ten-kilometre stretch through the barren fields, across the dry riverbed, past the school of giggling, chanting children and he is striding ahead now, ahead of you all, free of your grip and you are stumbling after him; he knows where he wants to go now, and father, reprieved temporarily from the rain of blows, follows cautiously behind.

You are there, almost, when he charges into Babamukuru Tachiona's yard, the chickens flap-flying from under his boots; he catches Babamukuru Tachiona staggering open-mouthed out of a hut and he gives the old man a mighty kick in the crotch so that his bags burst and a wing of urine flies towards his aged head; the old man tumbles onto his back on the ground, his face screwed up with pain, his white hair drenched in urine. Maiguru Mai Ratidzo his wife wrings her hands and enscribes, with her quick diminutive steps, a half-moon around her fallen husband gasping, *'Yuwi! Yuwi! Yuwi!'* and Kelvin swings a foot at her so that her skirts fly; he butts at the mud walls with his head, hitting out at everyone and everything in sight, mother and even you – mother has a black eye and you a sprained arm to show for it.

'Sekuru Kelvin, *please.'*

Yes, Mai Tariro, you are there when the village men help father and Babamukuru Tachiona trap him behind the kitchen and rope up his legs and fell him, like they do young bulls to castrate them; they bind him up and bundle him into a hut and lock him up.

'Who are you?' Babamukuru Tachiona, catching his breath, challenges him through the slit in the wooden door.

'Sabastin,' he replies in a young man's thin, breaking voice.

'We don't know anyone called Sabastin here. What do you want, Sabastin?'

'My spirit needs rest.'

'We don't know you here. Go back to the person who made you like this.'

'I'm Comrade Tekere.'

'Tekere who?'

'You know me from the war.'

'We don't know anyone like that here.'

'I'm Mhokoshi!' This in an angry man's voice.

'Mhokoshi who?'

'You know me.'

'What do you want?'

'I want my weapons back.'

Silence, then a half-familiar, snarling old woman's voice, 'I'm Njiki.'

'Njiki who?'

'Fool of a son. Who gave birth to you, Tachiona, and your brother Dunge?'

'If you are really Njiki what do you want?'

'My spirit is roaming in the forest.'

'If you are really Njiki, you should know what ceremony was held for you two months ago, in this very homestead, to bring you back.'

'You lied to the soil, Tachiona. You forced my name onto your daughter Shuwiso. The soil is not happy.'

Then again, whispering, 'I'm Zevezeve.'

'Zevezeve who?'

'Fool child, questioning your forebears. You are too young to know. All is mist and dust.'

'If you are really Zevezeve, what do you want?'

'You soiled my good name with human dung. You closed your doors in my face when I visited your homesteads.'

'But how can we be sure you are him, and not some evil spirit out to destroy us?'

'Fool child, touching your lower lip to your upper lip to utter such folly. Child, seek the counsel of those whose eyes see better than yours.'

***

And so they – Babamukuru, Maiguru, father and mother – leave Kelvin locked up in the hut and go to consult *n'angas* but you are not there to go with them, Mai Tariro; this matter is now beyond you, and you are now smelling gusts from the Gwanangara's buried past. You say to mother, 'Mbuya Shingai,' and go to catch the last bus to Gweru.

I'm not there and you're not there, Mzukuru Mai Tariro, and this mother tells us later that of the three *n'angas* they visit, none mentions Sabastin or Zevezeve, one vaguely alludes to Mhokoshi and two deposit the matter squarely on Njiki's doorstep. A fierce argument follows between Babamukuru Tachiona and father, Babamukuru insisting that two more ceremonies be held, and father arguing that the ceremonies and consultations be skipped altogether and, this half-reluctantly, that a herbalist be found to help Kelvin back to his senses.

In the end they agree to urgently summon their in-law Mkwasha Phiri, a renowned medicine man, hailing from Malawi but currently living on the other side of the river, who happens to have married their *mzukuru* and, more recently, Babamukuru Tachiona's third daughter Chenai. And while they wait mother feeds Kelvin, still bound hands to feet, bitter porridge, water and pills.

Mkwasha Phiri arrives the next day and promptly sets to work on Kelvin. He unbinds and frees him, smokes out the hut with scented grass, feeds him, covers him with a blanket over a steaming pot full of roots, cuts *nyora* on his hands and chest and legs and gives him potions to loosen his bladder and his bowels. Kelvin at once stops being violent and does as he is told. Mkwasha Phiri has recently become a *n'anga* and he is powerful, still untainted by the scandal, greed and abuses that often ruin mortals in his profession. The fame of his prowess has spread far and wide; he treats cancers, fevers, mental illnesses, ulcers, *mamhepo* – bad spells – and so on with amazing success. At any one time there are a dozen patients in his homestead receiving treatment. Because there are sick people waiting for him and many more arriving he cannot be away from home for any stretch of time, so he decides to take the now compromised Kelvin to his homestead where he can monitor him more closely, and mother goes with them. Kelvin and mother are there for a good three weeks and there is no news from them – an anxious time for all of us.

Two days before Christmas, mother turns up at the plot with a sober, laughing Kelvin!

***

Gwanangara did not marry again after the departure of Maribha. After giving birth to Dunge, her second son, Njiki did not have any more children.

After the stillborn births of her two daughters, Njiki became irritable and moody. What had started off as her tolerable sarcasm and youthful nonchalance soured into bitterness and unpredictable fits of short temper. She felt wronged by nature and yet, without Maribha to humour and counsel her, without the conspiracy of the older woman's company, she was alone, adrift in her own sorrow and confusion. The gossip in the air hardened her young heart. She was now the sole wife of her husband, this man called Gwanangara, but ironically, instead of condemning her co-wife and moving closer to him she resented him. She refused to feel guilty for having been the cause of the separation between Gwanangara and Maribha. She was deeply convinced that her husband had something to do with her loneliness, that it was he who made her feel like a widow, that despite all those thousands of years of existence, men were fools.

She would go gathering firewood in the forest, or collecting mushrooms or chakata or mashuku alone, singing old ballads to herself, and in the middle of a verse she would stop, fling a rotten shuku over her shoulder and laugh, 'Laugh, Laugh, Chibga's daughter. There is no laughter in the grave.' She aged twenty years in ten; became VaChivi, the lioness of Chivi.

***

Tachiona was a tall, lean, knock-kneed boy with a round face, obedient and companionable, but given to unpredictable bursts of tears; crying when he was happy or sad. He looked after cattle and goats; trapped birds and mice, and fought and swam with the other boys in the river.

Now those were the late 1920s. The Dutch Reformed Church had been setting up mission schools and churches in the district since the 1890s. White missionaries were hunting down boys of Tachiona's age and forcing them to learn to read, write and count.

One day when he was about fifteen Tachiona was herding livestock in the vlei with his peers when two familiar but now infamous white men on bicycles burst out of the forest and started rounding up the boys.

'Vanamuneri avo!'* *rang the cry, and the boys took to their heels, fleeing into the forest. Abandoning his whip, Tachiona scurried across the plain, but he was too late, one of the riders singled him out and followed him. Tachiona let out a cry,* 'Mhai! Mhai! Mhaiwe!'† *like someone who has seen a lion or a leopard and bolted homeward but still the rider followed him.*

Njiki heard her son's cry and came out with a pot in her hand, the young Dunge following behind her.

'Chii Tachi? Chiiko?'‡ *she gasped, seeing the white missionary riding up the path, straight into her yard.*

'Vanamuneri!' *Tachi yelled, helplessly.*

'Jump into the granary!' said his mother.

Tachiona hoisted himself up and squeezed into the granary hut through the small opening.

Njiki confronted the white man and said, 'What do you want with my son?'

'He must come to school,' *the white man replied, in a strangely intoned Shona.*

'And must you chase him like that?' *snarled Njiki, boldly, for no one spoke like that to white people and this was the closest she had ever stood to a white man.* 'What if he breaks his leg?'

'Your son must come to school,' *repeated the white man. He calmly stood his bicycle against the wall of the granary, rolled up the sleeves of his white shirt and dipped a hand through the small hole to reach for the boy. When Tachi felt a hand grabbing his foot he let out a scream, thrashing about in a sea of unshelled groundnuts, crashing and bumping his head against the mud walls of the small, dark granary.*

'Come out, child,' *said the priest, fishing out a leg.*

'Imwi, imwi, Vamuneri,'§ *if you hurt my son you'll bring me a new one,' Njiki swore.*

'Out, child!' *said the priest, fishing out another leg.*

---

* 'The white priests are coming here!'

† 'Mother, Mother, help me!'

‡ Who is it Chiko?

§ 'You, you, Mr Priest!'

'Mhai ndofa,'* bawled Tachi, kicking out at the cleric with his naked feet. The priest eased out one shoulder, pressed out a head. Tachi tumbled out and as soon his feet landed on the ground, he leapt behind his mother.

'Your child must come to school,' repeated the white man, undeterred by his now soiled white shirt or the small crowd gathering at the edge of the yard.

'Mhai ndofa kani,'† bawled Tachi, burrowing deeper into his mother's skirts. She slapped him on the head. 'Shut up, Tachi! Do you think white people bite like dogs?' Then, turning to the priest, she asked angrily, 'Why must you force our children to come to your school? My son will come to your school when he wants to do so. When I want him to do so.'

The priest took one step forward, aiming to extricate Tachi from his mother's skirts but stopped, surprised by Njiki's daring.

'Go on,' said Njiki. 'Go back to your school. I'll bring my boy to you when I want.'

Laughter rippled through the crowd and the priest, stunned and humiliated, mounted his bicycle and rode away.

When Gwanangara returned home from hunting rabbits, Njiki said to him, 'Baba Tachi, I think Tachi must go to school.'

'Why?'

'Are you going to have other people's children read and write your letters for you?'

'Who has been putting such silly ideas into your head, my wife?' said Gwanangara. Njiki told him about the incident with the priest and he laughed and said, 'But who will look after the cattle and goats if we send Tachi to school?'

'Dunge is old enough to go herding animals with the other boys.'

'What? A five-year-old boy?'

'He'll be six next harvest. He can learn. And besides, school takes up only half the day. You can go with Dunge to the vlei the first few days until he's used to it.'

'What will we do for relish if I go?'

'Who says there is no more derere or nyovhi in the fields?'

---

* 'Mother I'm dying!'

† 'Mother I'm dying. Help!'

Gwanangara laughed again. 'All right, Mai Tachi. Do as you please.'

And so next morning Njiki bathed Tachi in the chilly stream, dressed him up in his best patched shorts, dragged him, sniffling and whimpering, to the door of the classroom and said to the priest, 'I have brought him. You can have him,' and the priest smiled with incredulous delight. When Tachi pleaded, 'Mhai ndofa' she gave him a back-handed smack on the head, like a mother baboon hitting her young and said, 'Stay here!' and she walked back home to shell her groundnuts for the mouse and peanut-butter gravy while the priest found the still sobbing Tachi a place on the mud benches, between two big boys.

And so for a month Gwanangara accompanied Dunge to the grazing fields with the cattle and goats, and the rabbits and mice of Chivi got an unexpected truce.

And so Njiki, the wife of Gwanangara, became Njiki the Great, VaChivi, Mwana waChibga, the woman who dared to answer the white man back and tell him off, the first mother in those parts to willingly deliver her own son to the doors of the white man's school.

And so Tachiona Gwanangara disabused himself of his earlier conviction that schools were lairs where indescribable monsters lurked, and that the white priests were disguised dip-tank masters who cracked salted whips at you if you said three plus three is seven; he went to school and learnt to read, write and count. He recited the letters of the alphabet, practised scribbling his name in the dust with the big toe of his right foot and counting up to one hundred and seven – the next number, one hundred and eight, somehow caused problems and made him wrinkle up his forehead in confusion. He sat between two bearded men who were old enough to be married and gladly chanted:

Ona baba
Ona mai
Ona mai nababa

Ona Punha
Ona Pesvu
Ona Punha naPesvu

Cha Che Chi Cho Chu
Chari, Chigaro, Chuma
Hawa mashoko amunoziva zvino

Ahi emu e boyi
My nemu izi Tachi Gwanangara
Godi sevhu tha Kwini*!*

He was the reserve goalkeeper for Sub B class team and he en-joyed strutting about in the field and shaking his limbs singing:
Tinozunza zvose, mavoko namakumbo.***

He was at school for three years at most, then he dropped out, perhaps because there were no further classes to go to, or no teach-ers available, or because his parents could not afford the school fees.

***

Mkwasha Phiri, Babamukuru Tachiona's in-law, intersected, inter-sects, with our lives without warning, in a way that is to irrevocably affect us.

After taking Kelvin to his homestead and bringing him back to his senses, after making him eat, sleep, talk and laugh, he declares that there is a deeper crisis at work in our household, one that needs to be urgently solved. He sends word with mother that our family needs to be thoroughly cleansed, and its every inmate fortified against evil. Because of the gravity of our situation and the impressiveness with which Mkwasha Phiri treated Kelvin, the need for debate on the is-sue falls away and father, for once, readily complies. Mkwasha Phiri is summoned to Gweru. Tragedy blinds its victims to rationality.

And so on New Year's day Mkwasha Phiri arrives at the plot with his bags and his first wife, Aunt Mai Jonasi, our father and Uncle Tachiona's cousin. Now Mkwasha Phiri is the traditional in-law, the kind who will crouch on the ground as far away as he can from his mother-in-law (mothers-in-law must never be seen masticating) and clap his hands in respect loud and long even in a crowded market place, the sort that will refuse to eat and drink in the presence of the

---

* We shake everything, hands and legs.

revered mother of his wife. He is sharply aware of his two disparate roles, one as the in-law, and the other as the professional healer.

After supper we assemble on the floor of the lounge, like so many chickens come home to roost from our various pecking fields, our jobs, schools and colleges, all we Dunge's children, mother and Maiguru Mazvita, Mai Nda, Rindai's wife. Mkwasha Phiri sits on a stool in front of the fireplace with his tools on one side and his wife on the other. He ties a white cloth over his shoulder, plants the head of his *tsvimbo* under his chin, closes his eyes with deliberate slowness and, mumbling a few indistinguishable words, summons his *mudzimu*. He mixes snuff and water in a wooden bowl, drinks from the bowl and then blows a fine spray over us. He shudders as the spirit possesses him.

He cuts *nyora* with a razor blade on our necks, chests, hands and feet and rubs the now familiar black powder into the cuts. Thank goodness AIDS is still unknown. While we sit bleeding and smarting, waiting for the next move, Kelvin suddenly reaches for Mkwasha Phiri's *tsvimbo* and tries to break it on his knee. Unalarmed, Mkwasha Phiri takes back the *tsvimbo*, dips the thin end of it into a pot of mud and holds it up to Kelvin's face. Kelvin flinches as the stick is pushed into his mouth but slowly, mesmerised like a chameleon, he eats the mud from the stick. Mkwasha Phiri feeds him the stick for a while, lets him swallow the stuff till he is subdued, then lays the *tsvimbo* at his feet. He pinches a yellowish powder into twisted bits of khaki paper which he hands to mother, with instructions for making porridge for everyone. He speaks in ChiChewa with a slow, unaffected ease and his wife translates into ChiKaranga for us.

'You do not do things together with your brother,' he says to my father. 'Your brother Tachiona does his own thing in Chivi in the middle of the night and you sit here bathing in your electric lights doing nothing. Your household is open to *mamhepo*, evil spirits cast away from other homesteads. Your homestead is the open, steep slope down which rocks will roll unimpeded, crushing the heads of your children. Your *midzimu* love you and have showered you with many blessings but they have been blindfolded like mules and led astray by your enemies. Now your *midzimu* do not know good from evil. Your spirits are like the mother hen which drinks the yolk of its own eggs. Your enemies work day and night to harm you and they are driving your *midzimu* ahead of them and hiding behind them in order to confuse you. Now even your *midzimu* have been turned against each other.'

'What needs to be done?' Rindai interjects, casting an accusing eye at father, then glancing back at the medium. 'We are tired of illness!'

'Your *midzimu* need to be cleansed,' says Mkwasha Phiri.

'What about these illnesses?'

'You need to eat herbs and bathe in special waters.'

'Can you do that?' says Rindai. 'How much will it cost?'

'Baba Nda, imi!' Mazvita protests at this irreverence. *'Ndo zvadii kanhi? Ko mukamirawo mukaterera?'* *

'There is a lot to be done. You must work together with the people in Chivi. First, you have to sort out his case.' Mkwasha Phiri points his muddied stick at Kelvin. My brother casts his head quickly aside, away from the stick, his face stony. The medium continues, unperturbed. 'You need to brew beer and let the *midzimu* speak their wish. You must act fast. But even before that, we need to fortify this plot against evil. Why don't you listen to others for once?'

And so at midnight Mkwasha Phiri, father, Rindai and I go out to plant things around the plot. Using a hoe, I dig holes at the corners of the plot, by the gate posts, behind the garage, in the chicken run and at the base of the windmill. Into each hole Mkwasha Phiri drops two smooth egg-shaped stones, the kind you find in the bed of a river, and Rindai covers up each hole up with his farmer's shoes. I think to myself, what a bizarre sight we must seem, three men led by a seeming prophet in a white robe, whispering, digging and planting stones in the dark!

In the morning Mkwasha Phiri is himself again – unpossessed. Like a true son-in-law he wakes up before dawn to weed the maize crop. I join him at daybreak and we converse in ChiKaranga as the January sun starts to sting our backs.

'So when did you become a *n'anga?'* I ask.

He stops to knock the soil off a thick clump of grass and replies,

---

* What's the matter Baba Nda? Why don't you stop and listen to others.

58

matter-of-factly, 'Two years ago.'

'How did you become one?'

'I became sick, with a painful chest and swollen feet. I couldn't move for a year. Your aunt, my wife, tried everything – hospitals, doctors and *mapostori* but nothing worked. No one could say what the problem was. I was a staunch member of the Seventh Day Adventist Church and did not believe in *n'angas* or *midzimu*. One day as I lay sick in bed an old, old man came to me in a dream and said, ''You have to accept me if you want to get well. Brew beer if you want to be cured of this illness.'' This man was my father's dead grandfather but I didn't know that at the time. I told your aunt about it and we discussed it. My parents and grandparents were dead and my last living relatives were in Malawi. I was born in Zimbabwe and have never been to Malawi. We consulted an old woman in Mberengwa who is good at these matters and she agreed to help us. We brewed the beer and at the *bira* I started writhing and foaming at the mouth and speaking fluently in deep ChiChewa. I had never spoken in deep ChiChewa before, let alone fluently. The spirit of my father's grandfather was possessing me. After that *bira* I recovered my health, gave up going to church and started treating sick people.'

'Do you think someone is trying to possess Kelvin?'

'That's possible. But it's also possible it could be an enemy hiding behind the guise of your *midzimu*. Or a jealous relative tying up and gagging the *mudzimu* so that it cannot speak.'

'So how do we know?'

'If you brew the beer the *mudzimu* itself will speak.'

At this point Kelvin comes out to the field to join us, walking with his slow, drug-dazed but determined step, a hoe on his shoulder. Mkwasha Phiri and I change the topic of our conversation.

***

When he dropped out of school Tachiona was eighteen, just old enough to be conscripted into the labour camps. He had to find money to pay tax as required by the district commissioner. He was forced to work with the other men on the roads, cutting down and destumping trees, smashing and hauling rocks and digging drainage trenches, from dawn to dusk. The men lived in tin shacks and were fed sadza and salted beans. In winter the chilly wind whistled through the shacks; in summer the men ploughed knee-deep in the red mud, like oxen. They were paid very little and were allowed to visit home only once in three months to see their parents or wives, and then only for two days. On his third visit home Tachi, lean as a gum tree pole, wept openly and said to his mother, 'Mother, I'm not going back there.'

His father Gwanangara was coughing blood, sitting at the fire in the December sun, covered by goat skins. Njiki planted a large wooden plate of boiled mushrooms between the two men and said, 'And if you run away from the road camps, Tachi, who will be there to answer the white man? Do you think there is much life left in your father? Who will look after this home? Dunge? And besides, where will you go if you run away from the road camps? Where will you get money to pay your taxes?'

Next morning Tachi woke up at the second crow of the cock, fetched his goatskins and knobkerrie and left his father's household. He did not go back to the road camps. He walked to Shabani, braving the leopards and hyenas, and asking for food, like a vagabond, in strangers' homes. When he got to Shabani they gave him a vest, a pair of shorts and a helmet, and he built himself a small grass hut in the compound. Mine work was hard, no better than the roads; the white asbestos dust settled in his chest but he got a few shillings at the end of the month. He met people from other places, strangers from other countries – Nyasaland, Northern Rhodesia, Portuguese East Africa – who did not speak ChiKaranga and they taught him songs, languages, customs and stories from other lands. He had a few friends, one of whom lived near his village and through whom he sent word home to say he was alive, but he rarely heard from his people.

He must have worked for two or three years and when he had saved enough he bought a blue cotton dress for his mother and a woollen blanket for his father and set off, homeward, to see his parents. But when he arrived people gathered round him wailing and shaking his hand and his mother was wearing a black dress – he knew at once that his father had died. He threw himself in the dust, crying, 'Mhai ndofa! Mhai ndofa khani!'* and Njiki sobbed back,

* 'Mother I'm dead, I'm dead, I say.'

60

'Tachi-weeee, Tachi-weeee!' *After the chorus of cries had relented a little they led him to the fresh mound of earth; he knelt down and planted a small stone at the head of the mound and an uncle said, 'You are the man of the house now, Tachi, you have to be strong.' His father's elder wife, Maribha, was there and his half-brother Chari, Maribha's one and only son, was there too, only much older, with a beard, a wife and a little son. Tachi greeted his brother Chari curtly, begrudgingly, the quarrel between his father's two wives having got the better of him. Nothing but jealousy and bitter words had ever been exchanged between them, as a result of which Chari had named his son Tavengwa* – 'they hate us.'*

When the crowd and the crying and the formalities let up a little he presented his mother with the dress; the blanket would have to be given to one of his uncles, later. His mother thanked him warmly and he grinned, proud tears streaming down his face.

'So when will you be back? Your brother Chari and his mother were only here for the funeral and now there's only Dunge to look after the livestock and help with the housework. And Dunge must go to school.'

He could not stay long because he was wanted at the mine.

On the day of his departure his mother cooked him a chicken.

'Thank you mother, but no, I don't eat chicken any more.'

'What do you mean you don't eat chicken any more?' Njiki demanded, alarmed and hurt.

'I mustn't eat chicken.'

'Since when did a Gwanangara not eat chicken? I knew you were up to no good, Tachi, going off to that mine and living among people with strange customs. What fetish did they give you that demands that you don't eat chicken? And don't think I didn't notice the nyora *on your head. Where did you get the* nyora *from? What did they put in your bloodstream?* Zvatichaona pamusha pano!* † *You, Tachi, are going to bring a curse on us all.'*

Tachiona did not say anything. He shrugged his shoulders guiltily and asked his brother Dunge to fetch him his blanket and knobkerrie.

***

---

† 'We shall see unusual things in this homestead.'

Sisi Ratidzo, Ratidzo Gwanangara, Babamukuru Tachiona's daughter, the new Mhokoshi, Mhokoshi the hunter, dances at the front of the assembly. She challenges the song with a mocking sideways prance, and takes an admonitory, eagle-eyed sweep of the gathering. When the drums bark she suddenly leaps into the air like a warrior, and, in mid-air, hurls a spear at a lion. She stabs once, stabs twice, lands lithely like a tiger on the mud floor and spins round so that her black cloth flies to her face. She shakes the raining sweat off her face. Kelvin totters beside her, heavy, restrained and drug-dazed, a white sheet strapped over his shoulder. He takes each step carefully, weakly aping her. Immediately behind Sisi Ratidzo and Kelvin is a half circle of the Gwanangara children – Chari's child, Tachi's children, Dunge's children. We, Dunge's children, we townies, we Dutch-Reformed offspring to whom these tunes and rhythms are completely new, are bouncing, twisting and shaking, earnestly, totally out of step, as if we are at a disco, but no one minds. Everyone seems to be enjoying themselves and we try not to be too solemn. The hut is thick with dust and the smell of the cow-dung floor, heavy with a sense of purpose and full of people: neighbours, well-wishers, relatives called from afar – uncles, aunts, cousins, nephews, nieces, in-laws; names long lost to time and distance but now transformed into living faces, rhythmical figures, dancing, singing, sweating in unison in the flickering yellow light of the oil lamp.

Mhondoro dzinomwa muna Zambezi
Mhondoro dzinomwa muna Save
Mhondoro dzinomwa muna Zambezi
*Mhondoro dzinomwa muna Save**

Babamukuru Tachi sits on a mud bench near the door of the house with other grey-haired men. They're drinking seven-days brew from a large mug and taking snuff, Babamukuru occasionally elbowing his urine bags into place. Father sits sombrely in his grey overalls two men away from him, touching the mug to his lips and discreetly passing it on when it is his turn to drink. Mkwasha Phiri squats on the floor with other *vakwasha*, those of his rank, a vague, distracted look on his face. The women stand singing and clapping opposite the men – there's mother between two women and Maiguru Mai

---

* Great spirits drink from the rivers.

62

Ratidzo kneeling over her pots, serving beer and water. There's the woman with the shaved head from the adjoining yard who confided to mother, who'd arrived earlier in the week to help prepare for the ceremony, 'Mai Rindai, let me bite your ear a little. Your Maiguru, Mai Ratidzo, Tachiona's wife, is laughing behind your back and saying, "*He, hede!* The white people from the town have finally come to the bush to brew beer and dance to drums!" Beware of her. I don't think she means well to you.'

And there's Baba Tariro, Mzukuru Baba Tariro in his corduroy shirt and denims, closing the door of his Mazda in the moonlit yard, yawning and squeezing his face through the doorway to have a look.

'It won't be long now,' says Mhokoshi, Sekuru Ratidzo Mhokoshi pinching snuff onto Kelvin's palm. 'It's very, very close. It won't be long now.'

But Kelvin does not speak. He doesn't fall, writhe and foam at the mouth as he is expected to, gasping out who it is inside him, who it is has been making him sick, who it is wanting to inhabit him, who it is summoning people from their fields in January, when weeds are choking the millet: whose name, what name, what reasons and why?

Kelvin stamps on the floor with his heavy, drug-dazed feet, like a baby elephant, and does not speak. It is hard to dance when you've been taking sedatives.

'It won't be long now,' says Mhokoshi, and the women start another song.

Mhokoshi sits down on a stool and the singing fades away. Everyone in the hut sits down. Mhokoshi drinks deeply from a mug and clears his-her throat to speak. Everybody listens.

'It won't be long now,' he-she says, nodding at Kelvin. 'The spirit is very close now. Meanwhile we can talk. Tachi, are all my grandchildren here?'

Babamukuru Tachi is startled to attention and he answers back, 'Eh, Sekuru, they are all here.'

'I don't see Dzenga, your first son, here, Tachi,' says Mhokoshi.

'I sent word to him Sekuru, but he didn't ...'

'That son of yours needs to be watched, Tachi. And Dunge, are all your children here?'

'Yes, Sekuru.'

'You did well to come, Dunge. No one can escape from his people for ever. Now we will teach you everything, show you the way. Are Chari's children here?'

Our cousin Tavengwa Gwanangara, son of Maribha, the cousin we left at our dew-in-the-morning home in Gokwe when we moved to the plot house, answers, 'I am here, Sekuru.'

'Did you bring your family, Muzukuru?'

'My wife is here with me, Sekuru,' Tavengwa replies. 'But it was too far for the children to come.'

'I see,' says Mhokoshi. 'And is everything well with you in the home your father Dunge left you, Tavengwa?'

'That I can only hear from you, Sekuru. You who can see everything from above.'

'Is your wife well, child?'

'I think so, Sekuru.'

'And your wife's young sister, your muramu who came to live with you in the home your Babamunini Dunge left you, is everything all right with her?'

'I think so, Sekuru.'

'Let me give your ear a little bite, child. I know as your forebear I must not be a snake which spits venom into your food but I cannot watch fire consume your huts.'

'But what do you mean, Sekuru?'

'This, child. That everything is not well with your *muramu*. There are ill winds that have followed her into your father Dunge's house. *Mamhepo*. Your *muramu* needs to be taken away at once, back to her people, to be cleansed.'

'We heard it said before that my wife was a witch,' says Tavengwa, his voice rising bitterly. 'Right here, in this very hut, just a few years ago. So now it's my muramu who has a problem.'

'Tavengwa!' Father admonishes him from the bench.

'Nobody in this family ever loved me,' Tavengwa continues, unrestrained. 'My grandmother Maribha was called a witch. My father Chari was driven out of his father's home. Why else was I named Tavengwa? Why would anyone give a child a name like this?'

'Tavengwa!' Babamukuru Tachiona shouts from the bench, and Mhokoshi shakes his-her head in silent despair.

'Don't think I don't know.' Tavengwa contines. 'The whole world knows it. You hated my father and mother and you hate me. And now, though you took me out of here and dumped me in Gokwe, you hate me even more. You banished me, didn't you? You wanted my miserable face out of the way. And now you can't even allow me to breathe a little fresh air.'

'Who taught this child to answer back when his elders speak?' Mhokoshi interjects. 'You, Dunge?'

'Tavengwa, listen!' urges father.

'Come, Mai Hamu,' says Tavengwa, beckoning angrily to his wife among the women. 'Let's catch the first bus and be gone. We have no business listening to folk tales like these.'

'Tavengwa, sit down and listen to your elders,' father urges him, but it is too late, for he is already stepping through the crowd, towards the door, his flustered wife, Mai Hamunyari, behind him. Outside a door opens, shuts and feet hurry away into the darkness.

'Some children spin fire in their own eyes, ' says Mhokoshi.

'Imi Vamutazviona,' Maiguru Mai Ratidzo, from among the women, remonstrates with her husband. 'How can you let them go like this into the night?' But Babamukuru Tachiona pinches snuff into his nostrils, flicks some towards the door and slaps his palms clear of the dust.

'The troubles of this family are many,' Mhokoshi resumes, after moments of suitable silence. 'We in the winds are watching all the time but you people of flesh and blood do not heed the signs we show you.'

'What do you mean, Sekuru?' Babamukuru Tachiona asks.

'These signs that we make, don't you see them?'

'Tell us, Sekuru.'

'Sometimes we pinch a child on the arm just to give you a sign. You Dunge, how many times have I pinched your children's arms these past sixteen moons?'

'Explain to us, Sekuru,' says father.

'First, I pinched this one on the arm,' Mhokoshi announces, tapping my sister Vimbai on the head with his stick. Vimbai the *menija* of 33 Hoffman Street, wearer of burning curtains. 'You couldn't understand why she hiccupped and bled through the nose for two days.' Next, the stick on Rindai's head. 'And I pinched you on the night of your wedding. Don't think it's your wife or bad neighbours who did it to you. I wouldn't allow them to touch you. It was me, and only me, who did it.' Next, the stick flies onto Kelvin. 'And this one was pinched by several hands.'

'Please explain, Sekuru?' Babamukuru Tachiona interjects.

'This one was pinched by several hands,' Mhokoshi, Ratidzo Mhokoshi repeats, shaking his-her head. 'When I held up his arm it was puffed up and there were already several sores on it and I said, "Child, did mosquitoes bite you?" and he trembled and cried. I pinched him and I did not pinch him.'

'What do you mean, Sekuru?' father demands, drawn now into the intrigue. Kelvin swallows, his head trembling silently under Mhokoshi's stick.

'You're a child, Dunge, and your head is as empty as a gourd. You ought to come to your people more often so that you can learn the language of your elders.'

'But why would a good father pinch a child on the arm?' father asks again.

Mhokoshi throws his head back and laughs, two or three aged heads guffaw from the bench. 'I pinched him and I did not pinch him,' Mhokoshi repeats, placing the stick back at his-her feet. 'He is the chosen one, the arm with the sweet blood which attracts mosquitoes. He shall himself tell us before this ceremony is over who pinched him.'

'What do you want of us, Sekuru?' Babamukuru Tachiona asks, in an attempt to bring some purpose to the situation.

Mhokoshi stares up at the sooty roof of the hut and says, 'I want my weapons back.'

'But your real weapons were never found, Sekuru. You died in the mountains. Your brothers and sisters bought you others in their place.' Babamukuru Tachiona retorts, speaking almost familiarly and conspiratorially with this voice from the other world. Or so we thought.

'You know what you did with those new weapons, Tachiona? You and your mother Njiki?'

Babamukuru Tachiona's face falters in the lamplight and he

promises recklessly, 'We can pay for that, Sekuru. We can find you new weapons, and more.'

'*Imi Vamutazviona,*' Maiguru Mai Ratidzo interjects from the female half of the hut. 'Stop making promises you can't fulfil!'

'Yes, we can find the weapons *and* a shield,' Babamukuru Tachiona says. 'I know somebody who makes shields as they were made in the past.'

'Do you have a beast to sell to raise money to buy the weapons?' Maiguru Mai Ratidzo shrieks at her husband. 'And would you know what to do with the weapons if you got them?'

'You said it was you who pinched us and made us sick,' Rindai challenges Mhokoshi, with startling directness. 'Tell us, now, will you make these illnesses go away?'

Mhokoshi stares at the roof, untouched by Rindai's brashness, and repeats, 'I want my weapons back.' He shudders, closes his eyes and leaves this human pocket that has contained him. He floats away through the open door into the night, into the forest and the mountains where he belongs.

Babamukuru accompanies Sisi Ratidzo out of the hut and then comes back in. A woman starts a song and the drumming and dancing resumes. Outside the east is aglow with the promise of dawn and sleep is tugging at my eyes.

Still, Kelvin stamps on the floor with his heavy, drug-dazed feet, like a baby elephant, and does not speak.

***

In the morning Sisi Ratidzo, in an ordinary dress, serves tea and bread to the gathering with the other women. Half the people are gone, and the remainder sit or lie under the eaves of the huts, trying to catch some sleep. Mkwasha Phiri is administering some medicinal herbs to Rindai and Kelvin, behind the grain hut. Father sits with Babamukuru Tachiona and an elderly neighbour under a mango tree, discussing family matters.

'Godifiri!' Babamukuru Tachiona calls me over when he notices me. 'Come and sit here, my son.'

I sit under the mango tree and greet them.

'You are my heir, Godifiri,' Babamukuru announces, putting his hand on my shoulder. Hiccup. 'When I die I want you to take everything I own.' Hiccup. 'My huts, my cattle, my goats, my plough, everything, Godifiri.'

'You hear that Godifiri,' laughs the elderly neighbour, 'You'll have to take this mango tree, and that paw-paw tree too, and this kraal and this arid soil.'

'My clothes, my blankets, my snuff, my knobkerries. Everything, you hear.'

'This broken stool, that blanket with holes ... and shouldn't we give him your urine bags too, Tachi?'

'You think I am joking? Here I am, making my will and the two of you witnessing it.' Hiccup. Sob. Sudden stream of tears coursing down the black unwashed face. Elbow the urine bags into place.

'And should we squeeze a bucketful of tears from your eyes to give him too, before you die, Tachi?'

'No one else will touch my belongings as long as I am Tachi Tazviona Gwanangara.'

'And why are you choosing this one and not the others, Tachi?'

'Because he came to find me in the hospital where they fixed me up with these plastics ten years ago and he said, ''Babamukuru, here is twenty dollars.'''

'So for twenty dollars you will disinherit all the other boys – Dzenga, Jonah, Tavengwa, Rindai? Shall we give him your name too, before you die?'

'I have spoken.'

'Tachi has spoken,' says the elderly neighbour. 'You may go now, boy.'

Should old people's words be taken seriously? What was Uncle Tachiona scheming?

After the morning meal our cousin Jonah, Babamukuru Tachiona's third born, invites me to go and have a bath in the Runde river.

It's an hour's walk and the dry unploughed fields that we cross should have been green with crops but it's been a bad year and the rains are late. Chivi is anyway a dry, cruel district and good rains are the exception rather than the norm. I wonder why people choose to live in this harsh environment, how the land apportionment act could so callously banish people to this desert, why Babamukuru Tachiona declined to move with us to our fertile, more sustaining dew-in-the-morning village in Gokwe, fifteen years ago.

My cousin Jonah is a quiet fellow who does not speak much. He's a year younger than me. An ex-combatant who fought to free Zimbabwe. Before leaving for Mozambique, he had lived with us at 33 Hoffman Street, working temporarily in a smelting factory. He has just returned from the independence celebrations in Harare and is waiting to be recruited into the new national army. When we were young, long before there was tension between our families, he slipped off into the bush without warning. At one time we corresponded regularly with all the enthusiasm of cousins who like each other. But now he is strangely reserved, speaking with an unfamiliar ChiManyika accent in an odd, high-pitched voice. He won't be drawn to explain how he acquired the accent or how he fared in the war. I am wise enough not to interrogate him but I suspect he was operating in the eastern district of the country, where new idioms and vocabulary grafted themselves into his speech. He has returned home with his spoils: black denims and a small transistor radio that he listens to endlessly. I wonder if the impressive watch on his wrist was slipped off the hand of some dead white soldier. I wonder how many close shaves he had with death and how many people he killed and if Babamukuru Tachiona took him for ritual cleansing after his return.

The Save River is dry. I wonder where the hippos and crocodiles that once inhabited it have vanished to, or if perhaps they died off, one by one, but Jonah finds us a pool in the river bed, behind a clump of rocks. The water is green and stagnant; he strips, wades in up to his knees and starts soaping himself. He assures me that the water is OK and that no women come here as this is a designated bathing place for men, but I am not persuaded to join him. Perhaps I should be sociable and forget the health risk, but I am wary of bilharzia, hookworms and what have you. This pond is a sad comparison to Lulu's copious clear stream in our Gokwe village. I sit tight in my trousers, waiting for him to finish.

Suddenly, Jonah bolts out of the pool, stark naked, and charges at me. 'Take cover! Take cover!' he yells, pushing my head down to the ground, behind a bush. He is breathing like a train. He flings his muscular black body onto the bare ground next to me.

'What is it, Jonah?'

'Quiet!' he whispers. 'They're there, behind the rocks.'

I raise my head very slightly and look towards the pool. I see nobody, nothing except the shallow water and the rocks. Jonah pushes my head down again. I can smell him, all body musk and carbolic.

'The water,' he gasps. 'Red with blood.'

He begins to sob, his body shaking and heaving over me. Scared and confused, I listen, bewildered. Then he sits up, dries his face, holds his head in his hands and breathes deeply, gently. After a few minutes, he stands up slowly and goes down to fetch his clothes.

***

When we reach home in the afternoon we find everybody in a state of panic. Jonah's young brother, our cousin Taurai, who was out herding cattle has come running home to report that a young bull in the small family herd has inexplicably collapsed and died in the forest. It feels like an omen.

Portent number one.

***

His only bull has died. Threatening to hang himself, Babamukuru makes for the mountains. Father and the elderly neighbour, fearing he really means it, have gone after him.

'How can they have a *bira* without slaughtering a beast?' Jonah says to no one in particular, shaking his head sadly. 'Something is amiss. The soil is not happy.'

It strikes me only then that there has not been any meat served on this occasion, one at which people were supposed to eat meat till their teeth ached.

Maiguru Mai Ratidzo orders that the bull be skinned and the meat brought home. Jonah and I go to the forest and find the bull indeed lying on its back with its feet in the air, freshly dead, with its eyes open. A group of herd boys are already waiting on the scene, obviously excited by the prospect of meat. Jonah takes charge. The bull is skinned, chopped up into sizeable pieces and carted home. When we return just before sunset, Babamukuru has also come home, but his distress is palpable – as only those who've nurtured a beast in

70

harsh conditions can understand. Trying to find reason in his misfortune he asks again and again, 'What if such evil had struck a human being, and not a beast? What if this had chosen a person?' Father, his face downcast, walks round and round the cattle pen, singing strange ancient songs I have never heard him sing before.

That evening we have a supper of sadza and fresh beef and the *bira* resumes. We are not done yet. Kelvin, or whoever it is inside Kelvin, has not spoken and has to speak – the mystery must be sung, danced and sweated out. The hut fills again with people. Mhokoshi returns and leads the singing and dancing. Kelvin stamps the mud floor stiffly, heavily with his bare feet. I check with mother if he has taken his sedatives and she discreetly confirms that he has done so. Tranquillisers are weighing him down. Everybody dances less energetically now, feet are strained from last night's performance and voices are slurred but Mhokoshi urges us on.

'Are you tired now?' he-she challenges us, shaking the sweat off his-her face. 'Your things are very, very close. It won't be long now.'

But Kelvin does not speak. He doesn't fall or writhe or foam at the mouth and say who it is has been holding up this ceremony for two nights, robbing a hut full of people of their sleep.

***

By the second cock-crow half the heads are nodding into their laps and the hut resounds with a cacophony of snores. A lonely determined voice tries to pick out a broken tune. The drum falters to a stop. Mhokoshi sits down and surveys his-her shrivelled flock. Babamukuru Tachiona leans his head against the wall, saliva dribbling from his mouth.

'*Imi Vamutazviona imi!*' Maiguru Mai Ratidzo's voice calls from the female half of the hut, wakeful as ever. '*Vamutazviona*, wake up!'

It's time for Mhokoshi to go.

Babamukuru Tachiona starts awake, looks around, yawns, dribbles, elbows his urine bags back into place, staggers to his feet and escorts Sisi Ratidzo out to the yard and the purple dawn. Today, I painfully remember the scene and wonder who duped who, or if we were simply overwhelmed by emotion and exhaustion.

***

We leave next morning with dubious goodbyes. Our departure is clouded by uncertainty. This time, thankfully, there is no stinking leg of bull in the car at our feet. Babamukuru Tachiona sprinkles snuff round Baba Tariro's Mazda and says, as we reverse onto the path, 'I am Tachiona. No one sees anything as long as I am alive.'

As soon as we alight from Baba Tariro's car after the long, weary trip home, mother, Shuvai, Vimbai and Tendai's eyes puff up and their faces swell like footballs – like people bitten by a swarm of bees.

Portent number two.

6

O *ne day when he was six years old Dunge Gwanangara woke up*
in the morning and said to his mother, Njiki, 'I dreamt I was in
a big white house sitting at a large table. I was surrounded by white
people. We were eating food together.'

'What kind of food were you eating?' Njiki asked.

'Meat.'

'What kind of meat?'

'I can't say. It looked like chicken, but also like goat.'

'You were surrounded by white people?'

'Yes.'

'Were there other children with you?'

'No. I was the only child there.'

Njiki knew Dunge had seen white people before – the priest who
rode after Tachiona wanting to take him to school, the same man
who had accepted Tachiona into the school, and the one or two ma-
joni, policemen, who had come to the village. But she knew it was
bad to dream about white people. It was a sinister omen. Gatherings
in a dream – weddings, beer parties, harvest feasts and so on – were
equally ominous. They portended funerals. And to dream about meat
– or any flesh – was terrible: it contained an irrepressible whiff of
putrefying human corpses. But Njiki knew her son was not given to
having unusual dreams and she decided to keep the matter to her-
self.

A few days later Dunge reported another dream.

'I dreamt of those white people again.'

'What were they doing?'

'They were sitting around the table, talking. I tried to talk to them, but my voice failed me. They laughed. But one of them came over and gave me a piece of chicken with mhiripiri on it. When I tasted the meat the mhiripiri was so strong that I sneezed. They laughed at me again. Another gave me a vest, a pair of shorts and shoes.'

'What were they wearing?'

'Some of them were dressed like vanamuneri. Others were dressed like majoni. The one who gave me clothes was darker than the others and he was wearing a white shirt and a chitirobho on his neck.'

Now white majoni were considered bad too, perhaps for the practical reason that they came to haul you off to the stocks for not paying your taxes, or for some petty crime or other. But majoni in a dream – the meaning eluded Njiki. As for the vest and shorts and shoes, that was beyond her.

'Go to the dare and tell your dream to the elders,' she said.

The elders were sitting in a semicircle, roasting maize. His father was among them. Dunge crouched on his knee, and greeted them.

'Du-nge-dunge-dunge-dunge,' an elder cackled familiarly like a fowl. 'What brings you here so early, child?'

'I came to tell you about my dreams,' Dunge began, and falteringly repeated what he had told his mother. The men roared with laughter and teased him.

'Perhaps you are going to be a bhurakuwacha when you grow up,' said one, 'and arrest us all for not paying our poll tax.'

'You'll be a teacher. Tichara Dunge,' said another.

'No, a priest.'

'You'll wear a vest and shorts and shoes and be a kukara for white people.'

'Go away Kukara Dunge, and prepare a mhiripiri stew for us!'

Dunge fled from the dare, humiliated, and returned to his mother, who had overheard the comments.

'Idiot men,' Njiki swore to herself, 'Idiot men, thinking they know everything. Seka hako mwana waChibga.'*

***

---

* Laugh, laugh Chibgwa's child.

74

Dunge did not go to school until he was twelve and by that time his brother Tachiona was already in Shabani, working in the mines.

He, Dunge, did not have to be dragged to the classroom door by anyone. On the contrary, he kept asking his parents that he be allowed to go to school. When he was given permission he washed himself in the river, scrubbed the cracked heels of his feet with a stone, put on his best shorts, and presented himself, bare-chested and shoeless, to the head teacher.

He was a very enthusiastic pupil and was soon made class monitor. It was he who carried the books to the teacher's house, dusted the chalkboard and wrote down the names of those who were late, or made noise.

He loved all the subjects. He was fast at mental arithmetic and sums, accurate at spelling and his handwriting was neat. Scripture he loved, and he went home and recited to his mother wondrous tales of Joseph, Mary and Baby Jesus, Shadreck, Misheck and Abednigo, Daniel in the lion's den and Jonah in the belly of a fish. By that time there were black teachers at the mission school, and there was no separation between church and school matters – school was church and church was school. By the time he finished Sub B and proceeded to Standard 1 he had already started his Boka 1 Katikazi class, getting ready to be confirmed and later baptised in the Dutch Reformed Church. Best of all he loved reading – he was smitten by the magic of words printed on paper, the inexplicable connection between print, sound and meaning. He was a voracious reader – he would chase the whirlwind to catch a flying piece of paper just to read what was on it. And he relished reading letters aloud to his father, or writing them on his behalf.

Thus he went through Sub A, Sub B, Standard 1 and Standard 2. During his Standard 3 year his father Gwanangara died and he had to drop out for a while because there was nobody to pay his school fees. His brother Tachiona was earning very little and was rarely home. His half-brother Chari could not be counted on to help. Luckily, a sympathetic uncle offered to patronise him until he completed his Standard 3 year. After that he had to return home to help his mother with the work in the fields.

He badly missed school, but he attended church regularly. He *sang tenor in the church choir. He worked hard on their small farm: ploughing, planting, weeding, harvesting and looking after the small herd of livestock so that his mother never needed to beg. He rarely left home, but on one occasion his mother sent him with a letter to a* muzukuru *of his late father. This* muzukuru *was a renowned* n'anga *and his huts were full of horns, animal skins and the other parapher-nalia of his trade. During the few days he stayed at the* muzukuru's *place Dunge heard thudding, squeaking and muttering voices in the hut in which he slept and one night he woke up screaming, con-vinced that a hand on his throat had choked him. He was relieved to return to his mother at the end of his stay.*

***

I am sitting in the staffroom, marking a pile of exercise books, when I see Baba Mhlanga, Maiguru Rindai's father-in-law, waiting for me at the door. I put down my red pen and get up to greet him.

'Is everything all right, Father?' I ask after exchanging greetings. He does not say much; he tilts his face morosely. He lives in Harare but he has never visited me before, neither at my flat nor at the school where I teach. I repeat, perhaps too soon, 'Is everything all right?'

'Everything is fine,' he responds, then adds with customary under-statement, 'Well, not quite.'

We move away from the door into the privacy of the car park. He is a short, strong man with powerful, experienced hands. I am a foot taller than him, lanky and awkward in my suit and tie.

After a moment, he says, 'Your brother, Baba Nda, has been taken ill.'

Where? How? When? My mind races. And why is it Baba Mhlanga who is telling me this?

'He's been taken to Harare Central Hospital by ambulance. I think it's best you come.'

'What happened? Is he all right?'

'He's OK. Just – not well. I think you should call your father and ask him to come up right away.'

He's all right. Well, not quite. Come over right away. I try to ap-pear calm. Is it the usual thing? Or an accident perhaps? But why the note of anxiety? I ask the headmaster for permission to leave. He looks at me over the rims of his aged bone spectacles. 'But the visit-

76

ing hour is only at one o'clock. Can't you attend to your classes first?'
Of course. The visiting hour is at lunchtime. It's only ten-thirty in
the morning. I am new to the school, new to the profession. I have a
class in thirty minutes. I'm teaching Macbeth. Rindai is 'all right'.
He can wait.

Baba Mhlanga hurries away to catch a bus and leaves me to follow later. I'm nervous throughout the lesson. I make my students
dramatise the murder scene. It contains strange echoes. Time creeps.

I arrive at the hospital soon after one. Rindai is in the corner
of Ward D2. He is surrounded: Maiguru Mazvita, Baba and Mai
Mhlanga, Mai Mhlanga's younger sister and her husband, Mai
Mhlanga's youngest brother, Maiguru Mazvita's brother Tobias.
Some faces I do not know. Women sit on the benches. Men stand
behind them. They stand aside to let me through. He is on a drip.
His breath is shallow, raspy. His eyes are closed. He's unconscious.

'What happened?' I ask, looking at Maiguru Mazvita. She's wearing a coat over her nightdress. Bedroom slippers. She starts sobbing.
Her mother's younger sister pats her hand kindly. There is a khaki
file at the foot of the bed. I finger it cautiously. A young nurse comes
in and sees me. She takes the file away before I can read it.

'I'm his brother.'

The nurse shakes her head and leaves. Nobody says anything.

'What happened, Maiguru?'

Mai Mhlanga says, 'Come, Mazvita, tell your *muramu* what happened.' Silently my sister-in-law hands me a piece of paper covered
in Rindai's writing.

My dearest Mazvita

I'm sorry to do this to you, but I feel there is no hope left for
me and that I have become a burden to everyone. It's time I gave
everybody a little peace of mind. Thank you all for trying.
Please look after Nda and after yourself. I leave everything to
you. I love you very much.

God bless you.

Yours

Rindai

Maiguru Mazvita picks up two large empty bottles of Rindai's
pills. Three months' supply of phenobarb.

***

I phone father. It's a task that only I can undertake, as the oldest Gwanangara around. There hasn't been time for Maiguru Mazvita to do anything. Besides, what would she say? How would she broach this embarrassing subject? I call father at work. He's busy with some customers and takes a while to answer. The phone steadily swallows my coins. His voice drops when he recognises mine. Why should it always be me delivering the unhappy news? I can feel the pain in his silence, the dilemma in his hesitation. It is month-end. A very busy time at the store. He promises to come as soon as his boss lets him off.

At lunchtime the following day there is the same crowd at the hospital. Rindai is conscious, staring at the ceiling. Only one bag is suspended over him and only one drip remains in his arm. *'Hes blaz,'* he says in a brave, casual voice, swallowing guiltily and looking at me with wide, apologetic eyes. I now know that two days after our return from the *bira* in Chivi, he had attacks all night; that mother then arrived and took him to Mberengwa to consult Mkwasha Phiri; that after that trip he had terrible attacks five nights in a row; that in despair he had swallowed three months' supply of pills; that Maiguru Mazvita had woken up in the night to find him comatose and had called an ambulance.

Still no father. Rindai jokes bravely with the nurses, discusses his prescriptions knowledgeably with the doctor, and drinks Maiguru Mazvita's rich beef soup which was smuggled in in a basket, past the unsuspecting hospital guards. Ironically, the authorities think home-cooked food might poison their patients.

On the third day, not long before visiting time ends, father shambles into the ward, dishevelled and wrapped up in a grey winter overcoat on a sizzling summer afternoon. We make way for him. He kneels at the end of Rindai's bed, buries his face in his hands and weeps – or prays, perhaps. No one offers support. No one can help Dunge Gwanangara – his peer Baba Mhlanga stands at the head of the bed fingering his faded purple priest's collar and his king-size Bible. I am distraught, the women are embarrassed but relieved. We allow father his silence, his misery, his loneliness. I know that he is struggling with anger and pity, anger at the precipitous decisions of youth and the excesses of disobedience, and pity for his wounded family.

***

Whenever Tachiona returned on one of his rare visits from the mine, his mother Njiki would say, 'So Tachi, when are you planning to get married? Are you waiting for your beard to turn white before I can have a muzukuru *from you?'*

'No, Mother,' was the only response she ever received.

'Zvauriwe, you'll bring us a stranger from the mines who can't speak our language and whose customs we can't understand.'

'No, Mother.'

'So where is your girlfriend?'

'I don't have one.'

'How can a big man like you open his cave of a mouth and say "I don't have one"? Isn't there anybody in this whole land who has caught your eye? Are you blind? Or do you think women bite? Or who is she you're afraid to bring here and show us? Is she ugly like a three- legged pot? Is she a witch that you're ashamed to introduce to us? By the time your brother Chari got to be your age he was long married and had a son.

One day Njiki came from the field and found a young woman sitting in the yard, near her kitchen hut. She invited her into the hut and gave her water to drink. She was barely a woman, seventeen at most, and it did not take Njiki two glances to realise that she was pregnant. She had no bag with her and she sat silently beside the fire. Dunge came in after shutting up the animals, shook hands with the visitor and sat on the bench, squinting into the firelight. Njiki prepared supper and gave the young woman some food. 'Forgive me child, but I don't seem to remember who you are. Perhaps we've never met.'

The girl stared into the fire and said nothing.

'What is your name, child?'

Silence.

'Pardon me, but is there somebody you are looking for?'

No response.

Njiki called Dunge outside. 'You know the girl, don't you?'

'No, Mother,' Dunge replied, surprised.

'You are the only man here.'

'Perhaps she lost her way.'

'I wasn't born yesterday. She is pregnant. Are you the father of her child, Dunge?'

The young man shook his head.

They went back into the hut and Njiki said to her, 'Look, child, it's dark now and there is nowhere for you to go. But we can't keep you here if you don't tell us your name. Suppose something happens to you within our walls? What is your name?'

The girl whispered into the fire, `Chipo'.

'Are you a relative of ours, perhaps?'

Silence.

'Listen, child. Stop playing nhodo *with me. If you are not a relative of ours then who do you want here? Is it him?' This pointing at Dunge. No response from Chipo.*

'Is it Tachi?'

The girl lowered her head.

'Are you pregnant? Answer me! Did Tachi make you pregnant?'

The girl burst into tears.

'Where do you come from? Who are your father and mother? If you are pregnant why have you come here alone with nobody to escort you? When did you get pregnant? I am a lion and my sons are porcupines. What is your totem? Well, you'll tell me by and by. You'll stop this tearful nonsense and tell me as long as I am Njiki, VaChivi, mwana wa*Chibga, Mai Tachi, wife of Gwanangara. Dunge, go next door and borrow two shillings from Mai Tsungi.'*

Dunge went out to borrow the money and when he came back Chipo was talking softly to Njiki, answering her questions, silence defeated.

'Dunge, tomorrow you go to Shabani to fetch your brother Tachi,' Njiki announced.

***

It was Dunge's first ride on a bus. It creaked and lurched from side to side, slowly chewing up the gravel road. It was packed full. He sat between a fat, bearded mupositori *in a white robe who yawned endlessly and beat his chest with the curved head of his staff, and a young woman who held two chickens in her lap. He clutched the bar of the seat in front of him; the smell of diesel and swirling dust* choked him and made him cough whenever a bump threw him off his seat, the hens pecked savagely at his crotch. On the roof, pots, buckets, suitcases, hoes and ploughs rattled; outside in the rolling countryside half-naked herdboys whistled, waved and beat their livestock off the road, out of the way of the iron monster. Every now and then the bus would stop to disgorge a passenger or two, then grind on, churning through the muddy waters of shallow streams, groaning up hills and humming across the scrub-land.

He asked the conductor to show him where to get off, and after what seemed an eternity he wormed through the crowded aisle, down the treacherous steps, back onto the ground again. He waited a while to get his feet firmly on the earth, to shake the roar out of his head and get his bearings right. He did not have to ask where the mine compound was. It was right ahead of him, a half-eaten white mountain, a couple of dirty white-washed buildings, cranes and Caterpillars. Men in shorts, vests, gumboots and white helmets were moving about. He went to the building marked 'office' and greeted the short man standing behind the mud counter.

'I'm looking for my brother Tachiona,' he said.

'Tachiona who?'

'Tachiona Gwanangara.'

'What is his number?'

'I don't know.'

'If you don't know his number we can't find him. Where is he from?'

'From Chivi.'

'There are several people from Chivi. What is his totem?'

'Ngara.'

'You mean Misodzi? The tall dark man with a bucket of tears in his eyes?'

'It could be him.'

'Wait here. He's down in the mine. He'll be out at six.'

At sunset a team of men emerged from the mine and the man in the office called out, 'Misodzi! Misodzi!' and there was Tachi: dark, lanky, knock-kneed, his head white with mine dust, wearing a faded vest, khaki shorts and black gumboots, Tachi laughing and licking his brown lips and weeping freely with surprise and joy, 'Dunge,

81

Dunge mwana wamai vangu!'

They ate sadza and salted beans together in his small grass hut in the mine compound. Then they bedded together between two thin blankets on the mud floor. Fleas kept Dunge awake. Tachi slept soundly enough, snoring all night as if his skin was made of cast iron. In the morning Tachi went off to a shift and Dunge helped himself in the pit latrine and washed his body in a grass enclosure that was so low that he had to crouch to stop people outside seeing him. As he was drying himself with his vest a pregnant woman passed by and said, 'Hello there!' giggled and disappeared into one of the small grass huts.

They spent another night together in the compound, then Tachi borrowed four shillings from a friend because it was mid-month and he had nothing in his purse. Dunge was surprised to hear Tachi conversing easily in ChiChewa with his mates.

They caught the first bus to Chivi and found their mother at home eating lunch with Chipo. It was a Thursday, chisi, *the traditional resting day when no one was allowed to go to the fields. Tachi gave his mother the presents he had been saving for in the six months since his last visit home – a blanket and a doek.*

Njiki thanked him but did not waste time. 'Tachiona, do you know this woman?' She pointed at Chipo. 'She says she is carrying your child,'

Tachiona's mouth fell open. Tears filled his eyes.

'No use crying, Tachi. Do you know her or not?'

Groan. Nod.

'She told me about herself. Is she carrying your child or not?'

Sigh. Sob.

'If this is your doing then you have to move fast. Her people have to know. You hit their lamb with your knobkerrie and broke its knee. Now the lamb is walking lame. You have to account for your deeds,'

Sneeze. Sniffle. Confused hand-wringing. Another avalanche of tears.

'Stop crying! Are you the first man in this wide land to make a woman pregnant? Are you a man or what? You men call yourselves men but you are no more manly than women!'

***

A maternal uncle – Njiki's young brother – oversaw the negotiations. A munyai *was found and Chipo's people were contacted. The damages were charged and the lobola set. Because Chipo had not left home through the straight doors of propriety, but sneaked off on one and a half legs in the night, her people disowned her, at least until the preliminary fines were paid up. Njiki sorted the matter out.*

Tongues wagged. Tachiona had married a prostitute. Tachiona had married a ChiChewa woman from Shabani Mine. Tachiona had been duped by Malawian magic into marrying a girl somebody else had made pregnant, a desperate girl who had thrown herself at him. Tachiona had been forced by his mother to marry a woman without a home or a past.

Tachiona this ... Tachiona that ...

Njiki braved the gossip. She weathered the storm of malice with characteristic defiance. After all, nobody had approved her decision to snub offers of remarriage from Gwanangara's brothers when Gwanangara died, when she had cut herself off from her in-laws, and they had punished her by grabbing half the livestock of her deceased husband. The possibility that the pregnancy might not be her son's nibbled at her conscience, but she secretly hoped that Chipo would cure him of the wandering disease and make him settle down. Besides, she seemed a good girl, industrious and obedient. What did it matter if the child really wasn't Tachi's? 'A child is a child,' she mused. Didn't they say, after all, 'Gomba harina mwana'*? Tachi and Chipo could have more children.

Njiki was taking her revenge on the world. She believed in subverting men's rules without appearing to be subversive. She was a woman, but she was a man too.

Chipo got on well with Dunge. They were age-mates, almost. Perhaps she was even younger than him. He looked after her as he would his own sister. But he respected her, called her Maiguru, Maiguru Chipo. She called him Babamunini, Babamunini Dunge. Perhaps he felt close to her because he had never had a sister of his own. Together they went to the fields and to the church; he accompanied her to the river and to look for firewood. When she was not well

---

* 'A hole cannot bear children.'

he even cooked for her. Those who did not know them were likely to think they were betrothed. Like most girls of her time, she had not been to school, so he wrote her letters for her, while she dictated her thoughts. Most of the letters were to Tachi.

Now that he had reason enough to do so, Tachi came home more often, once a month perhaps. He did not earn much and the trips were expensive – there was very little left after the taxes, the bus fare, and the small presents for his mother and his wife. Often his mother had to sell a hen or a goat to raise his fare back to work. When Chipo delivered he was there. The baby was a puny thing, with a tiny, undecided face, stubby fingers and vague brown eyes. Njiki touched the baby's toes and palms and carefully turned him on his side to examine his profile.

'These aren't Gwanangara fingers,' she snapped, unfurling the child's knotted fists.

Chipo sat against the wall, fatigued, staring blankly into the fire, waiting for the accusation. Tachi wept as he always did when he was overcome by feeling.

'Dzenga,' he announced, sobbing through a smile. 'The boy's name is Dzenga.'

7

Arriving home, I find Kelvin striding around the house and the cottage, opening, closing and banging doors. Mother has called me home because she thinks that only I can make him listen. He shakes my hand without looking at me, tosses clothes into a suitcase, overturns the suitcase and starts packing again. He skims through a book and closes it; leafs through his files. A photograph and an unopened condom fall from a jacket pocket. Bella is a university student, a campus girl to whom he once proposed.

'I loved her,' he says, picking up the photograph, tearing it up, and throwing the pieces on the floor. He pockets the condom. A naked bulb hangs from the low ceiling of the cottage. He has lost weight, and in the hot, bright, yellow light his short hair is thin and lustre-less. He goes out of the cottage and pauses on the veranda. Our dog Shumba licks his ankles but he kicks it out of the way. He strips petals off a crop of roses and stuffs them into his mouth. He proceeds to the garage and starts moving things about in the dark. With maniacal strength, he loads bags of chickenfeed into a wheelbarrow and pushes it out towards the hen-coop. It is nearly midnight.

'Kelvin,' Mother speaks gently from the kitchen door, 'You can do that in the morning, *mwanangu.*'

He opens the coop and fills the troughs. I let him finish, then I say, 'Let's try and get some sleep.'

He lies with me on the three-quarter bed in the cottage, in his trousers, staring at the ceiling.

'I loved her,' he says again. Ten minutes later he gets up, as if going to the toilet, and unlocks the outside door. I hear footsteps outside, the gate clinking. I listen for a moment, then pull on my trousers and go out after him. I see him running across the asphalt road and into the bush behind our plot.

'Mother, he's gone!' I shout towards the main house and run after him, shirtless and barefoot. I follow a dust track through the bush and stop to listen. He's ahead of me, thumping through the grass. I see a grey blur moving through the thorn bushes on my right.

'Kelvin, please!'

I leap after him. *Muunga* thorns stab my feet and snap at my chest. He is running towards the stream at the base of a cluster of trees. I chug through the mud and plunge into the water. On the other side of the river I snag myself on a barbed-wire fence, and while I'm extricating myself, dogs start barking ferociously from the two houses up the slope. I hear the sound of glass breaking, a voice shouting and then the loud crack of a gun. The dogs stop barking and begin to whimper. Lights explode in the windows of the houses.

I run back home and meet father and mother coming towards me along the dust track. We hurry home and I phone the police. The phone rings for a full three minutes before someone answers. I tell them somebody unwell has run off into the darkness and there has been the sound of gunfire.

The police arrive fifteen minutes later and as their van is revving towards the gate who should stagger out of the bushes into the sharp beam of the headlights but Kelvin. He allows himself to be led into the cottage. His hands are bleeding, cut by glass, and there are lacerations all over his body, caused by thorns and barbed wire. But he has no gunshot wounds. There is a vacuous expression on his face. Father helps the two policemen bind his hands with strips of an old white sheet while mother, still in her petticoat, stands back, sobbing.

'But why don't you have him hospitalised?' says one of the policemen, who can't be much over twenty. He had the neat, clipped voice of the uninitiated. 'It's dangerous living with a person like this. He's a danger – not only to himself, but to other people.'

'It must be stressful for you,' says the other policeman, a kindly man of forty-something, with copper bangles on his wrists. 'You really ought to take him to a hospital where they can look after him.

Unless you're trying alternative treatment, of course.'

'*Mwanangu,*' says father, firmly. 'I know about places where in-mates are made to fetch water from taps using buckets full of holes to see if their minds are OK, places where the bedding is a flea-rid-den blanket on a cement floor, the diet a relentless menu of sadza and salted beans, and discipline a frequent sjambok on the back.'

'I understand,' says the older policeman quietly.

Father, Kelvin and I climb into the back of the van and we drive to the hospital. My brother is subdued. There they dress his wounds and give him a strong narcotic which puts him to sleep right away. They admit him into a ward for the remainder of the night. The po-licemen kindly drive us back home.

In the morning Baba Tariro hears of the latest mishap and drives over at once, with a woman he introduces as Mbuya Matongo.

'I have known you for over twenty years now, Sekuru,' he says to father. 'I'm not related to you by blood, I'm your *muzukuru* only by totem, but you are more like a brother than a friend to me. Your true relative is the neighbour who lends you a hand when your beard catches fire. We go to the same church, live in the same town and have raised our children together. I know about all the problems you've endured and have been party to all the trips you've made to try and solve them. So, this morning, I've taken it upon myself to bring you a woman who might help you. We black people go to church and to hospitals, but sometimes help is closer at hand. Mbuya Matongo does not know you and I have not told her anything about you, but she might be able to assist in her own small way.'

Mbuya Matongo nods slightly and slowly looks about the room as if dissecting our habitat. She is a lean woman in her forties, mod-estly dressed, with plain features.

'I see sickness in this house. It has been here for some time, mov-ing from child to child, shifting from head to head,' she begins with-out much ceremony, smoothing out the pleats of her dress with her palms. 'It is not for me to say what caused this, for the causes are many. The devil strolls freely in our midst; brother can harm brother, but even God in heaven can himself cause illness. At present this disease inhabits the head of a child who is a man, and yet not quite a man, and it is seeking to snatch him out of school and make him a vagabond. This child is well and he is not well, his actions confuse you. He is a very intelligent man, though those around him have not always perceived him to be so. All the children in this family are clever. Is this the reason why ill winds have chosen this household? It is possible that his intelligence is his problem – ideas bubbling in his head are seeking release – that he reads too much, drives himself too hard to keep up with his siblings. It is possible the roots of the problem are *chibhoyi* – there is a long-lost ancestor seeking to inhabit him, seeking to use him as his voice. An important ancestor, little known to you, who has chosen your untainted walls for his shelter. But it is also possible that you have jealous relatives, people very close to you, who would like to host this ancestor and receive his or her blessing. People with bloodstains on their walls, and rubbish in their yards. People who have gagged this *mudzimu* with bad medicine, so that it cannot speak, or have driven it ahead of them and follow behind, hiding in the ancestral shadow, so that they can perform their wicked deeds undetected. You've seen this young man eating flowers and wondered why. Do you have an ancestor who gathered flowers, or tried to be a healer? And I see a big mistake in choosing to use the same *n'anga* as you did for his brother. That *n'anga* is a powerful spirit from a foreign land, a capable man, but he has been bought by your brother to bring harm to you and confuse you. This *n'anga* covets your money. After all, no two families can have the same *n'anga*. Your ancestors have been turned against you, and yet they want to protect and bless you. I see one ancestor, a strong woman from not so long ago, your mother, who is fighting to protect you. But she cannot defend you single-handed. Your ancestors need to be turned around, and cleansed, so that they can defend you. I can perform the cleansing ceremony for you, if you wish. And then we will see if you need a further *bira* for the ancestors themselves to speak.'

***

Baba Tariro drives us to the hospital for the Sunday lunchtime visit. We drop Mbuya Matongo off at the bus terminus and find Kelvin relaxed and cheerful, discharged with medication, and waiting to go home. When we ask to speak to the doctor we are presented with the matron, who stresses that Kelvin must take his medication regularly. 'Prescriptions need to be managed with care,' she cautions. 'Medicine is not like sugar to take just when you feel like it.'

'You may have a *bira* if that pleases you. I am black too and know how you feel about such traditions. But sometimes *biras* will unsettle the patient and can only make him worse.'

After her long cautious speech that has carefully covered all the bases, mother seems reassured, father dryly quizzical, and I remain as uncommitted as an empty page.

***

After the birth of Dzenga, Tachiona did not stay long at the mine. He dropped out or he was retrenched; some rumours say he fell out with the boss-boy. He came home to stay with his mother, wife and brother. He became irritable and unpredictable. The gossip about his wife Chipo, Mai Dzenga, never eased up. He frequently wanted to wake her up in the middle of the night to challenge her as to who who had fathered Dzenga, the puny child with no Gwanangara features. But he could not bring himself to do it. He loved and hated his wife; loved her for ending his long bachelorhood and bringing a hearth to his hut, and hated her for humiliating his name, for what seemed to be her cunning. But had she been devious? Was she perhaps not a hapless victim, like most women of her time, like women of all times, of self-righteous patriarchal condemnation? But he could not send her away because that would only heighten what he perceived as his own shame. And another child – Ratidzo – was on the way.

The harshness of Chivi got the better of him. Its stark mountains, arid fields and desiccated air sapped his spirit. The rain was erratic and the harvests meagre. At least at the mine he had been assured of the daily ration of sadza and beans. Now he was just another hollow villager, scrounging for food from day to day. Between May and November, when the fieldwork was over, he became restless. He took to drinking, the strong seven-days beer brewed in drums over blazing fires. He went from village to village, hunting for beer, and sometimes he only came home at the crack of dawn. Occasionally, he brought beer home and drank with his mother Njiki. Njiki rarely drank, but when she did she liked to sing songs and dance. They bantered and quarrelled like brother and sister. At other times she

gathered Dzenga, and later Ratidzo and other children, around her
and told them stories. Sometimes Tachi sang and danced with her,
but always he wept in the end and she chided him. He wept because
he had nothing better to do, because no one would sing with him but
his mother, because drought and poverty had scorched his hopes.

Still he refused to eat chicken; he wore bangles, undertook strange
fetishes and had fresh nyora *inscribed on his body to ward off his de-*
spair. He befriended workers from foreign lands and learnt to speak
strange tongues.

He never got on with his half-brother Chari, or his half-mother
Maribha whom he rarely saw. When Maribha died he begrudging-
ly agreed to go and give his condolences. His brother Dunge he
tolerated, though he now accused Dunge of having connived with
his mother and wife to bring him home to get married, and tie him
down.

***

Mbuya Matongo stands waist deep in the middle of the river, arranging her fronds and dipping them in the water. We stand in a row on
the bank, barefoot, our trousers or skirts hitched up. Father, Rindai,
me, Kelvin, Shuvai, Vimbai, Tendai and Tapera. Shuvai holds baby
Nda, Rindai's daughter, in her arms. Mother and Maiguru Mazvita,
because they are not Gwanangaras and belong to totems of their
own, are sitting on the opposite bank, tending a small fire and roasting the goat meat.

Mbuya Matongo calls us into the river one by one. Father wades
out to her. She dips her fronds in the river, beats him on the head,
chest and arms and tells him to wade to the opposite bank, to the
fire. Once beaten with the fronds we must cross the stream, not look
back at the river, eat a piece of the unsalted goat meat, and proceed
up through the trees, back to the main road.

I feel the tadpoles brushing my toes, green weed floating around
my ankles. I wonder how many others have come to this river for
help. The water looks clean enough. Promising. Father wades out of
the water, dripping wet, his clothes sticking to his surprisingly lean
body. He collects his piece of unsalted meat, puts it into his mouth
and walks into the forest, towards the road.

Rindai next. He misses his footing on a slippery rock. Mbuya

Matongo catches his arm and rights him with a smile, then beats him with fronds and sends him away. I cross without mishap. *'Dlula ndoda, dlula Ngara, '** she says in Ndebele, the language spoken by her spirit. The current flows strongly, carrying away leaves and flowers, sweeping away the dregs of our distress. Mother holds up a plate of unsalted goat meat. Maiguru Mazvita throws twigs into the fire, under a sizzling strip of meat. I do not look at them. I put some meat in my mouth and chew it as I march into the trees, after Rindai. I hear baby Nda babbling, 'Tete Shuvai, Tete Shuvai, *handidi kugeza ini, mvura ine tsvina iyi.*'† My neck feels stiff but I do not turn my head. Father and Rindai are ahead of me and half a kilometre beyond is Baba Tariro's green truck where we are all going to reassemble.

I march ahead and do not look back. I am alone amidst the cooing of doves and the shade of trees. I am in the procession and I am alone, turning my back on our despair. I reach the truck and climb into the back to wait. Baba Tariro sits in the front, reading his newspaper, Rindai sits with him in the driver's cabin. Father stands beside the truck wringing water out of his wet trousers.

That night as we are having supper, we hear the sharp screech of brakes and then a bang and we troop outside into the road. A Mercedes Benz has stopped, its lights still on. A white woman stumbles out, nervous and shaken. In the bright beam of the lights lies the sprawled body of a whimpering animal.

Our dog Shumba is dying.

***

Dunge went to get a birth certificate for his brother's son Dzenga. He did so because he could speak English and spell names, because his brother's wife asked him to do so, because his own brother was drunk as usual, and could not in his doubt and lethargy be persuaded to do it. He went because he wanted to be the glue that kept Tachiona and Chipo together.

He, Dunge, sang tenor in the church choir and after his confirmation became a Sunday school teacher for the Dutch Reformed Church. He went around the villages asking parents to send their

---

* 'Pass on man. Pass on.'

† I don't want a bath. The water is dirty.

91

children to Sunday school – much like vanamuneri had done before, except that he did not use force. He preferred to teach the New Testament, for he found the God of the Old Testament too angry and vengeful, like his ancestors. For him the words of Jesus bore no grudges, invited salvation and forgave all manner of sins.

He had wanted to be a teacher, but had gone no further than Standard 3 because there were no higher classes in the district. His only opportunity had been at a mission boarding school, which was too expensive. Once when a Sub B teacher fell ill, he was asked to teach the class for a few weeks and was nicknamed Teacher Mfana. He was sad when the stint came to an end.

Strange things now happened in Njiki's household that no one can explain. For some reason Njiki and Tachi both converted to the mapositori *sect. It is said that Njiki fell seriously ill and could not be cured at the mission hospital. She was saved (so it's said) by the waters and prayers of the apostles and after that she donned a long white dress and a doek; Tachi had his head shaved and he too put on a white gown and together they would go to the mountains to sing and pray with their new colleagues every night for several months after Njiki became well. It is said that the prophets asked them to put out all the traditional paraphernalia so they could be destroyed, and that among Gwanangara's spears, axes, knobkerries and shields, which they surrendered to the bonfire, were some articles which Gwanangara had procured for his late uncle Mhokoshi, the hunter. No one is sure why, but after Njiki became well she and Tachi reverted to their old ways, as people are known to do when a crisis is over and the prayers ceased to have the same meaning.*

***

OK, OK, maybe I'm leaving things out. It's too easy when you're telling a story about strife and striving to focus on nothing else. Much else had happened. For example, I'd married Vongai. It happened like this, like every other campus affair.

She falls pregnant – yes, falls pregnant at the beginning of her second year. She comes to my flat at the beginning of the second semester looking every inch with child, her skirts and blouses full, her face round and glowing, her hair shining. She looks at me uncertainly, guiltily. I love her, value her. She's a sweet girl, honest, patient, reliable and unpretentious. I've known her for three years but I'm scared to death. I feel angry, sorry and confused. I hold her tight that night and in baffled tones we plot what to do. We wrench ourselves out of murderous possibilities. Fortunately the university won't send her away because it's not their policy to expel pregnant students. If everything goes well she will make it through the academic year and deliver during the Christmas break. But her parents have to know. I have, as my good old grandmother VaChivi would say, fractured their lamb in the knee with my fat, ill-disciplined knobkerrie and wantonly stepped on their bare backs and broken them. I've snatched their child away just when she was on the brink of a career after a long, expensive education. She's the only one in her family who has managed to go to university and now she won't be able to work and re-pay them for their toils. They're a poor family who have scratched sandy soils to send her to school. There'll be damages, fines. And then there will be the inevitable question, 'So what do you want to do?' The idea of marriage frightens me. I have only been working for a year and a half. I want to help my parents, and to enjoy myself a bit. The thought of weddings, especially after what happened to Rindai, only stimulates my apprehension.

There'll be nervous consultations with father and mother. Our family's reputation, Dunge Gwanangara's reputation, is at stake on the fires of patriarchy.

There'll be relatives to be consulted, journeys to be made. I already have visions of Muzukuru Mhungu, Vatete Mai Farai, Babamunini Wanisai and Baba Tariro, that firm contingent of our urban relatives, racing across the country, with a suitable *munyai*, in Baba Tariro's car, to negotiate on my behalf.

So we get married, face up to our responsibilities. I go through the routines and take the way of all flesh, become the bespoken husband of somebody's daughter. Vongai's parents are level-headed. Her father is a modest, soft-spoken man, the deacon of our church and his two elder daughters have been married this way – he is not vindictive. Her mother, a renowned peanut farmer, sobs her child away. And so we are wed, and after work every day I go to the campus with yoghurt, peanuts and apples to see Vongai, and monitor the progress of our child. The idea that there are three beings between the two of us sends a tingle up my spine.

We move together into a bigger flat with a sitting room and a phone, and we buy a lounge suite, a stove and a fridge and I shut my eyes to the flowers of Harare.

Did all this take place during our troubles? I forget – but Vongai is not in the thick of it yet. She knows about Rindai's problem, about Kelvin, but Mkwasha Phiri and Mbuya Matongo make their secret entrance before she joins our family. I do not even tell her about Rindai's suicide attempt – this she only learns from Maiguru Mazvita, Rindai's wife, whom she quickly befriends. I set the wrong precedent for our marriage by not talking, by assuming the role of the strong man of the family unit.

***

One morning, a month or so after Mbuya Matongo's cleansing ceremony, I'm involved in an accident on my way to work. I'm travelling with three colleagues in an old bullfrog Citroen along a busy, two-way road when a bus in front of us crashes into an overtaking combi, laden with passengers. We hit it. Another bus hits us from behind, pushing us under the bus in front. Two collisions in quick succession. We duck instinctively, then scramble off the collapsed seats, through the mangled doors, coughing in clouds of dust and exhaust fumes, and squeeze out through the narrow space between the two buses. The roof of the Citroen has been sliced off. Two people in the combi die on the spot and the driver of the bus in front is badly hurt. The combi driver runs away.

'You've been very lucky,' says a policeman, marshalling us off the road through the gathering crowd. 'If I were you I'd go straight home to brew beer and thank the spirits.'

An ambulance whisks us to hospital where we're examined and discharged. None of the three of us is hurt.

Vongai comes back from her lecture at four o'clock and finds me lying on the bed. I tell her what happened.

'Have they taken X-rays? Have you phoned home to tell them about it? Maybe you shouldn't burden them with the news given what they have been going through – after all, you are safe, unhurt.'

'I *have* to call them,' I insist. I try to sit up but my body aches. After supper I pick up the phone and talk to father. Mother doesn't answer the phone any more. Father hears me out, then he says, 'Are you hurt?' I tell him, no, and he repeats his question.

I ask him, 'Is everything OK at home?' and he says, 'A little.' I lean against the fridge to support myself.

'We received bad news from Chivi. Babamukuru Tachiona is no more. He died early this morning. He'd been ill for a week. His old urine problem. They sent for Mkwasha Phiri but by the time he arrived your uncle had died. We received the news from a passenger on the morning bus.'

'No more...? When is the funeral?'

'Tomorrow afternoon. Your mother and I are leaving for Chivi first thing in the morning.' Pause. 'You don't have to come right away. We'll organise a trip for everyone once the rains are over.'

I put the receiver down and Vongai asks, 'Who is it?'

'Babamukuru Tachiona.'

'Your father's brother?'

'Yes.'

'I'm sorry. Was he ill?'

'Must have been his urine problem.'

'So, what are the arrangements?'

'Father says we'll all go together – after the rains.'

'Aren't there any buses which go straight there from here? You can't put this off until after the rainy season. If he's your father's brother, we ought to go tomorrow and give our condolences when everybody is there, together.'

I am silent, winnowing my thoughts. I can't reveal to her the hollowness I feel at the news of Babamukuru's death, what a nightmare Chivi has become to us, our secret dread of the place and its people. I can't begin to mention the strange parallel of my accident and Babamukuru's death, the baffling coincidences which have characterised the last three years of my life. I'm silent, sifting my thoughts. I will not weep but my soul aches for this man with his urine bags, this unwashed man who looked like me and wept ten thousand times in a lifetime, my father's brother, who declared me his heir – did he really mean it? – now waiting to feed the hungry earth, this man who sprinkled snuff round Baba Tariro's car and said nothing would happen to anyone as long as he lived. This man who woke our sleeping ancestors with his *biras* and his drums and left us, ignoramuses, to do the rest. My heart cries for the void that he has left, which father must now fill. I know father's motive when he procrastinates, that we will not go to Chivi even after the rains. I know how he wants to shield us from the tragedies of Chivi.

'You're not going to your father's brother's funeral?' Vongai says, surprised. 'I would have accompanied you.'

No, I'm not going to mourn him in Chivi tomorrow.

8

Njiki had prepared him mbwire-mbwire *and said, 'If things don't work out, come back home,' and yet here he was, sleeping at the bus station among beggars and lunatics in the bitter cold. In the morning he did the rounds, his thin blanket tucked under his arm, looking for work in shops, factories, on building sites and even at schools. The supervisors looked at his Standard 3 report, shook their heads softly and said, 'Sorry, we don't have anything for you at the moment. Try again next week.' He fingered the few shillings left in his pocket from what his mother had given him after the sale of a precious goat and reflected ruefully that if he did not find a job soon he would be stranded. Once, while standing within an eager, almost frantic crowd outside a factory, he had only just missed being handpicked for a temporary assignment – sorting out and cleaning empty bottles. At a building site a white boss boy who wanted two* dhaka-*boys had looked at his certificate and reference letter and said, 'You don't need this here, Mr Teacherboy!'*

One afternoon a rotund Indian wholesaler with a balding head fingered his papers, looked him up and down and said, 'Can you sell shoes?' and he said, 'I can try.'

'What do you mean, you can try?' The wholesaler goaded him, 'Can you or can you not?'

'I can try, Sir.'

'What is your name again?'

'Dunge Gwanangara.'

'What kind of name is that?'

97

'Just my name, Sir.'

'You're a very tall man. I'll call you Longman. That's much easier to pronounce. So, Longman, you taught Sub B for three weeks?'

'Yes, Sir.'

'Are you honest and hard-working?'

'Yes, Sir.'

'I'll try you for a week.'

'Thank you, Sir.'

And so Dunge acquired his first job selling shoes. All day he stood on the veranda, near the entrance of Mr Punjab's small dark shop, shouting:

'Shoes, shoes, shoes
Cheap shoes here
Shoes two' en six here
Shoes three bob please!'

He made up shoe poems, shoe verses and shoe songs, sweet-talked passers-by, waylaid and coaxed them, laughed at them, chided them, begged them, grabbed them by the hand and dragged them into the shop. Some were barefoot, others wore tenderfoots or faded tennis shoes strapped wretchedly together with bark-string. Some walked stiffly past him, some brushed off his advances with dry smiles, others took an obliging, polite peek into the shop and allowed themselves to be sung to or shouted at for a moment; a very few dusted their feet, put on the old socks he proffered them and tried on a pair or two. His first success – on his fourth or fifth day – was a dubious-looking, barefooted mama who strode down the pavement, grabbed him by the hand and said, 'Quick, quick, boy! My bus is leaving! Find me a pair of tennis shoes!' Trembling with disbelief, he had found her a pair which she hurriedly tried on, and watched while she slapped three shillings, warm from a handkerchief lodged within the ample cups of her dress, into his palm.

'Very good, Longman,' said Mr Punjab, laughing as he put the money into the till, 'Very good, boy.'

Little did Dunge know then that he would work for Mr Punjab for forty years, selling shoes, shirts and trousers, and that he would see the little shoe-shop expand into one of the biggest wholesalers, departmental and supermarket groups in Gweru.

Now that he had a job and his registration certificate was stamped, he found a room in the bachelor's quarter of the township. He quickly sought out the Dutch Reformed Church, presented his transfer letter to the pastor and announced himself to the congregation. He joined the choir and offered to help with the catechism classes. At that time the church was very small – a pole and dhaka affair which the authorities regularly threatened to close. So they had to build a proper church with solid brick walls, a corrugated iron roof and proper windows. Members of the congregation pledged money for the various components of the building – bricks, cement, doors, windows, frames, glass and roofing material. Progress was slow. It took years to lay the foundation alone, many more for the structure to rise. He contributed regularly to the construction – it was not uncommon to hear people talk of 'Dunge's slab' or 'Dunge's window' or 'Dunge's Door,' or, much later, 'Dunge's pulpit.' Over the years he was to rise quickly through the ranks – Catechist, Deacon, Central Deacon. He was a staunch member of the Men's Union; two or three times a year he put on his suit and carrying his red banner went out with the other men to sing, eat, pray, sleep, and testify in the streets. His favourite song was Jesu ibgwe rangu, Jesus is my rock. He had a way of starting the tune from somewhere deep within the crowd, stepping out into the aisle, thumping his Bible against his palm and sharing with the congregation a verse which had inspired him during a weekend of communion.

He went home to Chivi to see his people every month-end, taking his mother, brother and brother's wife sugar, flour, cooking oil, dried fish, salt, soap and clothes. Sometimes he took pickled onions or spicy dishes donated by his boss. He did not drink, and saved enough to buy first one cow, then another. Over the years those two cows would create a sizeable family herd. Njiki became the proud and well-nurtured mother of a son with a job in town. Later he would send school fees home for Dzenga, his brother Tachiona's son, and Tavengwa, his half-brother Chari's son.

He took himself to night school.

He befriended people who were related to him by totem, others who were only slightly related, and people he lived with in the township; they were many – Muzukuru Mhungu, Babamukuru Clever,

Vatete Mai Farai, Babamunini and Mainini Waniso, Vazukuru Baba and Mai Tariro. His job brought him into contact with many people. He enamoured himself to teachers, headmasters, clerks, hospital orderlies and bus drivers. They fired his ambition and his hopes for the future, they were people who steeled his belief in honesty and hard work. He had no time to waste. He worked in this way for several years while everybody wondered if he would marry or if, like his brother Tachi, he would marry late. One unexpected winter afternoon he took with him to Chivi a beautiful young woman and told his mother, 'This is my friend.' Njiki asked the woman what her totem was and where she came from and subtly inquired if she were pregnant. She was gratified that the woman had the same totem as Mai Dzenga, Tachiona's wife – water, the fish – that she came from the farms just outside Gweru, and that she had not yet known a man. Dunge had met her in church. Njiki at once approved of her. He brought her again at the end of the following month and announced his marriage plans. Muzukuru Mhungu was to accompany him, with a munyai of her choice, to begin the marriage process.

That woman was Hilda. Hilda Dolly Tsvangira – the woman destined to become Masiziva, Mai Rindai, the moon huntress.

***

We did not, do not go to Babamukuru Tachiona's funeral. We do not go to our father's brother's funeral. Oh, how unAfrican! It is a guilt that is to haunt me all my life. Father and mother go, of course; father has to be there to mark out the spot where his brother is to be laid to rest and to oversee the burial and distribution of his property, but when he arrives in Chivi, half a morning late, they are already covering up the grave. Maiguru Mai Ratidzo has deftly taken charge of affairs. Father and mother are there but we, the children of Dunge Gwanangara, are not. The rains end, the dry season comes and goes but still we do not go to pay our condolences.

The best time to attend a funeral is soon after the death, before the body is buried, when people are still together in one place and the embarrassment of death can be swallowed up in the crowd, in the inconspicuous shaking of hands, in the faceless spectacle of shared grief. Going to visit the bereaved after a funeral is complicated, a cross-country marathon to meet dispersed members of the family, in their disparate homes. Going through the motions of grief again and yet again.

We hide behind father's procrastination. The guilt of not going slowly wears off, or seems to. We convince ourselves that funerals are for other families, distant tragedies. We're still untouched by death. The truth, however, is that the family in Chivi, the associations with Chivi, and the memories of Chivi are an embarrassment we have avoided for two decades, a raw wound that nobody knows how to heal.

We do not go. We are freshly bathed, or so we believe, in the waters of Mbuya Matongo's river, the ill-luck beaten off us by her fronds, our bodies fortified by the roasted, unsalted goat meat and bitter porridge, our lives turned irrevocably away from tragedy, the malice of previous healers washed off, our homestead cleaned, our path cleared, our true ancestors turned around so that they no longer pinch us on the arms at night or strike us on the head with their staffs; now they can come home to protect us. We now need, says Mbuya Matongo, to brew more beer and hold another *bira* to invite the spirits to confirm the cleansing, and invite whichever spirit is trying to inhabit Kelvin, to now do so.

'But the Gwanangara homestead is black,' father argues, inevitably. 'Babamukuru Tachiona has not been dead a year yet and it would not be right to hold the ceremony in a black homestead.'

'Now that we've come so far with Mbuya Matongo we might as well go the whole way with her,' counters mother.

'If Chivi is not the right place then why don't we do it in Gokwe?' argues Rindai.

And so Gokwe it is. I am not sure if Mbuya Matongo is told about Babamukuru Tachiona's death.

***

We descend from the bus at two in the morning, at our dew-in-the-morning bus stop – Kelvin, Shuvai, Vimbai, Tendai, Tapera and I – and begin the long trudge to our dew-in-the-morning home in the moonlight. Our cousin Tavengwa and his family are waiting for us. Mother was there a week ahead of us, to help with the preparations. Rindai, his wife and child are driving from the research station; father is to follow with Mbuya Matongo, in a hired car. No one is coming from Chivi – I coldly suspect no one has been invited. Vongai is with us, heavily pregnant, and I point out, with some romance, the stream, now heavily silted, where we went swimming, the dam where we went fishing, the small primary school, the 'township', the village 'line' and the fields.

The moon is almost round, one night short of full, the vista is clear. Kelvin stops now and then for a deep inhalation of snuff, a habit he has acquired since being in Chivi and the more recent insinuation that he is the new Sekuru Zevezeve. The dogs bark lazily from the homesteads – we must seem like a strange multicoloured army marching through the night. There are new homesteads, corrugated iron roofs gleaming, cattle pens stinking richly of cowdung, *tsapi* full of maize, owls flapping out of muhacha trees, fresh graves. I haven't been there in almost eight years – the denuded landscape tells a strange tale of the once leafy place in which I spent half my childhood. I wonder if Vongai is impressed.

Rindai's white 404 – not Baba Tariro's Mazda this time – gleams in the midst of the huts. Our cousin Tavengwa and his wife Mai Hamu open the gate, followed by mother and Maiguru Mazvita; little Nda wakes up at once and clamours for Tete Shuvai's arms. We gather in the kitchen. Hello's and how are you's criss-cross the air, a moth explodes in the flickering lamp light. Bhudhi Tavengwa stares solemnly at the wall and mother buttons a jersey over her nightdress. We talk in low tones for a while – we have a long day ahead and must soon sleep. Maiguru Mai Hamu surrenders the bedroom to the men. The women bed down companionably on the kitchen floor. Rindai is already stretched out on the sagging, squeaky three-quarter bed that used to be mother's – snoring and immovable; I squeeze onto the narrow space between him and the wall and close my eyes.

In the morning the people of the line flock to greet us: totemic relatives, family friends. Some we remember, others not. Mbuya Sibanda, whom my father calls *mainini*, a niece of Mbuya Njiki who lives on the other side of the river, attends to the brew in huge drums. I go to the kraal and look at the cattle. I enjoy the fresh air and my reminiscences.

One, two, three o'clock and father has still not arrived.

Four, five, six and still no father. He had said he would take the day off and should have been here by midday. Have his reservations got the better of him? Has he got cold feet?

It's growing dark. The beer is ready and the sacrificial ox is awaiting slaughter. The village folk are milling in the yard, waiting for the party to begin, hungering for beer and beef. But nothing can begin without father.

Seven, eight, nine and he still hasn't arrived. We're anxious. Father is usually reliable. What can have happened? We eat supper, hardly talking. It's too late to start anything now. We sit around a fire in the yard, waiting. We eventually go to bed.

In the morning we're sitting at the fire and the villagers have begun to gather again when father suddenly emerges at the gate in his winter overcoat and woollen hat, without a bag or a briefcase. We shake hands with him, give him a chair and wait for his news, but he just picks at his teeth and smiles at his flock.

'Did you have a good trip, Ngara?' Mbuya Sibanda asks and he nods slightly and laughs. He whispers something into Bhudhi Tavengwa's ear and calls Rindai and me to the bedroom.

'I had an accident,' Father says, slipping off the woollen hat to expose a freshly shaved head. A long cut runs down the left side of his head.

'I was driving with Mbuya Matongo and her husband in their car when the car hit a donkey and overturned just outside KweKwe. Mbuya Matongo broke a leg but her husband wasn't hurt. The car was a complete write-off. They detained us at the hospital most of the night but I insisted on leaving. They had treated my wound. It didn't need stitches. I hitch-hiked all the way here.'

We stand up to examine the cut. The blood has blackened on the edges. I slip out to fetch a little water and a clean rag, and wash the cut gently. I don't remember touching father's head before.

'So can the *bira* go on without Mbuya Matongo?' asks Rindai, eventually

'She told us to go on without her. Don't tell the women, not even your mother. We might panic them and the villagers. We'll just carry on as if nothing happened.' He puts the hat back on his head.

So we go out, conspiratorially, back to the fire and the women serve breakfast. The news of father's arrival spreads fast and the yard is soon milling with people.

We go to the kraal and father points out the ox to be slaughtered. Its name is Blantyre. I remember him from when Kelvin and I used to yoke him to another ox during the ploughing season. Blantyre swishes his tail lazily and turns his sad eyes away from us when father's stick prods him on the belly. There is no shortage of hands to help, no lack of advice. Blantyre is roped by the horns and dragged out to the bushes to be felled. Rindai and Kelvin are in the midst of it; the women are waiting with their dishes for the tripe and the intestines. I turn my head away from the dull thud of axe on bone and the choking moaning as the beast falls. Is this how God singles us out in the shuffling crowds, knee-deep in our own dung, prodding us in the belly with his long stick and marching us off to accidents or asylums, or condemning us to urine-soaked, soiled deathbeds? Are we all God's little Blantyres, obliviously awaiting our turn at his abattoirs?

***

Everything that can go wrong goes wrong that evening. First, there is a scramble for meat. A whole limb disappears in the dusk. Father orders the remaining carcase to be locked up in the spare bedroom and Bhudhi Tavengwa spends half the night patrolling it for possible miscreants.

The tunes and rhythms in the kitchen are not quite right. Strangers lead the singing; north and south disagree. The throng is unruly. The footwork clashes. There is discord between Gokwe and Chivi.

The beer is excellent, but too much of it is given out at once. Participants get drunk too quickly. There is no one really in charge, who knows how things should be done. Mbuya Sibanda calls for order, Maiguru Mai Hamu, Bhudhi Tavengwa's wife, starts an optimistic refrain, father sits open-mouthed on the bench with his face in his hands, and a group of elders near the door quaff the seven-days brew and guffaw at each other.

'Midzimu yepi yaDunge? Midzimu yepi yechiKristu?'*

Kelvin totters uncertainly in front of the group, adjusting the white cloth over his shoulder, occasionally waving Sekuru Zevezeve's ap-

---

* 'Dunge's spirits. Dunge's Christian spirits.'

pointed walking stick to the earthen shelf and to himself.

Rindai grabs a mug from an elder, imbibes deeply and shouts, to nobody, 'Today they will speak. We are tired of illness, we are.'

Bhudhi Tavengwa, who is normally quiet and reserved, has obviously had quite a bit to drink. He says, 'Yes, we want to know if our path is clear.'

Kelvin does not speak. He doesn't fall, writhe or foam at the mouth and say who he is, or who is trying to inhabit him.

Kelvin does not speak; instead, a young man falls down in the crowd, screaming. A youth with a black headband and a white cloth tied over his shoulder, a man from across the river who calls us cousins, and whom I should certainly remember from our dew-in-the-morning days. The crowd catches him and plants him, panting and sputtering, against the wall. His father, whom we call uncle and whom I should certainly also know, hands the young man – or whoever it is possessing the youth – his stick and tries to calm him.

Kelvin does not speak, but instead, he turns and moves towards our frenzied cousin, opening a way through the crowd. The singing falters to a halt. My brother leans down in front of him and offers him snuff. Still whimpering, the youth holds up a limp hand. Kelvin shakes snuff onto his upraised palm and then steps back to the front of the hut. Someone offers him a stool and he sits down, facing the crowd.

Kelvin feeds his nostrils from Zevezeve's appointed *chipako* and empties the snuff into a wooden bowl full of water. He invites first Rindai, then me, then Shuvai, to drink from the bowl. The water is acrid with snuff; already my head is singing with the seven-days brew.

'Drink, Rindai.'

'Godfrey,' he says to me. 'You are strong. You fear nothing.'

And to Shuvai, 'Are you well, child? Are you well?'

There is a pause, then Bhudhi Tavengwa shouts from the crowd, 'And am I safe in the home that my father left me? Am I safe?'

Kelvin will not be hurried. He does not reply. I think Kelvin is acting. He hasn't said who he is. Either he is imitating Sisi Ratidzo at the Chivi *biras* or he is acting out a role he read about in his Shona literature or sociology classes. Perhaps it's the effect of his drugs.

That and the seven-days brew. Perhaps he's acting out a role people have expected of him all along.

'Am I safe in the home my father left me?' Bhudhi Tavengwa demands again. 'Am I safe?'

Pause. Maiguru Mai Hamu hurriedly begins a song to drown out her husband's voice and several voices take up the tune. The dancing slowly resumes. Kelvin leaps off his stool, throws Zevezeve's appointed *chipako* over his shoulder and snaps Zevezeve's appointed walking staff in two with his knee. He tears Zevezeve's assigned white cloth off his shoulders and rips it up. The singing stops. He breathes heavily, fists clenched and trembling, like somebody facing an adversary. The crowd edges back towards the door, the women gasping, *'Yuwi! Yuwi! Yuwi!'* The hut quickly empties. Mbuya Sibanda kneels in front of Kelvin clapping her hands, 'What is it, Ngara? What is it now, Ngara?'

***

In the morning, in the aftermath of the night proceedings, when the villagers have left us to ourselves, we are rudely shaken out of our frayed sleep and father gathers us together in the kitchen before our various departures. He starts off with a Dutch Reformed tune.

'Tofara sei, munyika yakadai?' *

And then he prays, 'Jesus, show us the way in this moment of darkness. Jesus, show us light in our dilemma ... ' The prayer is broken by a thud. We open our eyes and Rindai is face down on the floor, having a fit. Mother, Bhudhi Tavengwa and I grab him and hold him up while he stiffens and shakes. It is half a fit, almost noiseless. He slowly regains consciousness with a confused, guilty expression on his face. Mother makes him open his mouth to see if he has bitten his tongue and Maiguru Mazvita searches in her bag for his pills.

Mbuya Sibanda wipes the tears from her face. 'What is it, Ngara?'

Father says, earnesty, 'Let this be a lesson to them all, Mhai.'

Mbuya Sibanda wipes her face again and asks, as if it's an afterthought, 'Were the people in Chivi informed, Ngara?'

Father adjusts his woollen hat over his forehead.

---

* 'Where is happiness in this sad world?'

'Shouldn't there have been somebody to help, Ngara? Somebody who knows what to do?'

Father fingers the cut on his head, adjusts his woollen hat again, and with an almost triumphant glint in his eyes, says, 'Let this be a lesson to them. Two lessons. That Gwanangara blood and alcohol don't mix. And that the dead are best left alone.'

***

Her name was Hilda Dolly Tsvangira and she was neither pregnant, nor had she run away from home. She was sixteen, barely half his age. Her people were workers on a farm just outside Gwelo. She had just completed Standard 2. She met him in Mr Punjab's shop and he was selling shoes. It was a week before Christmas. Her mother's brother, the tractor-driver on the farm, had given her some money with the words, 'Here is your Krismas. *Get yourself a new dress,* umzukulu.*' She wasn't sure whether she wanted a dress or a pair of shoes. This man standing in the veranda outside Mr Punjab's shop stopped her and sung her his strange shoe songs. He took her into the shop and showed her a pair of gleaming brown shoes. Only Sthandazile had a pair like that on the farm. Now she could show off to her friends. So she bought them. He wrapped the box up in a sheet of khaki paper, the kind used by children at school to cover their exercise books. This tall funny man also gave her three pink sucking sweets and said, 'Come again soon.' Mr Punjab was watching and smiling. Dunge Gwanangara had followed her a little way out of the shop and asked her for her name. She was foolish enough to tell him, and to give him her address. Then the letters followed. One after another. He said, 'I want to marry you,' and she said, 'Do you mean it?' and he said 'Cross bible.'*

That was how it all began. Almost too fast. Now he had met her aunt – her father's sister – and persuaded her to visit his people. At first she didn't like Chivi. People said it was a cursed land of drought and hunger. She had heard strange stories about it. Stories of the hungry old woman who boiled stones until they became soft and edible. His mother was VaChivi but she wasn't like the old woman in the story. His mother sang, talked and laughed to herself, but she didn't give her too much trouble. His brother Tachiona was nice too, except when he wept. And his brother's diminutive wife, Mai Dzenga cautiously tolerated her, watching to see how they would relate.

She lived with Dunge in the township, first in one room in a jha-radha, then, much later, in a little four-roomed house. They visited Chivi perhaps once every three months. Soon after she was married, her people all emigrated to Northern Rhodesia. She cried a great deal but could not go with them because she had chosen to marry Dunge and stay behind. Her children were born in the small clinic in the township. The first five were two years apart, then the gaps widened. Rindai, then me, Godfrey, and Kelvin; then, when she had almost given up hope of daughters, she had three girls in a row – Shuvai, Vimbai and Tendai – and much later Tapera, the boy who completed the circle. It was said that if your womb began with a boy, it would end with a boy, to tie the knot. If you started with a girl, you would end with a girl.Rindai, her first son, was a bright, good-look-ing little boy. At three he could read and write simple words; at four he could do simple arithmetic; at five he could read the newspaper to his father. When he went to school he was so far ahead of his mates that the headmaster had to be called in to intervene. After a few weeks he was allowed to skip the first class and proceed straight to the second. I was bright, too, so they say, but I wasn't asked to skip a class. Perhaps the headmaster did not want to make class-skip-ping too much of a precedent. Or perhaps I wasn't as bright as my brother.

Rindai and I were alike, and yet different. He was light-skinned and soft-featured like mother; I was dark and strong-boned like father. Rindai was prone to headaches and nosebleeds; I to vomiting and a running stomach. Rindai loved mutakura wenyemba *while I happily dug into* mutakura wenzungu. *Rindai was a wizard at arithmetic, I at composition. We both read voraciously. Rindai adored Biggles and the Hardy boys, I was in love with Enid Blyton. When we made our weekly music hit parades the Rolling Stones topped Rindai's charts while the Beatles headed mine. At the church we both loved Sunday school, and reciting verses in front of the congregation. Rindai liked hymn 42, the gospel according to Mark, and the parable of the wise and the foolish maidens; I preferred hymn 90, St John and the prodi-gal son. At school Rindai belonged to Muleya House while I cheered for Lobengula. At home our mother ran cleaning competitions for us: Rindai cleaned the sitting room while I did the kitchen, and the winner walked off with a plateful of scones. We argued fiercely and exchanged hot little blows in ready, savage competition whenever we could, yet in public we were almost like twins; people knew us as the brilliant Gwanangara children and were wont to confuse one for the other and say, to either of us, 'Which Gwanangara are you, Rindai or Godfrey?' We set a reputation for ourselves and our siblings – a reputation for intelligence, neatness and obedience; those who came after us had to strive to keep up and do well, for father and mother, and for our family name.*

9

Father stays behind after the *bira* in Gokwe to take two of his remaining head of cattle to market. One is a healthy bull in his prime, worthy of being named Bhuru raGwanangara, the bull of the Gwanangara kraal. Bhudhi Tavengwa helps father drive the cattle to the market, some twelve kilometres away. Perhaps because of the unaccustomed distance, father returns home with a swollen leg and has to go to hospital for a week. I go to Gweru to see him. The swelling is on his shin, neither a wound or a boil, but still they give him antibiotics. He is impatient to return to work, against all our protests – I don't remember him ever reporting sick before – and he is clearly uneasy that people are journeying from all over the country to fuss over him in his bed.

At the plot Kelvin is restless, and demanding to return to university. I can see that he is not nearly well enough to sit at a desk. Mother begs me to let him try. So I accompany him to Harare. He is manageable but his face carries a hurt, distant look. Vongai accompanies him to the university doctor, and when I return from school, he has been referred to a specialist psychiatrist, and hospitalised. I go at once to see him. The place looks comfortable, and the nurses are friendly. Kelvin steps out from the sunny garden to meet me. He is co-operative in his green hospital pyjamas and striped cotton robe, quietly accepting his fate. There is TV and table tennis. The medication is regularly administered, and the progress of the patients closely monitored. I can tell at once, and with sharp regret, this is where we should have brought him to in the first place, and not dabbled with *n'angas*. He assures me he should be out in a few days, that at least the doctor has told him so. His worry is whether he is still eligible for his university grant, having missed the better part of his first year.

I make an appointment with his department to find out his status. The dean is a large Indian man, well reputed for maintaining high standards, and known for his intolerance for slack work. He opens Kelvin's file and shows me a chain of Ds and Es and says, sombrely, 'His performance was very weak, even before he fell ill.' I beg him to give my brother a second chance, especially in view of his illness, but he snaps the file shut. 'He'll have to re-apply if and when the doctor decides he is well enough to return.'

I tell Kelvin that the dean said he must get well first, but I don't tell him anything else. Vongai and I visit him frequently and play table tennis with him. The psychiatric wing is good for him, the medication is working. His drugged body straightens a little. I haven't seen him laugh like this in the past year. He makes friends with the other inmates. He tells us their individual problems; he knows who is from where, who does what, and so forth. There is an accountant whose mother has the same totem as us and at once addresses Kelvin and me as *VanaSekuru* and Vongai as *Mbuya*. A politician is brought in whenever the spirit of Soshangana rises up and frequents his office. And a shapely girl who calls Kelvin 'Darling K' and reads him stories from romantic magazines. Kelvin is busy all right, doing his alternative sociology and political science.

I call home regularly and tell our parents not to worry, Kelvin is improving. I feel responsible, happy to give them this reassurance. Rindai neither visits nor phones. I am afraid to ask about his health. Later, I wonder if a proper medication regime wouldn't have helped him more.

Weeks pass. Father says the doctors must decide when Kelvin should be released. Sometimes he is allowed out over weekends and visits us. One Sunday afternoon, all dressed up, he takes a walk in town, returning in a taxi, with the shapely girl from the annexe. They've been to a cinema together. I pay off the taxi and walk the two of them back. Later, when I'm alone with Kelvin, I drop a hint about using condoms, trying not to seem too bossy. I'm secretly relieved that Kelvin is making friends again, and the shapely girl is friendly. Would anyone know that she was mentally disturbed if they hadn't seen her at the annexe?

***

In those sweet years, my mother's babies came without trouble. And every time she gave birth, my father brought her presents to reward her for being such a good wife. Each time one of her children celebrated a birthday she cashed in her empty bottles to buy cream sodas and meat pies. Her children hardly went anywhere, apart from school or church. On a few occasions, she had insisted on travelling to Northern Rhodesia to show her children off to her relatives. The journey was bone-tiring: the trains were crowded and filthy with engine smoke and the stench from the lavatories. She always had heaps of luggage, bagfuls of nappies, a child in arms and several toddlers at her feet but men rushed to help her because she was young and pretty. Her mother, siblings and their spouses also made pilgrimages to visit her, this wonder from Southern Rhodesia. Her mother once slaughtered her a cow and her brothers brought her large river bream so that she could feast on tripe, liver and fish – her favourites – and let her mother spoil her.

We were almost too young to remember those visits but the stories lived on. When Rindai was barely four, and mother had just alighted from the bus with the three of us, a bull had frightened my older brother who fell down and broke his arm. He had to be rushed to the nearest clinic for a case of plaster of Paris, earning himself the nickname Mr Plaster. On another occasion, the train took off with father aboard hauling in mother's bags, leaving Rindai stranded on the darkened platform. He had reported himself to railway security and when father re-appeared hours later, my capable brother was reading magazines aloud to the bemused railway staff.

For me the scenes that gel are of father, tall and dignified in his black suit, the train jerking ahead without warning, hurried goodbyes, mother gathering us onto the seat beside her and feeding the youngest a shielded nipple; a big fat ugly white guard with flaking lips and sausage fingers flipping a towel off mother's breast and snapping 'Tickets! Tickets!', and banging sleeping passengers' heads against the windows, and kicking open lavatory doors; fitful

112

sleep, the train chugging on forever; the rinsing of mouths with sour
water from the chained cup near the lavatory, breakfast of cold fried
chicken and sliced brown bread, trees and grasslands spinning past,
sweltering afternoons and windy nights; and then, finally, the bus,
roaring through a forest of tall trees. Cattle. Kraals. Village huts.

Our northern relatives emerge from the blur of my memories –
grandmother VaMurozvi sitting solidly by the fire shelling ground-
nuts and laughing with her hoarse voice; Sekuru Elias cycling away
into the sunset with his fishing lines; Maiguru Mai Charity win-
nowing grain in the midst of a flurry of cackling chickens; Mainini
Nomsa bathing me in a huge tin bath; Sekuru Bhuru scraping out
the stings from the swollen face of a boy mobbed by a swarm of bees;
children gathering in the moonlight to sing:

Chimba chaSekuru Elias chineman'a!
Chimba chaSekuru Elias chineman'a wo!*

Strangely enough, I have no memory of our return trips.

One morning in 1965, when I was in Sub B, I heard that a man
called Smith had taken over the country. Everyone was very sad.
My mother sat at the kitchen table and wept. She said we could no
longer go to Zambia to see her relatives. I did not know who the man
was and what taking over a country meant, but I cried too. Bhudhi
Dzenga told me to 'Shut up!' When father came home from work, he
showed us a picture of Ian Douglas Smith riding a bicycle because
there was no petrol in the country. Father laughed and said, 'What
kind of a prime minister rides a bicycle?'

It was raining heavily that summer and a boy had drowned in
the Gweru River. Bhudhi Dzenga kicked my shin and said, 'Idiot! If
you go swimming in the river you will catch bilharzia and drown.'
I dreamt of the boy drowning, his mouth and nose full of bloody
water, fish nibbling at his feet. Strangely, in the morning, I wanted a
fish. Mother had gone to work on our small plot of maize outside the
township and there was no bread. Bhudhi Dzenga told Rindai and
me to fetch our rubber catapults and we went to Matroko bush to
hunt birds. We never shot any.

Later one day our neighbour Mai Kero came out of her house ulu-
lating and dancing and shouting, 'UVerwoed ufile! UVerwoed ufile

---

* Sekuru Elias's hut has cracks.

bantu! *Verwoed has died!' All the women in the street started ululating and dancing and shouting. I said to mother, 'Who is Verwoed?' and she said, 'Ask your father.'*

***

Four months later, Kelvin is released from the annexe. By then Vongai has given birth to a baby girl, Piwai Gwanangara. Mother offers to look after our daughter while my wife goes back to the university to complete her degree.

Father absorbs himself in his tomatoes, vegetables and mealies. With the help of his newly acquired master-farmer notes, he turns the plot green. He buys an order bicycle with a carrier and each morning he rides to work laden with tomatoes, eggs, cabbages and green mealies to sell to his customers at the store.

Vongai and I go home every month to see our daughter, Piwai. I now have a car, a good second-hand VW Golf, and when we drive back to Harare the boot is always full of crates of eggs that we sell for mother.

***

This is a time of reprieve. For a year the moon is magnanimous – we have not been happy like this in months. Rindai has no fits. Kelvin secures a place at a teacher training college. His letters bristle with enthusiasm; he claims he is doing well, but there is a recklessness to his style which makes me suspicious. Even his slipshod handwriting tells another tale. Half his letters are about girlfriends, or his quest for such – he seems desperate for attachment, even marriage. I tell him to take his time, but he seems to think that at twenty-four his time is running out. His academic performance is dubious. Because he has had one partial year of university education he seems supercilious, determined that he is a cut above his A- and O-Level mates. Inevitably he quarrels with his lecturers in his bitter way. I steal books and send him pocket money. Now with curriculum development, I'm in a better position to help him out. Father covers the bulk of his costs – I doubt if Rindai ever contributes. I somehow feel that as the healthy brother in the family I should do something for my siblings.

When we're together at home at weekends, Rindai buys himself a crate of beer and sits on the veranda, drinking steadily. Hypocrite

114

that I am, I don't join him. Mother lets him be; father keeps a wary eye on him. Father assaults us with his accounts and lodgers' rent sheets and his inexhaustible interest in politics – this is the time of dissidents. His interest in world affairs is a little too earnest, in our baffled, cautious environs. We are comfortable with far more mundane subjects.

***

It started in such a small way that we didn't even notice when it began. I was eight or nine, and the first thing I remember was seeing mother at the kitchen table holding up her right hand, brushing the tears off her face, and sobbing, 'Oh my thumb!' Father was holding her hand, sitting helplessly by her side as the church congregants streamed in and out of our house to pray, Rindai urged, 'Mother, why don't you go to the clinic?' Mother, shaking her head cried, 'My thumb! Oh my thumb!' Baba Rhakeri from next door was called in to assist. He was from Malawi and people said he knew how to fix such problems. He brought a jar of oil and poured some into a cup. A little black cork floated on top of the oil. He warmed the liquid on the stove and made mother dip her thumb into the oil, again and again. At first she shrank back from the hot liquid, but soon she began to feel better. That night she slept well. In the morning she was laughing again but I overheard her telling Mainini Waniso, 'I almost died. This little thumb nearly did me in. I felt faint, as if there was a needle moving in my heart. Then I went blank. I could hear voices singing but all was dark except for a little light at the end of a tunnel. It grew until I felt my heart lifting out of my body. It was outside me, floating above me. Then it became blindingly bright and I heard a gentle voice say, 'Go back, Hilda Dolly. Go back and look after your children." I felt a warm hand on my forehead. For some time I could still see the light although my eyelids were closed. I eventually fell asleep, and when I woke up I was well again.'

And then later Bhudhi Dzenga took Rindai, Kelvin and me to our mother's father's brother's home in Lower Gwelo. Bhudhi Dzenga was Babamukuru Tachiona's son, our first cousin. He was living with us and doing Standard 6. It was our very first trip to the countryside, apart from our journeys to Zambia. Grandpa slaughtered a goat but we did not like goat meat. We thought it stank. We preferred milk, especially creamy sour milk. His son Sekuru Mateu washed his hands in a pail of milk, stuffed his mouth with raw goat testicles and he said, 'Milk is for toddlers from towns! Goat testicles are for men!' That night Sekuru Mateu saw a ghost in a muhacha tree in the centre of the yard. It wore a black gown and fell out of the tree. Grandma said, 'Now, Mateu, no more ghost stories, please! Don't scare your cousins off.'

In the morning we went swimming with Mainini Nyembezi. She was grandma's daughter. She was my age but not shy. She took off her dress and walked into the river right in front of us. She had tiny black nipples. I wanted to hold her, to hold her hand and swim with her although she was my small mother. I was so sure I was in love with her. I often fell in love with my small maininis. Sekuru Mateu squabbled with her, kicked her on the buttocks and went off to find impfe, sweet cane. Grandpa had many fields and it was harvest time. We ate cane all day. There was plenty to eat. I was sad when we had to go back home. Lower Gwelo was nice.

That same year we went to Donsa, to see Maiguru Mai Elizabeth. She was my mother's sister, the first-born in their family. Elizabeth was our cousin, eight years older than me. There were always cousins, nephews and nieces staying with us, and once she did too, going school with us in Gwelo. Father paid her fees. She was older than all the pupils in her class. Then something bad happened and she was sent away. She stole something, or said something nasty to the teacher. Perhaps she bullied her classmates. She had to return to Donsa. She left hurriedly. Anyway, when we arrived in Donsa, Elizabeth said, 'Don't talk to Clarissa, or Mai Clarissa, either.' Elizabeth's father had two wives. Mai Clarissa was the younger wife and had three children. She lived on the other side of the yard. We hardly saw her. We never ate in her house. Babamukuru Baba Elizabeth belonged to the Apostolic Church. Every night he put on a white gown and took off his sandals and fetched his staff to go out into the dark to talk to the prophets and chase away evil spirits. He was a very quiet man.

I looked after the calves and goats which I enjoyed, despite one stubborn goat. One evening when I was chasing it, I fell over an old *grave near the goat-pen. I ran away spitting out grass and sand. I thought my skin would turn green. That night Babamukuru Baba Elizabeth was taken ill. They said he was poisoned; had eaten a poisoned melon. Nobody knew who was responsible, but they suspected Mai Clarissa. They said she'd done it out of jealousy, to spite Maiguru Mai Elizabeth or because Babamukuru was going to send her away.*

The whole village crowded in Babamukuru's yard. Everyone was crying. Women threw themselves in the dust. It was a terrible sight. A strange, sad smell came from the kitchen, where they kept the old man. Mother said we had to return to Gwelo. She said we were too young to participate in a funeral. She did not come with us. Sisi Elizabeth took us to the bus stop. Rindai was in charge. The bus was crowded, but we arrived home safely and found father's bicycle in the kitchen. I asked Bhudhi Dzenga where father was and he told us he didn't know. For four days we were without a father and when I asked Bhudhi Dzenga for an explanation all he said was, 'Shut up!' At night I couldn't sleep. I wet the blankets. I thought of the strange sad smell in Babamukuru Baba Elizabeth's hut, like that of a dead rat trapped behind a wardrobe. I prayed to God not to take my father away.

Mother returned on the fourth day. Her eyes were red, her skin pale and I could tell she hadn't washed or slept for days.

'Where is Baba?' she asked Bhudhi Dzenga

'I don't know.' he repeated. 'I don't know where he went, or who he went with or even when he went.'

Mother went out to talk to the neighbours. I couldn't hear what they were saying. When she returned home she was very, very quiet. That evening father came back with Babamunini Baba Marks. He too was quiet. Very, very quiet. His white shirt had sweat and dirt on the collar. He'd lost his tie. He did not greet us but went straight to the bedroom. Babamunini Baba Marks took mother to the spare bedroom to explain. I could hear her sobbing. Two days later, father went back to work. I don't know what happened to him. I still don't know. Much later I sneaked a look at his diary hidden under his clothes and tried to decipher some meaning from the words recorded in his galloping handwriting:

He came at me with clenched fists. He punched me on the nose. He tried to hit me again. I ducked. The other people in the store said, 'Run away, Dunge! Run!' I ran out and didn't look back. People's faces leered at me on the street. I could smell blood in my nose. Everyone seemed to be shouting. I ran into Babamunini Baba Marks. He said, 'Let's drive away from town at once. There's evil here. I know a man who can help you ...'

I wonder who he was, the man with the balled fists. Some irate customer? Somebody father had caught stealing and reported to the security guards or his boss – a customer with a vendetta against him? Or somebody from his well obscured past? Was it somebody or something he had imagined? Where had he gone with Babamunini Baba Marks for four days? To seek out who? What?

I searched my father's diary for clues. It was a hotchpotch of daily minutiae, recorded dreams, diagrams, mini-budgets and Bible verses. In places it read like a personal manifesto, a version of Pilgrim's Progress exhorting him to soldier on conscientiously with life. It even had proverbs such as 'A large snake does not bite itself' with an accompanying illustration, or 'The wages of sin are death'. Now I realise that sloth and superstition were my father's biggest foes.

10

The prophet from Kwekwe adjusts his white and purple robes and commands us to take our positions around the garage. Rindai looks drawn. After seven vicious attacks in two nights, he has instigated this new mission to rid our family of evil and has personally sanctioned this man of God and driven him to our plot. Father has reluctantly allowed him in; he is dubious, mother optimistic. Kelvin, Shuvai and Vimbai are not in attendance. Tapera boyishly brandishes a thick stick to stave off any creatures that may burst out of the boxes in the garage. Maiguru Mazvita and Vongai linger on the veranda. Tendai stands loyally behind mother.

Oh, how strife can destroy rationality!

The prophet fishes among the cartons with his staff. Rats scramble out of the way, forgotten rags tumble out of broken cardboard, stained rotting mattresses burst open.

'It's in here somewhere,' the prophet declares. 'Look inside that box. No, this one.'

We fumble blindly in the half-light. I wonder what the lodgers are thinking on the other side of the hedge, or what visitors would say if they happened upon the scene. The prophet's voice acquires a new urgency: 'There, that one!' I stumble over a rusty wheelbarrow and dive towards an empty cooking-oil box.

'Yes, that one. Bring it out and turn it upside-down.'

I stagger into the sunlight and turn the box over on the lawn. A buck horn falls out and lies black and gleaming on the grass. A horn, no bigger than a man's thumb.

'Don't touch it!' urges the prophet, rushing forward with a bottle of holy water. He gives the horn a good dousing then turns to father. 'There's the source of your trouble, Baba. That's the horn that's been hounding your family for years. That's the work of your enemies. It's harmless now. You can pick it up and burn it.'

'Can we go into the house and say a prayer first?' father asks, and I detect a tremor in his voice.

We troop into the house. Father utters a long bitter prayer about betrayal, urging the Lord Jesus to punish charlatans who make money out of fools, urging us, his children, to beware of lies, imploring us not to believe in the venality of this world, or in superstitions planted by so-called believers. As soon as father finishes praying, the prophet rises from his seat, packs his kit-bag and leaves, without farewell. Rindai rushes after him. There is a scene. Rindai tries to drag the prophet back but the man of God strides defiantly down the road. My brother returns to confront father.

*'Hamubatsire imi!'** You've never been ill, that's why. Some of us are sick of illness. We make an effort to bring in somebody who can help and you send him away with your goody-goody prayers. Now look what's happened.'

Everything that can go wrong, goes wrong.

Rindai looks as if he will strike father. Maiguru Mazvita urges him to calm down. Half the house is against father. As usual, I refuse to take sides.

Father runs away into the bush behind the house. I imagine he wants to escape the hotbed of emotion.

'And what if your father hangs himself?' sobs mother. 'Go after him!'

By now it is growing dark. We go out to look for him. There is a fire in the forest, grass burning in late winter. Trees throw long shadows, the grass rustles, dead trunks burst in the glow. He might already be dangling from the twisted branch of a tree. Rindai rushes home to call the police. Three young officers in grey uniform arrive with torches, their light slicing through the gloom. They're businesslike, untouched by our anxiety.

'Has he ever run away before? Attempted to kill himself?'

---

* 'You're useless!'

'No.'

'Did he take anything with him – rope or wire perhaps?'

'No.'

'Then go back home. Suicide is not easy. He's probably just testing you.'

'Doesn't he work in the big Indian shop, selling clothing?'

'Yes, he does.'

'Half the town knows him. He wouldn't kill himself. He has a reputation to maintain. He'll be back in the morning.'

We hardly sleep. In the morning Tendai spots father curled up in a ploughed furrow without a blanket. Maiguru Mazvita and Vongai take him coffee and cake. Mother fetches him a pullover. He smiles nonchalantly.

Rindai keeps his distance.

***

Maiguru Mai Dzenga, Babamukuru Tachiona's wife, sat cross-legged on the kitchen floor of our little four-roomed house and ate sadza and tripe. She had probably not eaten meat for weeks. Chivi is a harsh, barren land – its people eat sparingly, carefully licking morsels from their fingers, contemplating the troubles of this earth. Now she was here, a hundred and fifty miles away, freshly arrived with nothing but her little bundle of clothes and two matamba, to help us out.

One of the most difficult aspects of childhood is when adults withhold information and leave their children to intuit matters.

I thought that father had asked Babamukuru Tachiona to come and provide some support to his vulnerable family and his brother had said, 'No. You go, Mai Dzenga, and help your Babamunini.'

Maybe he felt that God had not done enough, and conversation overheard in muted sitting rooms suggested that he was taking advice from troubled neighbours about asking his family for help.

Maiguru and Mother took us to a herbalist. The house had two rooms, loosely divided by a sheet, with a bed on one side, and two chairs, a small table, a bicycle and cooking utensils on the other. Sekuru, the herbalist, evidently worked for a milling company be-

cause his overalls and hair were white with maize meal. He greeted us warmly and called us 'Vazukuru'.

Who was there? All of us – Rindai, Kelvin, Shuvai, Vimbai, me, and Bhudhi Dzenga, sitting legs stretched out before us on the concrete floor as we were supposed to. You don't cross your legs in the presence of a herbalist as it might appear that you are negating their powers.

I guessed that father and mother and Maiguru had already spoken to Sekuru.

He made little incisions on our chests with a razor-blade and rubbed an itchy black powder into them, as had happened before and would happen again. He rubbed oil over our faces, arms and legs, joking with us as he did so to make us feel at ease. The oil smelt like ordinary cooking oil to me; I supposed the little powdery seeds floating in it were what gave it its power to ward off evil as Sekuru explained.

He said, 'There are banana trees in your yard, aren't there? They're safe during the day but in darkness they're a danger. Wicked little men hide in the trees at night, waiting to slap you on the face and breathe poison into your noses. These little men are also in your toilet, your shower room, and all over the yard. For the time being you must never, never go out of the house after dark. Use the chamber pot at night and empty it in the morning. You understand?'

We obeyed Sekuru's instructions – for some months anyway. Every Saturday we went to his house to receive the protective powers of the oil treatment. When he worked late, we had to wait for him. Sekuru was always cheerful and liked to joke with us. One day he even asked, 'Do you want to do well at school and always come first in your classes?' It was embarrassing. I thought we could manage to come first without medicinal powers. He noticed our lack of enthusiasm and never mentioned the subject again. We never talked about him to our friends, or at school. He was our big secret. We did not want people to say, 'The Gwanangara children are intelligent because they visit a herbalist every Saturday!'

We did not go out of the house at night. We used the chamber pot. It was not easy. If we wanted to pass stool, we had to wait until morning. Bhudhi Dzenga was defiant. After all, he was nearly eigh-

teen. In the middle of the night he would wake up, undo the bolts and kick the door wide open. He would whistle loudly as he went to the toilet. Through the open doorway I would see the banana trees shivering in the moonlight. I thought that perhaps the ghosts were put off by Bhudhi Dzenga's whistling and spitting, or else they thought he was too old to bother about. Perhaps they liked more tender flesh and were deterred by Bhudhi's lean calves.

We visited Sekuru regularly for several months and then slowly the gaps between each visit lengthened and finally we stopped going altogether. Perhaps it was because we were growing up or because nothing calamitous was happening to us, but mother had ceased to be so anxious. Each time I heard the banana trees rustle, though, I thought there was something out there, a supernatural being.

***

Kelvin falls out with all of us. After dropping out of the teacher's college, or rather more honestly, being expelled for poor performance and arrogance towards his lecturers, he returns home to haunt father. Like Rindai, he believes the old man is primarily responsible for his fate, perhaps for the simple reason of having brought him into this world.

Nothing can be crueller to a parent than when your sons turn against you with savage hatred, as if you were the sole cause of their woes.

Kelvin's illness takes him through various stages. It is almost cyclical. At one stage, he sleeps late, and doesn't raise a finger to make his bed, clear his plates away, or pick the ripe tomatoes rotting on the ground in the garden – the very fruits that sustain his livelihood, and pretty much everyone else's. He rarely goes into the garden, and when he does, it is to exchange a supercilious word with the gardeners, or to ask for cigarettes. He eats in the mornings and then wanders into the streets, pubs and shops, returning in the evenings to eat and sleep. He talks to no one in the family and his silence is oppressive. Sometimes he goes away for days on end without letting us know where to. He speaks shamelessly and disparagingly about the state of things in our household, railing about what he sees as parental neglect. He convinces people that there is a major family ancestral spirit trying to inhabit him, to speak to the family through

123

him, and that father, because of his goody-goody Christianity, is blocking the return of that spirit. He talks about the robed prophet and brags that the whole family rose against father and had almost driven him to suicide. He discloses stories about the many other *n'angas* and herbalists who have visited our home and tried to deliver us from whatever spirit is blighting us. Relatives and strangers, loving a good gossip, egg him on, and he fuels their contempt for my parents.

Some people, too many perhaps, gloat over the misfortune of households that are not their own.

Kelvin takes to heavy smoking and perpetually wants money for cigarettes. Father resents it when, with fraternal guilt, I leave him a few notes every month-end because he will spend it all on cigarettes. He is convinced that Kelvin is also smoking *mbanje* – marijuana – and traditional snuff taken by all those who believe they are possessed by ancestral spirits. Perhaps his voracious appetite and his taciturnity confirm father's suspicions.

To protect himself from despair, father tries to pretend that, 'All Kelvin needs to do is to stop smoking and drinking and do something with himself and for himself.' I am only now just beginning to understand the degree of his hurt and his shame, his belief that 'No Gwanangara need ever smoke or drink; they are taboo to the Gwanangaras'. Only now do I begin to understand how much he sacrificed on our behalf and dedicated his working life to improving ours.

Then, however, I did not understand. I felt ambivalent and guilty. I knew I could do more than dole out some pocket-money. I had even begun to feel guilty about being 'well' – or so I thought – unlike my two brothers. I want to make up for my well-being. Being 'well' obliges me to be more involved in events at home, to side with mother and father, to help out in times of trouble. I convince myself, foolishly perhaps, that I was cut out to be the appeaser in the family. Cockily, and because I also earn more money than the others, I think I'm superior, even indispensable, the only one capable of making decisions. Rindai has mentioned it, and his wife has hinted that I like to hold the family to ransom.

Rindai, the rational scientist, reads up the literature on schizophrenia and advises against philanthropy towards Kelvin; he argues that this will create a dangerous dependency syndrome, the belief that we all owe him a living. Rindai's rationality means that he offers Kelvin nothing. But why, I wonder now, was Rindai never similarly rational about his own condition?

Obstinately, and still eager to prove himself, Kelvin becomes an aspiring political commissar in the local branch of the people's party, a part-time catechist at a new spiritual church, and a youth counsellor on health. At one point he simultaneously tries to sell life-insurance and burial policies, peddles cent-cools and condoms and even joins the Red Cross as a volunteer.

I pity him, pity his craven ambitions, which like the assortment of boiled butter beans we planted together in the tiny gardens of our youth, the gardens our cousin Bhudhi Dzenga irritably ploughed up, never germinate.

When father realises that Kelvin's many and diffuse efforts are spent, he prays that he is ready to reform and enrols him at the local technical college to study book-keeping and accounts; and yet again, with the meagre income from his hard-grown vegetables, buys him expensive textbooks. Mother washes and irons his clothes, makes him egg and tomato sandwiches, and for a while he seems happy enough.

Before long, however, the remission is over – his hunger to be somebody, someone that we will all recognise, who has a girl on each arm, who frequents restaurants and is a natty dresser, means that again he lives beyond his means. He peddles his textbooks for pocket-money, his exercise books for cigarettes and dope. He drops out of college. *Shiri ine muriro wayo* – a bird never changes its song. Of course, we have heard this refrain before, but we never made the effort to really understand its meaning.

None of us understand the behaviour of a paranoid schizophrenic. We've heard the words; we know the diagnosis; we could have made more of an effort to find out and explain, to support and help our parents to understand, but we did not. Father becomes incensed, 'Look Kelvin. Your brother Rindai is not well but he can look after himself and his family. You just can't be helped. Go away!'

Mother watches and weeps helplessly while Kelvin packs his

suitcase. But our father has spoken.

Kelvin seeks out relatives: our totemic uncle Babamunini Waniso, our blood cousin Tafirenyika, newly married in his early forties, our mother's well-to-do cousin Mainini Hazvi and, inevitably, Sekuru Mhasvi, my father-in-law, who is a stickler for tradition. He lodges with each of them and their families in turn. They house and feed him, dutifully listening to his woes. While he is with them he seems to turn over a new leaf. It is convenient for him to do so. I explain his behaviour away. He is a Gemini after all. It is easier for me to put it all down to the stars than to schizophrenia, a word that fills me with horror and shame. Kelvin, this brother I love and hate and love and pity so much, this brother over whom I wield so much power, who has not once in his rages struck out at me, or challenged me.

Of course, for us, his good behaviour is almost as embarrassing as his bad. When he washes and irons his own clothes, makes his bed, waters the gardens, cuts the hedges and weeds the path, helps the children with the homework and speaks ever so gently to everyone, his hosts are truly baffled about the cause of his problem, and feel that we others can only be to blame.

Ever an expert on these matters, Sekuru Mhasvi consults father and attempts to mediate between them, but he will not hear of it. Neither can Sekuru Mhasvi, a retired policeman, believe the charges father lays against his son. Unwittingly, he is led to believe that father simply wants to get rid of his son. 'Where is this *mbanje* your father says the young man takes? Why doesn't your father bring us a twist so that he can convince us?'

So cunning is Kelvin that he goes to Babamukuru Tachiona's household in Chivi and stays with them for a good month, and when he returns, emaciated and dirty but unscathed, Sekuru Mhasvi is the first to insinuate that 'Dunge Gwanangara has always hated his relatives.'

In the streets of the town, the refrain is taken up. 'Kelvin has exposed his father to be a selfish snob who turned his son out of his home.'

Self-righteous gossip, ignorance, misunderstanding and a simple lack of compassion all contrive to make our problem a very public one in which my parents, particularly my father, are condemned.

***

Mbuya VaChivi, Mwana WaChibga, Njiki, the wife of Gwanangara, Mai Tachiona, Mai Dunge, my father's mother, my grandmother, the woman who dared answer back to the white man and tell him off, the first mother in those parts to willingly deliver her own son to the doors of the white man's school, came to live with us in Gokwe. Now let's retrace events a little.

A year or two after father's disappearance and mother's sore thumb, father decided, somewhat arbitrarily, as was often his style, that the family had to relocate from Chivi to Gokwe. He and Babamukuru Tachiona went on a preliminary trip to the new land and brought back startling stories of matamba *as big as footballs, forests teeming with* chakata, mashuku *and wild mushroom, vlei gardens wild with vegetables and* tsapi *sagging with produce. As evidence they brought with them a cockerel big enough to feed three families and half a bag of big round nuts. They had agreed to relocate but Babamukuru later changed his mind on the grounds that if he stayed in Chivi he might be given a junior chieftainship. Besides, he claimed, it was imprudent to abandon the land of one's birth and one's ancestral graves for another area, however alluring.*

Mother went first with Vimbai, who was not yet at school, and so our dew-in-the-morning days began. Babamukuru agreed to let Mbuya VaChivi and his daughter, Ratidzo, join mother at our new home in Gokwe.

Mbuya VaChivi came to Gwelo without notice, and our little four-roomed house was immediately full of her smell, the odour of trapped time. This stern old woman with white hair peeping beneath her doek was a stranger to us cultureless young townies fidgeting with our books. I don't remember who took her to Gokwe but we next saw her in the August holidays, when we went there for the first time to keep her company after mother had returned to Gwelo. She was feeding day-old chicks and we wanted oh so much to touch them, oh so much to fondle their little warm fluffy yellow bodies. She forbade us to do so because 'you will bring the eagles down upon them! Imi vana vaDunge, *you, Dunge's children, don't you ever listen? ' When we had given her the cowhead meat we'd brought with us on the bus, and thrown off our shoes, Kelvin lifted up a chick which pecked him*

127

so he dropped it. We thought the chick was dead, but after we'd said a quick prayer it miraculously wriggled back onto its feet and we sighed with relief.

The old woman was the totemic lion, classic huntress and feeder on flesh. She loved meat and would sit at the fire for hours, burning out worm-sized maggots from rotten meat so the whole hut was full of the smell of hot fat. She couldn't do this during the day because if villagers discovered that we had a box full of meat, they could bewitch us for being well-off.

Our grandmother loved coarse salt. She despised tea and bread, much preferring pumpkins and sweet potatoes. The smell of new clothes offended her, so did diesel and petrol fumes, and all forms of mechanical transport. She hated to bath but occasionally mother would subtly induce her to do so. Afterwards when she was sitting near the fire smelling cleanly of carbolic, Dettol and Vaseline, she would poke us in the ribs and cackle, knowing that we also had a bath coming.

The lionness of Chivi loved mother and hated her, hated mother and loved her: this thirty-year-old who already had five children and another one on the way, this young tractoress who conquered virgin fields with a mere hoe, this young wife who left her son alone in town to cook for himself every planting season, this young daughter-in-law who touched no herb and was as yet untouched by tragedy.

Mwana waChigba loved chakata and she would fill a mortar with the ripe brown fruit, pound it with a pestle until the pips were clean, and then pour the sweet juice into a cup for us to drink..

The well-known storyteller bedded with us in the kitchen and like many old people she slept badly. One stormy night she woke us up screaming, 'Nyoka! Nyoka! Snake! Snake!' and indeed there was a puff-adder near the door, its eyes gleaming. Rindai killed it with a piece of firewood.

The matriarch of the family saw things we didn't see, heard things that we didn't hear, and knew things that we didn't know. Once, when she woke us up, the door was wide open. She screamed, 'Silly children, sleeping flat out. Wake up! What animal can it be, kicking in a bolted door? Wake up!'

Our gogo loved Chivi. She was lonely in Gokwe. Tachiona was not there to sing with her after a beer-drink and she had no friends. She did not understand the secrets of the terrain and she could not converse with the spirits of the land. 'Zinyika rakaipa iri!' she swore to herself, 'What a terrible land!' But she stayed on. When other villagers accused mother of abandoning Mbuya for Gwelo after the harvest season, the old woman snorted loyally, 'Let my daughter-in-law join her husband. They're married, thank you.'

It is said that when an old or important person dies, their death is followed by a big harvest, and the year Mbuya VaChivi died, we had a bumper one. Gokwe killed her. She only lasted three planting seasons. She must have been sixty-three when she died, not very old.

She became sick. Father sent us to accompany her back to Gweru to take to her to the hospital. Mother had to stay looking after the homestead. Mbuya VaChivi sat stolidly at the front of the jolting bus, rocking to its motions, her defiant crop of grey hair peeking out from her doek. When we finally arrived in Kwekwe she joked about the driver , 'And was that his job, that man sitting up at the front of the bus, to jolt up old widows like me?' On the shorter train trip to Gweru she managed to doze, so that we had to wake her up and walk her to the waiting taxi – 'tortoise of a scotchcart' as she called it.

It was early August and the cold had not yet relented. Father fussed about, piling firewood into the mbaura *to keep his mother warm. In retrospect, I think father was trying to make up for all those cold years when he had neglected Mbuya in Chivi.*

That drizzling Saturday morning I set out with Mbuya to the clinic. Bhudhi Dzenga, after father's intervention, was working as a hand in another Indian shop. It was 1969. Rindai was already boarding at secondary school; Michael Jackson had several songs on the local hit parade, Neil Armstrong had just set foot on the moon. I was twelve and in Grade 6 and the 'menija' *at 33 Hoffman Street. Father was, of course, busy at the Indian shop.*

Mbuya trudged behind me at a snail's pace; we didn't have money for the 'Omen' – the omnibus – and a taxi was out of the question. Several times I had to stop to let her catch her breath and once I turned back to see her squatting, plump brown and naked from the waist, stopping to relieve herself behind a tree. She said, nervously, 'Iwe! Iwe!' and waved me on.

At the outpatient section I left Mbuya sitting on a bench and sought out Baba Kidias, the medical assistant who went to our church and to whom father had written a letter. The man helped us jump the long queue. The female assistants took the old woman's temperature, blood pressure, urine and stool samples and X-rays. After a good two hours she returned clutching a card marked with an indecipherable scrawl, and two bottles of pills. We had done well enough, I thought.

In the evening, father talked of a private doctor and injections, the golden words of health in those days.

Father sat long into the night with his mother, asking her about our lineage and taking copious notes, mostly names, places and dates which he later meticulously transferred into some kind of narrative family tree in his diary. I still have that precious book, going back perhaps a hundred and fifty years, locked in my wardrobe. Father stoked the fire and insistently, almost desperately, interrogated Mbuya, and she tolerated the inquest. I eavesdropped on them through a crack in the door as I sat in the yellow gloom pretending to read Jane Eyre.

On Sunday afternoon, after the church service, people came in their dozens to pray for her. I overheard father and our priest talking of baptism though, as far as I knew, Mbuya had never been inside a church. Unfortunately, Mbuya did not respond to the treatment and, in unaccustomed panic, father sent to Chivi for his brother, Babamukuru Tachiona.

He came quickly and perched on a stool in the kitchen; father sat on a chair and Mbuya sat on a mat between them. Behind them, we children squirmed, out of the fire's warmth. Babamukuru laughed, wept and staunchly refused to eat the chicken father had bought for the occasion.

Mbuya bit into her drumstick, and growled, like a lioness, at Babamukuru, 'You and your chicken vows, Tachi, will finish us all off.'

They consulted late into the night, debating the best course of treatment for Mbuya. Babamukuru was of the opinion that she should return with him to Chivi and seek the help of a n'anga or a herbalist, while father believed she should be hospitalised at once.

Babamukuru pleaded and sobbed, so that Mbuya chided him; 'Am I the first person to die, Tachi? Who on this earth was not born for the grave? Seka hako mwana waChibgwa! Mubgwiro hamusekwi!*

In the morning the debate grew more intense, father and Babamukuru arguing in the kitchen, in the sitting room and outside in the garden, now shouting, now consulting in hushed whispers. 'Munu'una†, let me take mother home with me,' Babamukuru pleaded. 'Let her not perish in the houses of white men.'

When we returned from school at lunchtime the house was locked, and father had left a note for us to collect the keys at Vatete Mai Farai's house. 'Your father and Babamukuru have taken Mbuya to Bondolfi Mission Hospital,' Vatete explained.

I dug up a tattered old map of Rhodesia to find out where Bondolfi was, among the obscure web of schools, roads, shops and dip-tanks.

Father returned two days later, tight-lipped. Mother arrived from Gokwe on the same day. After a week of scant news, our parents left for Bondolfi Mission. When they came back I spotted them at the shops, father in his brown ankle-length woollen overcoat, mother in her black and white church uniform and I ran out to meet them.

'How is she?' I panted. No one answered. My parents strode on past me towards the house. Hurt, and feeling brushed aside, I followed them.

Within minutes the alarm was raised and our house filled with neighbours and relatives. Babamunini Waniso and the other church people brought chairs and benches for the crowd. Vatete Mai Farai brought pots and plates and Muzukuru Baba Tariro got a big fire going in the yard.

'There was very little the Bondolfi Mission hospital could do for her,' father said. 'It was too late. All the mission staff did was to pray for her and prepare her to meet her maker. When my wife and I arrived my brother Tachiona had already laid her out in her new rest house.'

Later, from the diary, I was to learn four things. First, that Mbuya had staunchly refused to be baptised by the Bondolfi priests. Second, that because of the lack of funds to transport her to Chivi, she had

---

* 'Laugh Chigbwa's daughter! There's no laughter in the grave!'

† Little brother.

been buried in the mission cemetery. Third, that Babamukuru had buried Mbuya alone, without any of her relatives present. Fourth, that because the graves were unmarked, our uncle, who'd been drunk, had had difficulty in identifying Mbuya's grave to father and mother or to any of Mbuya's relatives.

ii

Ping, pong. Ping, pong.

Kelvin and Rindai alternate illnesses. When Kelvin is ill, Rindai is not; when Rindai is, Kelvin is not. It is as if a roaming affliction has camped within our household.

Kelvin, penitently back home, as if atoning for his crimes, is up at four in the morning in the light of the full moon to feed the chickens. He is loading bags of layer's mash and replenishing the troughs. He cleans the pen and carts wheelbarrows of manure off to the garden. The chickens flap and caw in their pen, alarmed by this disturbance in the dark hours of early morning.

Mother watches him from the bedroom window and calls, 'It's not yet dawn Kelvin, my son. Why don't you go back to sleep and see to the chickens later? Try and rest.'

Kelvin, for once, obeys her. He comes back and lies prostrate on the bed, next to me, his eyes glowering in the dark. We know it will be violence and another police truck in the morning; tranquillisers, sedatives, and a brief detention at the hospital.

'Why don't you try sending him to a halfway house?' the nurses will say, and mother will sigh and say, *'Mwanangu!'*

Rindai soldiers on. He has his plants, his trips home and abroad, his wife and his children, three now, all girls, to keep him busy. He does not stop drinking but switches to a milder beer, a Pilsener, but every day after work he drinks steadily. Still, he is up at six in the morning to get ready for the office. He's developing a paunch but when he's hit by a spate of attacks, it disappears.

Now the phone rings less and less often, and mother, the moon

133

huntress, worn with custom, wearied by a decade of moons, does not always hive off to Kadoma with a ready packed bag. But she keeps her ears to the ground, hatches new plans.

One morning she calls me to announce that she has been referred to an old woman in Gutu who might be able to solve Rindai's problem once and for all. There is a strange excitement, an urgency in her voice.

Father speaks to me quietly, careful not to worry or excite me unnecessarily, but he hints that mother has been having sleepless nights and feels the trip to Gutu must be taken soon, at whatever cost.

I know father is convinced that the real cause of Rindai's problem is his drinking. And he is right. I tell Vongai and she shrugs. I take two days off work, withdraw some money, throw a few clothes into a bag, fill up the car, and drive to Kadoma to pick up Rindai.

He is waiting for me with his kitbag. Maiguru Mai Nda says to him, 'Have you taken your pills? Purse? Toothbrush?' She fetches his ID.

We hit the road, Rindai and I. We have one third of the country to cover before dark. We chat in the shy, tangential way brothers express their intimacy, about jobs, cars, budgets, vocations, children – safe topics. We avoid contentious or irksome subjects: wives, politics, religion and women. I ask him about his plants and he inquires about my books. I realise for better or worse that our relationship has survived on our mutual tolerance, guarding ourselves from each other's deepest fantasies and fears. Not once do we touch on the purpose of our trip. At one point he offers to buy beer. I suggest we desist and he defers, companionably.

We find mother waiting for us, with her packed bag, egg and tomato sandwiches, roasted chicken and cool drinks.

'Did you bring blankets and warm clothes?' she asks. 'We might have to stay for the night.'

She shakes her head. Children will always be children, no matter how old they are. Mother brings out three blankets and father's ancient full-length brown woollen coat plus a newer grey one.

Again we hit the road.

It is early December and the rains are late. The sky is a dirty blue. The air is hot and dry. Leaves hang limply from the trees and the fields are covered with a meagre crop of grass, waiting for the plough. Last year there was a drought.

At Mvuma we stop at the garage to refuel and eat. Mother says little. I see her face in the driving mirror – her quiet, brown eyes meet mine and wander off anxiously into the distance. I play cassettes; Rindai and I discuss the jazz, blues and rock to which he, my musical mentor, had initiated me as a teenager. Mother taps her fingers on the sides of Rindai's seat and is content to let us, her two eldest sons, be.

Just after Mvuma we suffer the first mishap, a tyre ruptured beyond repair. Rindai and I change wheels with quick camaraderie and we're away again, without a spare wheel. Out in the country, we begin to consult the instructions scribbled in mother's Standard 5 cursive. It's nearly five, getting late. At a Growth Point we ask for directions to Mbuya Matope's compound. An old man with only three teeth and a blanket dangling from a walking stick says, 'I'm going where you're going, only nearer.'

I tell the old man to hop in. The car is soon full of his smell: tobacco, sweat, stale urine and seven-days brew.

'You're going to Mbuya Matope's?' he ventures, 'And what business do you have with the old lady?'

'We're visiting about a marriage,' Mother lies.

'I thought perhaps you were seeking her services,' responds the old man. 'She's a good herbalist. Anyway, marriage is good. I suppose one of you young men wants to marry into her family. She has three good unmarried daughters. The first one lost her husband a month ago. Which of you is searching for a wife?'

'Me,' Rindai answers.

We drive on through the swishing undergrowth for another five kilometres and see a large fire burning through the trees in the forest. The road comes to an abrupt halt. I stop the car.

'And where do you live, old man?' Rindai confronts our passenger with blunt suspicion.

'There, there,' says the old man, vaguely pointing towards the forest.

'And where is Mbuya Matope's compound?'

'Beyond us, in the valley. I didn't know if this road was any longer in use, but if you go back to the Growth Point they'll show you another way.'

'You tricked us into bringing you here,' Rindai wags a finger in the old man's face. 'Get out, you dirty fellow!'

He leaps out of the car, wrenches the back door open and drags the fellow out.

'No, Rindai,' mother says.

The old man tumbles out of the car, picks himself up, and shuffles away.

'Bloody hell,' says Rindai. 'Some people think cars run on river water!'

I reverse the car till I find a spot where I can make a U-turn. At the Growth Point a market woman points out a twin path leading towards a dark valley. Down this track we meet four young boys with a flock of goats and a pack of dogs. When we ask for directions to Mbuya Matope's place one of them offers to show us the way and climbs quickly onto the back seat. The remaining boys shout and whistle and the dogs chase after the car, barking madly.

As we approach the compound, women and children, startled by the whistling boys, the barking dogs, and the noise of an unexpected car, rush out of their huts. I park behind a large hut in the middle of the compound. As soon as the car comes to a stop, the boy on the back seat leaps out and bolts towards the approaching women.

The crowd from the huts surges forward, screaming.

'Kidnappers!'

'Child stealers!'

'Body-part dealers!

'Frogs in their brief-cases!'

'Stealing a child in its very home!'

'Today we have caught you!'

'Answer!'

'What do you want here?'

Mother struggles to roll down her window and pokes out her head.

Tisvikewo,' she says, clapping her hands.

Silence.

'Tisvikewo pamusha penyu,'[*] mother says again. 'We are looking for Mbuya Matope.'

'And what do you want with Mbuya Matope?' A woman with braided locks, demands.

'We're her visitors from Gwelo. We're seeking help from her.'

'Help? What help?'

'We have an illness.'

'And who sent you here?'

'We were given her name from her nieces in Mkoba, Gweru. They gave us directions.'

Mbuya Matope totters to the doorway of the large hut, her hands on her bent back, peering foggily at our car in the gathering gloom.

'Let them in,' she says, weakly.

***

'Futi, futi forgive us,' the dish woman with the braids laughs, serving us sadza and *mboora.* 'We seriously thought you were child kidnappers.'

'What with the boys whistling, and the dogs chasing after you,' says another.

'As well as the shiny white car,' continues a third, caressing her knees.

'A child was stolen in the neighbouring village last year and discovered dead, with parts missing ...' and I realise that this woman with braided hair could be as young as twenty-four. Village life is hard.

'You never know about these city businessmen.'

'Godwin always wanted a ride in a white car,' one child accuses another and all the children giggle.

Mbuya Matope gathers up a sleeping child and pushes a log into the fire. She is a small, slim dark woman with startling white hair. 'And how is Gwelo these days? I lived there before Ian Smith took over the country. My husband worked at Grey's Butchery until he sawed off two of his fingers and had to be retired.'

'Is he still alive?' I ask.

She shakes her head. 'He died ten years ago and left me this flock

---

[*] 'May we enter your home, please?'

to look after.'

After we've eaten and bantered for some time, the woman with braids sends the children off to sleep and Mbuya Matope gets down to business.

'Which of you boys is ill?'

With a start, Rindai raises his hand.

'The treatment is simple but I want you to follow my instructions carefully. It might work or it might not. It will depend on God, our maker, and the generosity of your ancestors. I have helped many and I believe I can help you too. Early tomorrow I will go into the forest to look for the roots with which to treat you. To work, they have to be freshly dug. With luck I will be back by noon. You boys can go to the Growth Point to wile away the time. But don't drink any alcohol, at least not until after my treatment is over. No alcohol, you hear? Now, Rebecca will show you where to sleep.'

The woman with braids leads us to a hut at the edge of the compound. It's small, neat, and probably hers, judging by the dresses on the hangers and the toiletries on the headboard. Rindai takes his pills at once, strips to his pants and burrows into the sheets. I take off my shirt and shoes, and sit on the edge of the bed listening to the night noises, the simplicity of village life which I once so intimately knew. Then, pondering our prospects, I blow out the lamp and squeeze into the little space left for me by Rindai's sprawling body. Hugging myself, I close my eyes and wait for sleep to claim me.

***

In the morning, when we've been served tea and fat cookies, Rindai and I stroll to the Growth Point to wait while Mbuya Matope and one of her younger granddaughters goes to the forest to search for the herbs.

This is probably the first time in recent years that Rindai and I have been alone together, two siblings pursuing one goal. We criss-cross unploughed fields and skirt dongas, stepping aside from the main road to let ox-drawn scotch carts and country buses pass, creaking and groaning with humanity and baggage. We chat quietly about erosion, deforestation and rural planning. I'm an artist and he's a plant pathologist; geography seems a safe, neutral subject. I am reminded, as always, of our dew-in-the-morning days when, still in our pre-teens, swimming and fishing in the river, and running about with our little axes, like wood-starved animals, we chopped down every bush in sight.

At the Growth Pont Rindai talks to a miller about grain supply and I chat up the ample-bodied hotel proprietress, rumoured to be an aspiring MP, about prospects for the Point. We do not drink any alcohol.

At noon we trek back to Mbuya Matope's compound but the old woman is not yet back. Mother is sitting with the young women, shelling nuts, talking and laughing.

We sit down in the shade of a stinking muhacha tree, and wait.

At four o'clock Mbuya Matope, dog-tired, arrives back with her little granddaughter. I fear the worst, that perhaps the precious herbs have not been found. But the woman with braids summons us to Mbuya's sparsely furnished hut. The old woman is leaning back against the mud wall and some bulbs are arranged at her feet.

'We had to go a long way,' she sighs. 'The forest almost denied us our quest. I kept praying to my ancestors to show me the bush, and just when we were about to give up, there it was right in the open, just where we'd been before, as if it was playing games with our eyes. My granddaughter spotted it, what a little doctor she is! This root is to be crushed and soaked overnight. Drink a mug of water in the morning and by noon you should start passing stool: hard, brown pellets at first, then black porridge and finally a slimy yellow stuff like egg yolk. Once you see the yellow stuff, you'll know the illness has been flushed out. Don't drink the water again. Now let me warn you. It is possible for the disease to pass from one sibling to another. This does not usually happen but if it does that would be very unfortunate indeed.'

At this point mother says very calmly, 'Mbuya Matope, if the illness should leave my son but has to inhabit another person, then let that be me, not any of my children.'

Rindai glances at mother, then at me and swallows hard. I stare at the ground.

Mbuya Matope kneads her stiff toes with her gnarled fingers and opens her mouth as if to speak, but says nothing.

I stare at the cow-dung floor and beat ants off my ankles and sandalled feet.

'I don't charge for my services,' Mbuya Matope says in conclusion. 'When you are yourselves satisfied that all is well again, then you can thank me as you see fit.

It is nearly sunset when we leave the compound, much against Mbuya Matope's protests. But we have to go. Without a spare wheel and with only a quarter tank of fuel, mother clutching the precious plastic bag of roots on the back seat, we set out for Kadoma.

**

There he was, my father's brother Uncle Tachiona, barrel-chested, dark-skinned, white-haired and huge between the blue hospital sheets, gigantic in the tiny bed, my uncle holding my hand in his stout brown palm, weeping and stroking the tears away with the back of his other hand, my uncle showing me the tubes that have been inserted to drain his urine out, the plastic bags at his waist. This was the contraption with which he was to live till he died. The nurses and other patients looking at the spectacle, at me, a precocious little Form 1 boarder come to seek out his father's elder brother, me counting out twenty dollars on the steel locker, me reading the letter father had written to him ... father was busy at the Indian's shop and so could not come to Harare to see him ... he was sending me instead ... my uncle weeping, showing me off to the inmates of the isolation unit and boasting, 'My brother's child, imagine! My very own brother's blood, all the way from boarding school to search me out in this city of iron lions, madmen and murderers. Doesn't he look like me?' Swearing, 'I'll never, never forget this day as long as I live, oh no! Oh yes, you wait, I'll make him my heir.' My uncle offering to share with me his midday meal of sadza and beans, and when I straightened my maroon school tie and declined, he spooned the food into his mouth with his soiled fingers, my uncle sobbing and smiling, saying, 'I nearly died but I'm now well – I couldn't pass water but they cut me open and fixed me up with these tubes.' My uncle chatting about everyone and everything back in Chivi, about drought, the scarcity of vegetables, dysentery, malaria, my cousins dropping out of school, one by one, graves appearing every season behind the cattle kraals, about how he and his family had not been able to move to Gokwe because he was about to be elected village headman and because it wasn't prudent for the whole family to leave the land of our ancestors where the bones of our forefathers lay, my uncle lecturing me about the largeness of life and the vitality of good health, kinship and obedience, my uncle moaning about my cousin Bhudhi Dzenga, his rogue son Dzenga who had caused him nothing but misery, Bhudhi who was working at the Indian supermarket and was now living with a woman and not sending a cent back to help the family. Bhudhi defiantly bringing home a 'slut' from the city whom he had married with my father's encouragement when he, Babamukuru, had arranged an honest girl from the next village for him. Bhudhi Dzenga selling off the family cattle one by one, without my father's knowledge or permission and causing bad blood between him, my uncle, and my father.

12

A week after our return from the dramatic trip to Gutu, mother is brought by ambulance to Harare Hospital. Her face is swollen like a football and she is hysterical. She swings from hysteria to delirium to triumph. She hugs Vongai's four-month pregnancy, her third (we have two daughters, Piwai and Tambu) and says, 'It's going to be a boy. Dunge's first grandson, and this one will be a true Gwanangara. I dreamt about him and I know. Mbuya Matope said so. He'll bring the power to shake the chaff from the grain of this family. It's a boy, Vongai, you hear? It's a boy, Godi, you hear? A true grain Gwanangara.'

I stand near her bed holding her hand, grinning painfully, as she digs her head into Vongai's belly. My wife stands back a little, holding her by the shoulders. I sit down on the edge of the bed feeling helpless. She has complained of a vicious headache and she hasn't been sleeping, alleging thumping and hissing noises in the ceiling. And now this, damn it! 'It's going to be a boy and he will bring with him the power to end our miseries. Mbuya Matope told me so. Meantime I will fight all the evil spirits myself. I have taken them on and I will crush them one by one with my willpower. There'll be no more suffering in this family. Kelvin will be OK. Rindai will be OK. Rindai is OK? Didn't we together see the black pellets, the porridge and the egg yolk in his stool, Godi? In Kadoma? Just as Mbuya Matope had promised? Did you tell Vongai? Rindai is OK, you hear? The bug is now in my veins and I am fighting it and will crush it with my willpower. None of my children or grandchildren need ever fall sick. Mbuya Matope said so and I dreamt about it. We are all going to be as happy as we were before.'

We were all so in thrall to our mother, her powerful belief in the moon and the power of the ancestors, their moody judgements and manipulations of us their living relatives, that no scientific information could persuade us that the health of the family was within our own control.

The doctor lets us take her home with a referral letter and a prescription. Once there she gathers together our two daughters Piwai and Tambu and hugs them.

'But what happened to your face, Gogo?' two-year-old Tambu asks. 'Did you get bitten by bees?'

Vongai cooks her a big fat fish, her favourite, but she does not eat much. Her tongue is swollen and it is difficult for her to swallow. My young sister Tendai, who is at university and living with us, beds with her in the spare bedroom. Mother cannot sleep and I hear her talking through the night. At two in the morning I knock on the bedroom door and enter. Mother is sitting in her nightdress, cross-legged on the carpet.

'Come in, Godi,' mother croons. 'Oh do come in and talk to me, my dear, dear son.'

'Now, Mother,' Tendai pleads with her, 'You're going to panic everyone. Why don't you try and sleep?'

'And who allowed you to talk to your mother like that, Tendai?' Mother retorts, severely. I turn to leave the room and see Vongai hesitating in the passage.

In the morning we take her to the psychiatrist who had previously attended to Kelvin. He remembers me and talks very pleasantly to mother, asking gentle questions, and when he inquires if she hears voices she nods and says, 'Yes, Mbuya Matope talks to me all the time.'

My heart sinks.

Later, he invites mother and Vongai into the reception area and, returning, asks me about Mbuya Matope. I explain as best I can, not without a sense of déjà vu. I do not tell him what I did not tell and will never tell anyone ever, that mother had challenged Rindai's bug to inhabit her. Somehow, I couldn't bring myself to talk about my family's intimate problems, even with my wife, without a sense of shame or disquiet. They kept me silent.

'She's very anxious and depressed,' the doctor announces.' I'm putting her on anti-depressants and valium.'

I put her on my medical-aid scheme.

That night mother sleeps deeply and when she wakes up she seems a little more herself.

We visit one more doctor, an oral and facial specialist; tissue samples and X-rays are taken. 'Her facial tissue is growing too fast,' we're told. 'She needs an urgent operation.'

'Is it cancer?' I ask, fearing the worst.

'I will only know when I see the test results.'

At home mother's spirit improves with the medication. Mbuya Matope speaks to her less often, and her appetite improves. She even goes to the garden to pluck pumpkin leaves and chats with Vongai and the maid in the kitchen. She beguiles us. I think of her dew-in-the-morning resilience and say to myself 'She's my mother, she knows herself better than we do. She knows what she's been through before.'

The swelling doesn't diminish. I'm scared to look at her. Her eyes are sunken, slits in the puffed-up ball that her face has become. She holds her head in her hands for hours, breathing through her mouth like an exhausted fish. She is furious and fatalistic at the prospect of an operation, 'It's the last thing I'll let them do to me, those good-for-nothing doctors. If the thing is inside me, it's in me and there's no use cutting me up and spoiling my face. I'll let you know if and when I'm ready for it.'

I'm angry with mother, angry about her self-assurance, her defiance, her daring to spit on the face of urgency. I, always the carrier of bad news, phone home. Father is quiet as usual, almost willing to let things take their course; too busy at the shop to come anyway. But I know he is suffering, eating himself up with worry. Rindai doesn't appear, only phoning once to say that it would not be wrong to force mother to go for the operation. But her blood pressure is too high and it needs to come down before she can go to the theatre. I am equivocal.

Mistake. Big mistake!

I feel confused, and angry. My siblings seem to think I can manage on my own – not that I do anything to discourage this – while I actually feel abandoned at the helm of this ailing ship of our affairs. Vongai says little. She is ready to bed my relatives, take days off from work to cater for their every need but she has no sympathy for the old women of Gutu, robed prophets or aspiring spirit mediums. A pastor's daughter, she has a mind of her own, not exactly rational but focussed, birthed by her three pet loves – accounts, medicine and the Bible. I know if I asked for her opinion she would say, 'She should have an operation at once.' I realise how the divisions engulfing the family have taken precedence over my self and my own family and made my wife and children temporary appendages; I know how, for better or worse, if somebody held a knife to my throat I would gasp 'mother', 'brother' instead of 'wife!', 'child!'.

Oh, the terrible ambiguity of it all!

***

Dunge Gwanangara believed in education. Had my father gone beyond Standard 6 at night school, he would probably have become a writer, politician or teacher. At that time teaching was seen as a noble profession and not despised as it is now.

He loved books. After searching through the flea-markets and second-hand shops, he bought us whatever he could afford: volumes as varied as the Reader's Digest, The Insolent Breed, The True Boy Scout, Feso, The Teenage Bible, The Adventures of Tom Sawyer, *the* Dutch Reformed Church Quarterly Bulletin, Munyai Washe, Biggles and Moto – *before the latter was banned. His biggest find was a leather-covered collection of the* Central Classics. *Like the protagonist who perfected the art of scavenging in Daniel Defoe's* Robinson Crusoe, *father believed in foraging for materials, some rare, some not so useful, and roughly cataloguing them for our use later. Cartoons of any sort were taboo for, he said, they encouraged laziness and bad language. But to spice things up a little, there was his own diary which strayed onto our little three-shelved 'library', juicily written in his galloping handwriting, aptly illustrated, and covered with card from the shirt boxes he salvaged at the shop.*

Father was a slow but meticulous reader. He would pore over a book night after night or finger through a borrowed newspaper, mouthing the words. He even read the classified advertisements. He was short-sighted and only secured glasses in the last two or three years of his life. He loved to discuss politics, or rather, to talk aloud to himself about politics, pondering the future, challenging us, now and then – alas, with little success – to comment on important matters. He was definitely the first person to tell us about Joshua Nkomo, Ndabaningi Sithole and the emerging Bishop Muzorewa during the 'No! No!' days of the Pearce Commission. We were not responsive, preferring to listen to music or read about sport, but he was not discouraged by our indifference to politics and did his best to keep us informed of affairs.

I found in my father's motley library a rich resource. I gladly recounted the exploits of Kalulu the Hare, the follies of Hyena, marvelled at Abdul's pointed shoes and cheered him on when he sold bags of ashes to gullible, sugar-starved customers. I sailed with one-eyed pirates, flew valiantly and often with Biggles over the stormy skies of England. I giggled over the Family Health Manual*'s encouragement to 'visit the toilet after every meal', coughed importantly with Samuel in Bernard Chidzero's* Nzvengamutsvairo, *wept with Jane Eyre after Mr Rochester lost his sight, and trembled with Giles Kuimba's* Tambaoga *in the cold, eerie nights at 33 Hoffman Street. By the time I was fourteen, I had read and reread the* Central Classics *and I hungered for more.*

Once father went on a month-long shoe-fitting course and brought back a photograph of himself with his course-mates in black suits, white shirts and black bow-ties and saying 'cheese'. His Indian boss and the white man who ran the course were sitting smugly in front of their standing class. Father framed the picture and hung it up. He was proud of it, about how he'd been chosen to go on the course because he was loyal and honest. He looked up to his boss and people of lighter colour, perhaps not in a servile way, but with the desire to learn from them and improve his own lot and that of his family. When there was a problem or a crisis at home, he would sit us down, hush us and say, 'Look, vanangu, *when things go wrong,* varungu vanodai, *– white people do this...' At work he built up a strong clientele for his boss because he talked to and mixed with everyone. Later, Rindai rather cruelly labelled him a colonial 'boy' and a so-*

cial climber. How ironic when we were all even more ambitious for ourselves, and our father was only ambitious for us.

Father not only sent us to school, but our cousins and more distant relatives from both his and mother's side: Bhudhi Pineas, Bhudhi Dzenga, Sekuru Peter, Sisi Elizabeth, Sisi Ratidzo and Muzukuru Maggie. He expected total obedience and hard work. If you failed he would warn you once, twice and on the third occasion, send you back to your people.

He sent us to the best schools in the country, he wanted the very best for us. He wanted us to rise up in life, to move out of the cramped, stained walls of 33 Hoffman Street, suckle the morning dews of Gokwe and masticate the books which would make us as solid and substantial as baobab trees. Like a consummate cartographer, he had our futures mapped out for us. Rindai would be a doctor; I an engineer, or so I learnt one hot Boxing Day afternoon when weeding the field in Gokwe. Kelvin's heavy silences and predisposition to argument seemed to make him a likely candidate for the legal profession. Shuvai would be a nurse, Vimbai an air-hostess and, judging by her dexterity with numbers, Tendai might try accountancy. As for Tapera – well, he was still wetting his nappies, too young to be assigned a profession.

Such were the dreams of our household, out of which father was, sooner or later, to be rudely shaken.

One wintry morning in the early seventies, father received an urgent call from the headmaster of Rindai's boarding school and he immediately cycled the ten kilometres to see him. Mr Knowles, was sitting at his desk, a file open before him.

'Your son Rindai was caught smoking mbanje *and drinking alcohol in the village with other boys,' the headmaster told him. 'This is a serious offence that normally deserves instant expulsion, but because he's a first offender, I am suspending him for two weeks. If he does it again I'll have to expel him straight-away. I have already given him six cuts. You can take him with you.'*

In the bush just outside the school premises, Dunge Gwanangara laid his bicycle and his son's trunk on the ground and leaned against a tree to absorb the shock, 'Why, why, why, why?' he hit his greying head against the trunk, his world in shreds. 'Oh Lord, why me?'

Rindai stood transfixed, watching his father weep.

Then, in a fit of inevitable rage, Dunge broke off a branch from a slim peach sappling and stripped it of its leaves.

'Bend down!' he commanded his son.

***

Mother's swelling does not come down; the pain grows too much for her to bear and she eventually agrees to have an operation and it is done immediately. I'm at a workshop in Malawi when Vongai phones me with the news and I fly home directly with twenty kilograms of fresh fish. Vongai picks me up and we drive straight to the Avenues Clinic.

Mother's face is bandaged up and she's resting on the pillows, awake. Half the family is there; they let me through and lamely I ask her how she is feeling. She swallows hard and Tendai reaches for her pain-killers. Shuvai tucks in her sheets.

'I brought you some lovely fish from Malawi,' I say. 'All your favourites.'

'She will eat when she is well,' Father says irritably.

A young nurse comes in to take her blood pressure.

'Is it still too high?' Rindai asks anxiously.

The surgeon who has operated on her comes in to see her, asks her a few questions, to which she nods or shakes her head, and scribbles in her file.

'Can we see you, please?' Father asks the doctor, leading Rindai and me into a discreet corner.

'I'm afraid it is cancer,' the surgeon, a slim man who seems younger than his years, says quietly. 'It has spread all over her face. Her blood pressure is too high and we very nearly aborted the op.'

'What are the options now?' I ask.

'I'd recommend chemotherapy once she has stabilised. She should also continue to see her psychiatrist. Her belief systems are undermining her and without a will to live, there is no hope. I'll refer you to a cancer specialist later, when I've discharged her. She'll need to be in Harare for some time, for the treatment. Do any of you live here in Harare?'

Father and Rindai look at me and I nod.

'Right now she is tired and needs rest.'

A week later she is discharged from the Avenues Clinic, and Vongai and I take her home. She shares the double bed in the spare bedroom with Tendai. Sleeping little at night, she spends the day dozing. Finding it difficult to swallow, she eats very little, a few teaspoons of porridge in the morning and soup in the evenings. But her mind is stable.

We wait for the wound to heal before we can begin therapy. The Jamaican radiologist carefully explains her problem to her and his method of treatment while I translate his words into Shona. He shows me the X-rays. The cancerous cells are in her skull eating at the bone, crooked cancerous roots snaking out from the terrible core, reaching down her spine. The cute, cheerful little nurses draw impressive diagrams of her head, like cross-sections of flowers in a biology textbook.

For months I drive her to the X-ray unit every morning so that they can burn out the evil cells. The therapy scorches her face, causes her tongue to swell, and induces nausea. The whole house soon becomes steeped in the smell of the odour of her rotting flesh. Visitors pour in to see her: our relatives, neighbours, hordes of the devoted from Vongai's church.

'Why don't you take her to a home for cancer patients?' we're asked. Rindai, Shuvai, Vimbai and I share the expenses. Tendai, who is still studying, washes her clothes for her. Braving the stench, little Tambu regularly visits the spare bedroom and pulls the curtains shut – light burns mother's eyes – and says, 'Do you want a glass of water now, Gogo?'

I go to the pub whenever I can, to escape the smell. Sometimes I come home late. One day mother complains to Vongai about my late nights, demanding to know why she lets me stay away so long. After all, Vongai is pregnant. Otherwise she does not say much. I visit her every morning and in the evening I bring her morphine and mouth-wash and talk to her a little. I know she wants me to stay longer, that there is something vital and urgent she wants to communicate. Nothing is more terrible than that, when you can't communicate with the sick and keep on postponing that last intimate conversation; when you can't discuss issues of life and death; when you are afraid your siblings will say harshly, 'You really want her to die, don't you?' but have they been there to watch her suffer?

Vongai gives birth to a boy, my parents' first grandson. Coincidentally, my fourth novel is launched that week. I take the little boy and the book to the spare bedroom and lay them on the bed. Mother touches the book and the boy and attempts a faint smile.

'What shall I call him?' I say.

'Ask your father,' she whispers.

I call Gwelo and father tells me, 'Takura.'

Mother's hair turns grey and falls out. Tendai shaves her head. I say to the radiologist, 'Please doctor, what can we do to help her? I'll do anything.'

The doctor closes the file and says, 'She left it too late. There's nothing more we can do.'

I'm angry, angry with mother, with myself, with medicine, with the world. She is now just a heap of bones, a skeleton in a nightdress. I'm angry with myself for feeling angry about how she is obstinately holding on, about how for months now she has lived on morphine, ampicillin, mouthwash and thin, thin porridge. Angry about how she has drained us all of our strength, sympathy and support. Superstitiously angry – and this I have not told anyone to this day – about how she challenged fate through Mbuya Matope to lodge Rindai's affliction within her own body.

Father visits once and sits on the carpet in our lounge with her. She says 'We can't sleep together when I'm like this. Oh no.' He busies himself with our house and yard, giving me tips about removing the rockery and felling the trees to turn the space into a vegetable garden.

In August, eighth months after the operation, mother's mother, VaMurozvi and her brother, Sekuru Bhuru arrive in Gwelo from Zambia. I decide, unilaterally, that it is time for her to return home. She's surprised by the decision, but says, quietly, 'Yes, I suppose I must stay in one place now.'

When we arrive in Gwelo, Gogo VaMurozvi, back bent and hoarse-voiced is waiting for her with her brother, after an absence of thirty years. Mother drags herself to her bedroom and collapses onto her bed, amid many cries and much weeping.

And so we leave her, washing our hands of her, only to return to her smell in our house in Harare; the reek of illness which hangs in the air and cannot be sprayed away.

'Where did you leave my *gogo*?' little Tambu demands.

I call home twice a week, feeling a terrible relief that we're rid of her, that other people have assumed the responsibility for fretting about her medication, morphine and mouthwash, the mere presence of her rotting flesh. I learn that Kelvin has moved in with his new 'wife' and supposed 'son' Kurai, and that his wife Mai Kurai is now in charge of matters at home. I later learn that Kelvin's return has the tacit approval of father who now harbours the conviction that a 'wife' and a 'baby' will anchor Kelvin to one place and one woman. Besides, no one in their right senses could overlook the convenience of having a young woman to manage a household of the sick.

Father is feeding all these new mouths.

Vongai and I drive down at the month-end to see mother. She is clearly much worse: a slow-eyed, brown skeleton drooling at the mouth, trapped inside a mosquito net to keep the flies off her torn face. Mai Kurai, a tall, thin, sly-eyed, long-legged woman in her early twenties, wipes her forehead with a cloth, touches a spoon of morphine to her lips and holds up a mug of water. Gogo VaMurozvi sits at the foot of the bed holding Kurai's squirming 'son'. Vongai and I poke our heads inside the mosquito net and father says to mother, 'Do you recognise them?'

Without nodding, mother turns her face towards us. She pushes a shaky, excited finger into a nostril and extracts – a maggot! Mai Kurai fishes a plastic tin from under the pillow, opens it and directs mother's hand to drop the maggot in the tin. Mother holds my hand. She wants to say something to me. I lower my head to her face and she gestures to her ears and whispers, 'Voices.'

You hear voices, mother?'

She inclines her head slightly.

'What do they say?'

'Let's go, Mai Rindai,' she whispers again and repeats, like a refrain, 'Mai Rindai, let's go'.

Sekuru Bhuru and I go out to the yard, to the fresh air and we exchange our how-are-you's.

'*Ndimi mune varwereka, imi* You are the ones with looking after

151

the sick,' Sekuru says, and I try to retrace the rugged terrain of his face from thirty years ago.

While Sekuru Bhuru and I are exchanging pleasantries, the cottage door cracks open and Kelvin comes out, shirtless, puffing at a cigarette, holding his 'son' Kurai, a puny mite without a single Gwanangara feature, and wearing only a grey nappy. I do not take the baby from him.

***

One Saturday evening, weeks later, I decide, not to wait for the jazz and leave the pub early for a change. Back home, I find the curtains wide open, lights ablaze. Vongai and Tendai are sobbing to Tambu's refrain, 'Why are you crying, Mhamha? Why are you crying, Tete Tendi?' There is no need to ask why.

***

'Mai Rindai is sniffing ash, for sure.'

'She thinks she's a tractor, ploughing up forests without oxen.'

'She has one dress that she washes every night. Chiwoma ndipfeke.'*

'Her husband hasn't bought her anything in years.'

'She has not tasted meat for months.'

'If the forests were not generous with madora *she and her children would be taking salt with their sadza.'*

'What a waste of energy, slaving away for a few bags of peanuts. She should try growing cotton, or sunflowers.'

'Oh, no. She couldn't afford the fertilisers and the sprays.'

'She thinks she's helping her husband, spending half the year away from him just to earn a few dollars.'

'Did you hear that her daughter Shuvai broke her leg? It became infected and nearly had to be amputated while she was planting sweet potatoes in Gokwe.'

'Yes, and her daughter Vimbai's nose bled through the whole night. Their wretched cousin Ratidzo from Chivi and Baba Tariro had to drive her to hospital.'

'Two homes never helped anyone.'

'Imagine all that travelling. All that duplication of duties.'

---

* 'Dry out dress, so that I can wear you again now!'

'It's the quickest way to lose a husband. No man wants to live alone for months on end. Have you heard about the woman who visits his house pretending to be a relative? She sometimes takes his little girls with her to Mtapa to feed and wash them. They call her "Mbuya, Mbuya".'

'She thinks he's a saint. She can't imagine him being unfaithful to her.'

'Imbwa nyoro. The soft dog doesn't bark, but bites.'

'No man is ever faithful to his wife. Especially the goody-goody ones like him. The ones who go to church every Sunday.'

'He's fed up with Gokwe. Three children at boarding school, two at primary, two more waiting; fees and uniforms wringing him dry. It seems such a mistake to invest all your hope in your children.'

'He's tired of living alone. He wants out.'

'She won't give up. The ploughing instinct runs in her veins.'

'They quarrelled once, all night. Poor soul, she was demanding new clothes. She threatened to leave. He nearly beat her up.'

'He doesn't go to Gokwe any more. It's been two Christmases now since he visited her.'

'Did you hear what happened to her peanut money last June?'

'No. What?'

'Well, she sold ten bags of shelled peanuts and made a tidy little sum. As the goody-goody wife that she is, she went to Gwelo to give the money to her husband and master. Her year's earnings. To help him with the school fees. To prove that the Gokwe home could help raise the children. Now they say that she left the money in the wardrobe to go to the women's Thursday church service. The house was locked. When she returned the money was nowhere to be found. No doors or windows were broken, no clothes thrown about, but she couldn't find a dollar of it. She suspected her neighbours, of course, Mai Ravi, Mai Fanwell and even Vatete Mai Farai. She reported the matter to the police but they couldn't help. She couldn't point a finger at anyone. Then Mai Ravi received an anonymous letter accusing her of having stolen the money. "I know you stole my hard-earned money. I have witnesses who saw you enter the house. Return it at once or you will live to regret the day you were born." There was no name or address on the letter and the writing looked

*like a student's. Baba Ravi was not amused. He complained bitterly
to Baba and Mai Rindai. He suspected that one of the boys, Rindai
or Godi, had written the letter.*

***

We weathered the gossip.

*Father held up the letter and said, 'You did this,Godi.' I silently
denied it. I knew Rindai was responsible There was no mistaking his
distinctive 'e's and 'r's, though he had tried to disguise his style by
printing the letters. He had once hinted that he might write the letter.
Now I was being blamed and was silently covering up for him. Or
perhaps I was being seen as a kind of hero?*

*I thought the matter had died but six months later, back in Gokwe,
mother called us to her bedroom one evening to witness a little ritual. She had, she said, obtained, from a sympathetic neighbour, a
powder which, when burnt and accompanied by the right incanta-
tion, would cause the thief to confess and return the money. Mother
sprinkled the powder over glowing embers and began the recitation:*

*'You who stole my money, return it. I never wronged you and by
this I mean you no personal harm. I only want back what belongs
to me.'*

*She had barely finished when a bat skimmed through the eaves
of the hut and criss-crossed it three times. I threw a book at it and
missed. Kelvin beat it down with an old newspaper. It plunged into
the embers, spluttered and exploded in the heat. Startled by this unexpected twist, we coughed in the smoke.*

*I gathered the ashes in a pan and went out into the dark to throw
them away.*

***

It is a gigantic funeral; mourners fill the house and yard. Rindai and
I run around shaking hands, buying bread, milk, sugar, tea, mealie-meal, meat and firewood. Tapera collects contributions and records them in an exercise book. The wife of father's Indian boss sits
in the kitchen with the women, singing and weeping. I borrow a grey
T-shirt from Kelvin and a dark jacket from father's wardrobe. The
jacket is too small and leaves half my arms bare. Squinting into the
blazing sunlight, I try to recall the faces of long-lost relatives: Sisi

Ratidzo from Chivi (Cousin Jonah and Maiguru Mai Dzenga come a week later) and others in the bus and cortege of over fifty cars. At the church, I glance at mother's face and look away. The mortician has laid her out, her face to the side to hide her disfigurement. The women are hysterical when they see the casket.

Father succeeds in getting Businessman Unesu, a provincial director of education, to give the main speech, and after the grave has been filled father makes his family step out from their scattered, unco-ordinated positions in the crowd, to introduce us to the mourners.

With Maiguru Mai Elizabeth and Sekuru Reuben, her cousin, Father connives to distribute mother's clothes and kitchenware in the conspicuous absence of his direct in-laws from Zambia. Gogo Vamurozvi is too overwhelmed, and too old anyway, to protest. Her brother Sekuru Bhuru watches from the sidelines. Maiguru assembles us all in the evening and shares out the property. Our sisters, *gogo vekuZambia* and Sisi Elizabeth are each given something, Maiguru Mai Elizabeth is given the overcoats and clothes. She leaves some items for her sisters – my aunts – in Zambia.

They say a dead person's clothes should be distributed in the morning, before midday, usually a year after death, after the deceased's spirit has been 'restored' from the grave.

I make photocopies of mother's best photograph and distribute it to every one. Shuvai buys Brenda Fassie's Mama and plays it all day on the hi-fi. Tendai takes out the bottles of morphine and crushes them, and cuts up the X-rays and doctor's cards with a pair of scissors. Vimbai sweeps out the house. Rindai phones Kadoma to find out about his plants. Tapera's classmates come in sorry procession to offer a song and a prayer. Kelvin holds his 'son' on his knees, borrows cigarettes from the lodgers and smokes openly at the fire. His 'wife', the new *mroora* of the plot, Mai Kurai, heats buckets of water for everyone, and with Vongai and Mai Nda tries to wash the smell out of the carpets. Father gives money to each of his three *varoora*, Mai Nda, Vongai and Mai Kurai, to thank them for looking after his wife in her sickness, as is required by custom. My little daughter Tambu brings me water to drink, sits on my knee and asks, 'Where did you put my *gogo*?' The elders say to me, 'This one is your favourite, for sure.' Mbuya Matope sends a message of shock and sympathy from Gutu. Vongai's boss calls to find out when she is returning to work.

It is time to return to our separate lives.

***

They say father unwittingly drove my cousin Jonah, Babamukuru Tachiona's son, to the war. Now let's see.

It was, I think, 1975 and the war against Ian Douglas Smith's Rhodesia was heating up. Young men and women, barely boys and girls out of uniform, were leaving schools, townships and villages to join the liberation forces in Botswana, Zambia and Mozambique. The country was under siege. Many books have been written about that war so I shall say little. In retrospect, I suspect that my cousin Jonah inspired the creation of one of my heroes, Comrade Shungu Dzangu.

Like Dzangu, Jonah was round-faced, dark and plump; his skin was a patchwork of nyora; he was contemplative, taciturn and given to abrupt laughter, a sad youth definitely destined to harvest thorns.

Well, there he was. My Chivi cousin Jonah. He appeared without warning, like nhedzi mushrooms after a storm, to live with us and look for work. We had just renovated our small house with floor tiles and, with her peanut money, mother had acquired a tiny fridge to grace our kitchen. We were slowly 'moving up'. Bhudhi Dzenga, Jonah's half brother, had, after allegations of theft, been relieved of his job at the supermarket and had gone back to his roots in Chivi with his wife. Rindai was now at university. For some time we had been blessed with a reprieve from visitors, so during the holidays Kelvin and I had had the spare bedroom to ourselves.

I welcomed Jonah with resentment because he came to share our three-quarter bed and our meagre meals, to sip coffee with us after supper, listen to our LPs and intimidate us with his silence. Like the false African that I was, I detested this new intrusion of our space.

Jonah woke up early every morning to do the rounds at the labour office and at the factory gates. I half hoped that he would soon grow tired, give up and return to Chivi. It was with some disappointment that I learned that he'd found a temporary job at Rhodesian Alloys, grading rocks. He would leave at four in the morning, returning at seven, dog-tired and as hungry as a farm labourer, to devour sadza

and spinach with amazing appetite. We boys ate from the same plate.
Every fortnight he would surrender his money to father for safekeep-
ing, retaining only a little for his needs.

He must have worked like that for six months, when tragedy
struck. He was caught smoking mbanje *at work, or so it was said,*
and he was fired on the spot. His employment officer knew father and
reported the matter to him.

'I can't keep you here, Jonah,' father said severely.

Jonah sobbed like his own father, Tachiona.

He appealed to me to intercede for him. 'It was just a match-
box-full in the urinal – the security man thought I'd been the one to
drop it,' he said. 'Please explain to father, Mukoma Godi.'

I smugly flipped through the book I was reading. I did not look up.
Mother was away in Gokwe.

'Is this it, then?' Jonah snivelled.

'Yes, Jonah,' said father. 'When you have learnt to be responsible
you can come back.'

Jonah went to the spare bedroom and packed his kitbag.

'I'm going now,' he said to me. And to father, 'Please can I have
the money I gave to you.'

'Where are you going at this time of the night?' father asked.

'Wherever I can. My money, please.'

'Do you think you've been living in a hotel, to demand your mon-
ey like change?'

'I want my money now,' Jonah said, his eyes glowering.

Father sent Kelvin to fetch Vatete Mai Farai from down the street.
He explained to her what had happened.

'This is not the way to do things, Jonah, mwanangu,*' Vatete im-*
plored. 'All you need do is apologise for your mistake, and your
father Dunge will let you stay.'

'I want my money,' Jonah insisted.

Father went to the bedroom and came back with an old khaki en-
velope. He counted out all of Jonah's money, had Jonah sign for it,
witnessed by Vatete and I. Our cousin picked up the money and the
envelope, and walked out into the night.

A week later Babamukuru Tachiona wrote his brother a bitter let-
ter from Chivi.

Dear Dunge

You sent my son away like a dog, without anything. You stole his money. Now you can live in
peace in your beautiful house. I shall not bother you
any more with my children. You will be pleased to
hear that Jonah left for Mozambique soon after you
sent him away. If he dies in the war, my dear brother, you will have his blood on your hands.

Yours truly,

Tachiona

P.S. Many thanks for arranging for Dzenga to
marry that prostitute from your street. Everyone in
the village is talking about her lack of manners.

î3

Kelvin's 'wife', Mai Kurai, is the new *'menija'* at the plot. Having looked after mother when she was dying, it would now be highly improper to send her away. She cooks, washes up, scrubs, sweeps and makes herself useful in this now wifeless house. There are strong rumours that she has done it before, looking for a roof over her head: yes, dumped herself and the same baby, Kurai, on a man, claiming he had made her pregnant, but he'd sent her away. Now the whole town knows that Kelvin is the willing victim of her cunning, or so the gossips say.

Gogo VaMurozvi sits on the lawn in front of the kitchen in her black mourning dress, her brother Sekuru Bhuru on a chair beside her, shelling nuts, coaxing time. The old woman nurses Kurai: a baby is, after all, a baby and besides, her eye-sight is faltering. Kelvin sometimes joins them and, snuffing out his cigarette, will pick up his baby and rock him on his knees.

Kelvin has sobered up, or so it seems.

Father returns to work, and afterwards tends his vegetables and chickens, works meticulously on his accounts, attends church and party meetings where he has been elected chairman of the cell. In other words, he keeps himself busy to forget. He buys shoes for Mai Kurai, nappies for Kurai, a dress for Gogo and a shirt for Sekuru. Sometimes he joins Gogo and Sekuru on the lawn, shelling nuts and giving his ideas an airing. He hints at the possibility of Gogo coming to live with him instead of returning to Zambia. After all, she has no passport and her emergency travel papers have long expired. But the old woman quietly declines. I am afraid that my Zambian uncles, stung by father's hasty handling of mother's property, will scoff at the prospect of their aged mother being taken off them, as if they were being accused of not looking after her properly.

I inquire about Gogo's travel status and am assured she will not have any problems with the emigration department at the border. And so we put Gogo and Sekuru on the bus to Zambia, and bid them farewell.

Left alone, without Gogo, Kelvin and his wife quarrel, first about Kurai's parenthood, then about the shoes father bought for Mai Kurai and then, inevitably, about Kelvin's idleness. The disagreement explodes into a fistfight and the glass in a display cabinet is broken. Father looks on helplessly. Mai Kurai goes away for a week. I pick up the phone and ask Kelvin, 'Do you want this woman back or not?'

'I don't want her back,' says Kelvin. 'She's a liar and Kurai is not my baby.'

'Then why don't you send her away?'

'Dad wants her to stay, can't you see? He's buying her shoes, dresses and all that, as if she was his wife.'

'But she looked after mother, and you don't have a job, Kelvin. You haven't married her. You don't even know anything about her relatives. You haven't even been to meet them.'

'Father said he would ask Sekuru Masvi to talk to her people.'

'Leave Sekuru Masvi out of this. She's your woman and you alone are responsible for her. Do you realise that your living with her is wrong, at least according to our culture, and that if anything happens to her at the plot *ingozi chaiyo.** You must make up your mind if you want to marry her or not.'

'I want her to leave.'

I ask Kelvin to call Mai Kurai to the phone and when she says, coyly, 'Makadii Babamukuru?' I say, 'What is this I hear about you two fighting and destroying mother's property? Look, Kelvin doesn't want you any more. You have to go away.' I am as blunt as it is possible to be.

'I'll only leave when the person who brought me to this plot tells

---

* We will truly suffer from avenging spirits.

me to do so,' she says.

'Who invited you to the plot?'

'It's not for me to say,' she says cheekily. 'And if I go, I will leave Kurai here, where he belongs, with his people. And you will have to pay me for washing and feeding your dying mother and picking those maggots out of her rotting flesh.'

'You fool! You think we're idiots, don't you? You did all that because you had nowhere to go and wanted to look good. You think we don't know you tried to do this to another man and he sent you away? Will you pay us for looking after you and your miserable baby?'

'Why don't you talk to your father?'

'Now listen. No one wants you. I'm getting into my car and driving over right away. If I find you still there in my mother's house, I'll … well, you'll see when I get there.'

I bang down the phone. I consider phoning Rindai but I don't. I consider phoning father but I don't. In the evening I phone Kelvin again and he says, 'She has gone. With her baby.'

I feel a strange mixture of worry and relief.

Three days later I receive a letter from father.

> My dearest son Godi
>
> Now that you have decided you know what's best for Kelvin and sent Mai Kurai away, I wash my hands of him and leave you to look after him. Rindai and you are old enough to decide for your brother. Please allow me the chance to mourn my wife in peace.
>
> Your father

A week later, on a Saturday morning, Kelvin arrives with his suitcase at my house in Harare. His face is black and his clothes are soiled. He sits on the edge of the sofa and rubs his eyes with sooty hands.

'What happened to you, Babamunini?' Tambu asks.

Vongai prepares him some breakfast.

'He sent me away,' he says. 'I had no money, so I jumped onto the goods train.'

'But Bhudhi Kelvin, suppose the guards had spotted you, or you had fallen off the truck,' says Tendai.

'Would it matter? You people would have got rid of me once and for all.'

'Now don't talk like that, Bhudhi Kelvin,' Tendai says. 'You know that we all care about you.'

'Talk about caring. You mean the cents you donate to me now and then.'

'And what have you ever done for anyone, Bhudhi Kelvin?'

'You sent my wife away just when I was about to pull myself together again.'

'You asked for it!' I hiss back. 'Don't say such things in my house!'

'Yes, it's your house, isn't it? Your house, your furniture, your swimming-pool and your cars. Fancy! One person owning two cars in a socialist state!'

'Excuse me, Babamunini,' Vongai trembles. 'If you mean the car that *I* drive that *I* happen to have worked for *myself.*'

'While you, Kelvin, were chasing women and sitting on your hands,' Tendai rubs it in.

'Money, money, money. It's the only word you know in this family. You people need to add the word "love" to your vocabularies.'

'Excuse me, but if your "love" means hankering after second-hand women and raising other men's babies then your dictionary differs from mine.'

'Shut up, Tendai or I'll slap you. I am your older brother and you shouldn't disrespect me just because I'm like this.'

'Slap me, ha, ha! What a laugh. You might have slapped my bottom when I was a toddler, not now. Just because you're a man wearing trousers doesn't mean you can treat me, or any woman for that matter, like a toy.'

'What makes you think you are special, Kelvin?' I say.

'So who is Sekuru Zevezeve to you? Who is Mhokoshi? Who is Njiki? Who is Gwanangara? Or have you forgotten already? Who do you think is guiding your every footstep and showing you the way? Who do you think has showered you with your so-called "success"?'

'Don't belittle God who made you and put the breath into your body,' Vongai counsels with her usual Pentecostal zeal. 'If your ancestors are that powerful why are they not looking after you?'

'Excuse me, Maiguru Vongai. Things may seem OK, for the time being anyway, in your cosy little family under your good father, the priest. But I don't think you're qualified to comment on *this* family!'

'Don't speak like that to my wife!'

'As for you, my dear brother. What herb has this woman given you to make you so blind?'

'Get out!' I yell, almost striking him.

Kelvin slams the cup of tea on the table, cracking it. The hot tea splashes onto his hands.

'That's it!' he grabs his suitcase. 'I'm out of here.'

He goes to the door, nearly knocking down Tambu.

I step out of his way. We follow him into the yard, as he struggles with the gate. Our neighbours watch, dumbfounded.

'Babamunini, wait!' Vongai calls out, suddenly conciliatory.

The gate bursts open and he strides out onto the street.

***

'I sold off all the cattle at the market,' father, back from Chivi, announced sombrely.

'And what will Maiguru and the family do for the scotch-cart, the plough, for milk and meat, Baba Rindai?' mother asked gloomily.

'I couldn't let it drag on. Dzenga was selling off a beast every six months, without my knowledge or permission. Babamukuru Tachiona and his wife didn't bat an eyelid – in fact, they encouraged him. I built that herd for them over twenty years, the least they could do was ask my permission to sell the cattle.'

'But how did you do it?'

'How did I do it? When I arrived, I called the headman and all the village elders together and said, "This is what my brother's son is doing in the homestead, destroying the very source of our livelihood and my brother Tachiona is doing nothing to stop him.

"I have my own children needing food, school fees and uniforms but all I hear is that the family herd is dwindling. Tell me Elders, am I wrong to do this, to sell the herd?"'

'What did they say?'

'They said, "Yes, your brother has wronged you, but why are you letting a child with milk on his nose come between you and your brother?" So I told them about how, every year, I have been sending

them mealie-meal and clothes, but instead of gratitude all my broth-
er's letters accuse me of having married Dzenga off to a prostitute,
stolen Jonah's pay and driven him off to the war. I said, "Elders,
haven't I done enough for my brother? When is enough enough?"'

'Don't you think you over-reacted?'

'Over-reacted? Hardly so. What would you do with a brother who
refuses to take your mother to hospital, and when that mother dies
he buries her alone, without you, other relatives or even her own
people present; and later can't even identify the grave?'

'What will you do with the money?'

'Why, send the children to school, or pay the deposit on a plot.'

'The soil won't be happy with this, Baba Rindai. Your brother
could appeal to the soil to revenge him, to bring you bad luck.'

'The soil knows right from wrong.'

'Not always, Baba Rindai,' mother repeated. ' The soil can be
swayed.'

I sat in the living room pretending to read, listening, filled with a
strange foreboding.

***

I never saw Bramson much during the days when mother employed
him to help with the housework. He must have been fifteen or sixteen then. Three or four times a year, when we dutifully trooped
down to the plot to spend the weekend with our parents, it was his
time off. He went to stay with a sister or relative, and we might
bump into him as he was leaving. Smiling shyly, he would open the
gate to let our cars through, tuck his paper bag under his arm, give
his half salute and then back off nervously, as if he needed to get out
of our way, we, the children of the house. Occasionally we caught a
glimpse of him wading among the eager chickens, replenishing the
troughs or collecting eggs, plucking a bunch of rape or spinach or a
pocketful of plums ever so gently for some visitor who had become
the victim of our parents' generosity.

'He's such a good boy, Bramson,' mother would enthuse, glad
that after a life–time of hard work she could allow herself the modest
indulgence of hiring a helper. 'He lives for his job and is no problem,
unlike the girls who are always giving trouble.'

Those weekend visits now seem like rituals with which we sought to stave off tragedy. When we left the little four-roomed house and moved onto the plot, we believed we were stepping up the ladder of success. With our children fluttering like butterflies in and out of the rambling house and we, brothers, sisters, wives, in-laws, lazing on the veranda, gossiping in unbathed languor, feasting on tea, sausages, bread, scones, cake, steak, sweet potatoes, green mealies, *nyimo* and God knows what else mother had stocked up for the occasion; father beaming in the background, trying, as always, not to interrupt our exchanges with too many questions, his politics, or his books of accounts; mother cooing contentedly among a forest of loving little arms, at the heart of our little tribe – who would have guessed in the midst of that apparent happiness, what awaited us?

Mother had her premonitions, though. Decades before, when we were still children rushing off to school on bare, cracked feet, scurrying in mindless poverty across frost-bitten grass in thirst of success, she would wake up to announce her dreams. Fires, pythons and weird gatherings peopled her sleep; we grew afraid whenever she said, 'I had a dream last night ...' Eventually, she learnt to keep her nightmares to herself.

Mother breathed tragedy. She scrambled to gather us up under her wings, squawking blindly at the eagles swooping down on her brood. She fretted through every pregnancy, every trip abroad, journeyed to set camp wherever a crisis loomed. Suspending her own life, she lived for us, rebuking the forces that threatened us.

'Take me,' she pleaded with the forces. 'Take me and leave my children alone.'

***

Bramson must have smelt death settling on her. Bramson, the calf that she had nurtured, who saw the visitors come and go, and heard their prayers. He saw men crush their hats to their chests and heard women click their tongues softly as they left her ill-fated bedroom. His young calf nose sniffed the air. The dank, sweet smell of rotting flesh and the devastation on her body terrified him. Or so I thought.

Taking only what was his, he packed his small suitcase and slipped into the night, quietly, glad to breathe fresh air once more, ready to seek out new pastures.

He came back months – perhaps a year – after the funeral, after

Mai Kurai had left. Father told us that he rescued him from the group of pilferers with whom he was hanging out, though it is also said that he returned of his own accord, half penitently, to ask for his old job back. Anyhow, he returned to the huge, now motherless, wife-less, womanless house on whose fringes he had once tip-toed. With mother gone and all her children called off to their various futures, father installed Bramson in the house, gave him his own bedroom and not only made him cook, cleaner, book-keeper, seller of eggs, fruit and vegetables and collector of lodgers' rents, but companion and manager of his emaciated household. Even given that power, though, Bramson remained humble, quiet, industrious and honest – and none of us had reason to complain when we came to visit.

***

Now, with mother gone, father launches into grand designs for the house and the plot. With nobody to say, 'We have worked hard all our lives, my dear husband, and we must rest and be contented with the small comforts we have gained,' he extends the building, piece by piece, adding five shoddy new rooms.

'I'm doing it for you all, for the family, if it's the last thing I do,' he promises.

The house becomes his obsession and we leave him to it, imagining that it will occupy him and ameliorate his loss, but when the bills start hurting he turns on us with fierce accusations of neglect.

'Talk him out of it,' our wives and sisters urge with feminine instinct. 'Why does he need to extend the house when he is now a widower?'

But with a new-found defiance, father soldiers on, brick by brick, as if the mere completion of the project is justification enough.

***

Vongai answers the phone and breaks the news to me. As we race across the country to Gwelo we hardly speak. The news is relayed over the air every hour. There is a huge crowd in the yard when we drive in. The house has been gutted by fire. Two sections of the wall have fallen in. Half the roof with it. Through the gaping holes of what once were windows we stare at heaps of sooty rubble and the blackened floors. As we get out of the car, Vongai and Tendai start

166

wailing.

'Shut up!' I hiss. 'What's there to cry about? This isn't another funeral, is it?' We stumble towards the line of outstretched arms and the blur of faces scouring ours for marks of grief. We have done it again, I think, angrily, struggling to look composed. Why does it always have to be us with our miseries catching the attention of this whole damned town?

Father sits on a sofa on the lawn, surrounded by neighbours and relatives, recounting what happened. Although it is hot, he is wearing a jersey and coat. He looks OK, but his hair is very white. I remember, now, that I have not seen him in four months. His handshake is slow, firm and searching; his looks tell us to be brave in front of the gathering.

'He was such a good boy, Bramson,' he resumes his narration once we have all settled down. 'He worked so well for my wife when she was alive. Being the young man he was, he became frightened and left when he saw she was dying. I took him back. He was looking after me so well and not once did we exchange bad words. He literally ran this plot – did everything: cooking, washing, cleaning, selling produce and collecting the rent. Every Friday he would give the money to me and we would go through the books together.'

He pauses, as if the thought has just occurred to him and says, 'He had become my paymaster.' But if there is a note of disbelief, or surprised recognition, in his voice, it is not the moment to ask questions. Two or three of the neighbours stir restlessly, almost suspiciously, in their seats. My father resumes his story. His voice has the hollow note of a tale too often told, at least to himself. 'Two months ago he brought home a pregnant girl and said, "Father, I want to marry this girl but my father and brothers are not helping with the lobola, though they said they like her." And I asked, "Do you really want to marry her?" and he said, "Yes".

'Then I said, "Very well, Bramson, you know you don't earn much and a wife is very expensive these days, so you'll have to save up as much as you can. She can stay here for a while, but because she's pregnant you have to introduce her to your parents and then take her to her own mother until she has the baby. We'll see what can be done once she has delivered."

'So the girl stayed six weeks and at the end of the month we arranged for Bramson's brother to take her home, since he was making a trip to that area, and the girl's time was drawing near. Bramson was busy in the house and had not saved enough for three bus tickets. We bought some groceries for his wife, Bramson and I, and she packed her things.

'Yesterday morning Bramson ironed the very clothes that I'm wearing now and said, "Father, take off that jersey, so I can wash it," and I did. His wife made me breakfast and then knelt beside the sofa and said, "Baba, I'm going now, but I'll come back once I've had the baby," and I said, "Very well," and left them preparing to go to the bus station to meet with Bramson's brother. I had things to do in town.

'The next thing I knew was that the police were at the shop. They asked, "Do you know what has happened at your plot" and I said, "No," and they said, "Brace yourself, man," and I said, "But why?" and they said, "The boy who worked for you locked himself up in your house, set it on fire and hanged himself in the kitchen." I didn't believe them. I said, "What? You don't mean my Bramson?" and they said, "Yes," and I said, "But I was with him only a few hours ago," and they said, "He's burnt down your house and now he's dead," and I said, "Take me to him!" I couldn't believe them. So they drove me to the mortuary and showed his body to me and I shook him and said, "Bramson! Bramson!" but they said, "He's dead, *mudhara*," and they showed me the note that he'd left and the long letters he had written to his father and brother...'

I see my father sitting in his chair dazed, puzzled and yet perhaps almost enjoying being the focus of attention. I feel a charge of anger that we are being made responsible for not visiting him often enough, for not taking care of him, for not monitoring his relationship with Bramson. I see the neighbours' upturned faces. Nothing so exciting has happened in this small town for a long time. They are greedy to become part of the drama.

I see my needy father naively allowing Bramson to become a companion, one that fed his vulnerable ego now that his children had fled his nest. I see that Bramson has never challenged him, never denied him. I see that Bramson has replaced us.

I realise how I have failed my father, how we all must fail our fathers as times change, values change, and we are greedy for success in a new age. How we do not understand each other.

I see Bramson hanging melodramatically from the kitchen roof. Was he hoping for more? Did he expect my father not only to treat him like a companion, a soft-spoken, uncritical companion, but to behave, in a time of his need, as if he were a colleague?

Suicide requires forethought. While he was ironing my father's clothes was he perhaps thinking of the rope he would tie round his neck?

Someone has a radio. It is muttering in the background. Another news bulletin. Perhaps there will be television cameras. I feel anger and revulsion and I want to stand up and shout: 'Go away. Go away. Leave us alone with our grief.' I already hear the voices: 'We were there. Did you see us on the news? Such a tragedy. The boy's tongue was hanging from his mouth. Poor old man. Extending that big house for his children. Not that they ever helped him. Treated Bramson like a son. Just like his own Indian bosses treat him. Believed in blind loyalty. But as I always say, it's a mistake to become too familiar with your servants. What could the old man do? He was lonely. The boy was good to him. Perhaps the boy was possessed. To take his own life like that. Bewitched. That family is bewitched. The mother died of cancer. Such a growth. Her whole face eaten away. One of her sons went mad; the other is epileptic. And now this. Too much Bible and book education, that's what. Who can make them see sense? The spirits are angry and will not be appeased....'

I do not want to hear the voices. If you had been here, Bramson, I would have wrung your neck. I take a deep breath and try to clear my mind.

Bramson, why did you come back from wherever it was you went when you saw that our mother was dying? Why did you come back to kill yourself in our house, in our mother's kitchen? Were there not enough trees to carry the weight of your shame? If your life had become too heavy for you, why did you bring our house down with you? Or did you believe it was now your house, because we kept out of your way? Even if you had stolen our late mother's dresses, our sisters' shoes and blankets did you think the fire would wipe away the evidence? If it was something your brother said to you at the bus stop, why take it out on us?

What about all those bitter words you wrote to your father and brother in those unposted letters? If you feared the drought and all those hungry mouths in the village, if your own mother was sick in hospital and you had to pay lobola for the girl you made pregnant – why did you lie? Why did your suicide note say you killed yourself because father owed you money?

If it was your dreams – the dreams you had of running amok and burning down your in-laws' huts – why did you pick on us? Was it because you knew people would say, 'Strange things are always happening in that family. This is nothing new.'

Why was your suitcase packed and ready, and the cash-box empty, when the fire-brigade axed down the door and found you dangling from the roof? If you had wanted to spite father for sending your girl off to the drought-stricken countryside, why didn't you just run? Did the fire get too big for you, get out of hand? Did you panic?

After you left your girl and your brother at the bus stop, why were you seen by Vatete Mai Farai sprinting back with your shirt tied round your waist, your chest dripping sweat, your eyes staring? What was driving you? Who recruited you to destroy our home?

***

We're still waiting for Bramson's people. It's been five days now. We're waiting so that we can show his people this charred shell that was our house, this electric wire that tore down the ceiling when the rope snapped, the remains of the ladder he mounted, this box of matches and the clever trails of sugar, still unburnt, he sprinkled through the remaining rooms. Nothing has been moved.

Bramson is still in the mortuary, his eyes hard and cold as glass.

The gathering in our yard has dispersed; only a few relatives visit us in the evenings. We're on our own.

The police have sent several messages to Bramson's father. His address was in Bramson's notebook. Record-keeping is something Bramson meticulously adopted from our father. Rushinga. The police say the drought is very bad there. The war in Mozambique has left people without livestock. Bramson's old man is probably trying to sell off the last of his possessions to raise money to hire a van.

The old man will at least come, the police say. But we've heard too many stories these days of corpses rotting in village huts while people argue about restitution and they say it always begins with the aggrieved family refusing, or delaying, to attend to the body, to the funeral.

If they don't arrive, convicts will bury the body, the police say. A docket for arson has been opened although the boy is dead. The police think it's true Bramson stole mother's dresses, left for my aunts in Zambia, and sold them. They suspect he set the house on fire to wipe out the evidence. The police think father was a fool to trust him so much. They have read his letters and inspected father's scrupulously kept wage books where Bramson signed every month for his pay. They think, as we all do, that the suicide note is a cunning lie, perhaps an attempt to salvage something for his family in the aftermath of his death, but inside their tunics and helmets and gleaming boots, the policemen are black people with totems and villages. They know the word of a dead man cannot be dismissed. They know suicide is not simply something that can be cut off, like a rafter, and loaded into a metal box.

We stay up very late each night – three brothers, three sisters, one father, two wives and a brother-in-law. Only Kelvin is not with us – he is in some half-way house or jail and nobody has suggested how or when we might alert him of this new tragedy. Like mother's, Bramson's death has afforded us, precocious siblings, starved of spontaneity, the opportunity to vent our souls upon each other. We argue back and forth, fiercely and bitterly, till our souls glow like hearth-stones. We argue about everything – about Kelvin whom we have dubiously sought to reform by banishing to the streets; about father who has been ruined by trust and what we can only perceive as ambition. We squabble about the tombstone we still have to erect on mother's grave and the attendant ceremony which we all secretly dread and don't know how to perform. We challenge father to prove that he did not indeed cheat Bramson of his pay. Rindai entangles himself in vain hypotheses, I am hypocritical, Shuvai introduces a note of laconic naivety, Vimbai parades her saintly airs and domestic martyrdom, and Tendai stings us with a new smugness that has come with recent financial independence. Our wives smirk in the firelight.

Young Tapera is quiet, taking it all in; Shuvai's husband, Baba Simba, takes another swig from the shake-shake and tipsily asks father if he has any plans to remarry. The women sleep in what was the dining room, and our good Uncle Mhasvi beds with us men in the kitchen. The place might fall down on us at any time, but we've exhausted ourselves and there is hardly any room for nightmares. We've done with herbs and bones and fears. We're past that now – or are we? A boy called Bramson hanged himself in this kitchen and his body is in the mortuary – and so what? We challenge Bramson's ghost to disturb us during the night.

***

We are still waiting for Bramson's people. It's been a week now.

Last night I dreamt of the boy running back, bare-chested, sweating and wild-eyed, from the bus station. The extensions to the house had been completed and the place was newly painted. Bramson's bulging suitcase and a huge cardboard box bound with black rope stood on the veranda. Inside the house a strange, large woman was fitting new curtains. Kelvin, hair unkempt, a cigarette jutting from his lips, came charging out of the house, exchanging angry words with the woman and then walking dejectedly down the road. Mother, swollen-faced and wearing her church uniform, lumbered out of the trees and, seeing Kelvin, stopped and shook her head. She waited at the gate of the extended house, gazing at the large woman inside it. Bramson approached the gate, panting, and saw mother. He froze, the sweat dripping guiltily down his face.

'Come here, Bramson,' said mother ominously. 'Come right here, boy.'

In the soft breeze, the crowns of the pine trees overlooking our plot gently heaved.

***

Once upon a time Father called us all into the sitting room of our small four-roomed house and asked Vimbai to open the registered letter and empty its contents.

'Forty dollars,' he said, picking up the four notes, straightening and thumbing through them, as if there might be an extra note stuck to the back of one of them, and again checking the envelope to make

172

sure that, apart from the short note, it was empty.

'Forty dollars,' he said again, re-counting the notes. 'The money your brother Rindai sent us from his first pay. Read the letter, Shuvai.'

Dear Dad (Shuvai read)
I have started work well and am enjoying the job. I am a research officer at the station. Here is $40 from my first pay to help the family. I hope you are all well. I am busy at the office. I will write again.

Your son
Rindai

Then dad brought out a brand-new exercise book and got Shuvai to print on the cover:

CONTRIBUTIONS FROM DUNGE GWANANGARA'S CHILDREN

and to write RINDAI GWANANGARA on the first page and enter the date, amount and registered envelope number. Then father said a short prayer and we all clapped our hands.

'There will be a section in the book for each one of you to be filled in once you start working,' he announced.

The next day father bought a new blanket with the forty dollars and summoned Vatete Mai Farai and Sekuru Mhasvi to the house.

'Rindai has started work and he sent some money,' he told them. 'I bought a new blanket with the money. The blanket is for my brother Tachiona to say Rindai has finished school is now working, as is required by custom. Tachiona is the eldest in the family.'

'Ndizvozvo chaizvo,'*said Vatete Mai Farai.

'Hear, hear!' said Sekuru Mhasvi. 'But did you sprinkle snuff on the ground and on the blanket and say a little word of thanks, muzukuru?'

'My brother in Chivi will do all that. He knows what to do.'

'Oh,' said Sekuru Mhasvi, a little surprised. 'But as Rindai's father you can do that here, Dunge, and then pass on the blanket. Just to make sure you say the right things.'

'My brother will know what to do.'

---

* That's as it should be.

'All right, then.'

'It's a good blanket,' said Vatete Mai Farai. 'The very best.'

'I am going to Chivi this month-end and I can pass by Tachiona's home to drop it off,' volunteered Uncle Mhasvi, ever so generously.

***

Later Babamukuru Tachiona was to weep, 'It's the best blanket in the world. When I die I want my body to be wrapped up in it.

14

Sisi Ratidzo (Babamukuru Tachiona's daughter, alias 'Mhokoshi') and Sisi Elizabeth (my late mother's sister's daughter) scrub the walls of the house and salvage what they can from the rubble. Only the main bedroom and the kitchen survived the flames; the ceiling of the lounge caved in. Sisi Ratidzo stops to blow her nose as she rinses her rags in blackened detergent for another attack on the walls. Then she straightens her back and says to father, 'We'll get the walls white again, Baba.'

Bramson's people eventually arrive with a van to take away his body; we're not there when they come. Bramson's father – a rational man, we are later told – tours the ruin with little comment or argument; his younger brother pees in his trousers when he sees the ladder and rope in the kitchen, left in place for Bramson's relatives to see.

A municipal truck comes to take away the rubble.

Sekuru Mhasvi sends over his gardener to help us.

Insurance sends an assessor to check the damage and, as always, promise little, claiming that the house was hopelessly under-insured. Father at once hires a builder to repair the damage; we each offer what we can, not much. What with our own mortgages, school fees and household bills, we more or less leave father to himself. We always did.

Slowly, month by month, the house rises out of its ruins: a room here, a passage there, a veranda somewhere else; a sprawling, sagging monster of a building with dark, sunless passages and tiny, paneless windows. I try to reconstruct the pretty little house we had once inhabited. I wonder where father is getting the money or the energy to rebuild. He is determined to defy the odds. Lanky, lonely and withdrawn, his fridge is always nearly empty. Tapera, who is now doing his 'A-levels at a boarding school, cooks and washes up during the holidays. We're at a loss as how to help. We decide to pool money together every month for him to buy groceries, with tacit instructions not to use it to purchase bricks or cement.

Widowed men who've been married for a long time often become almost helpless when they're bereaved: moody, aloof, or angry with the world, they grope for a reason to live. Perhaps widowed women are more resilient and survive longer. They have their children and grandchildren to live for and to keep them busy.

Father stops going to church and to party meetings. After work he inspects the progress on the house, and then goes to the garden to attack the weeds with his hoe. Sometimes he comes home late. Sometimes, at weekends, he is away all day. Most nights he does his accounts. He is lonely.

Mother has been dead over three years. Slowly, inevitably, there are rumours of women in his life. First we hear that he is interested in a woman – long divorced – with whom he works at the shop. Then there is news of Vazukuru Baba and Mai Tariro bringing a young *misi* from the church to pray with him in the evenings. Then, yes, there is a widowed teacher in Harare and once when I'm away he actually comes to Harare and Vongai drives him to her house so that he can meet with her.

Then, steadily, practically, he settles on one woman – a vegetable vendor who comes regularly to buy spinach and tomatoes from the plot. She is divorced with two young sons living in the rural areas with her mother. She's about thirty-five, but because of her large body and broad features looks older. First, she takes up a room in the lodger's quarters, and then she moves into the main house. She locks up her possessions in two new rooms and makes herself at home in mother's kitchen and the main bedroom. Father summons Rindai and me to Gweru for the introductions. Vatete Mai Farai, Sekuru Mhasvi and Muzukuru Baba Tariro are there, in attendance.

'*VanaSekuru*, this is your new mother MaNyoni,' Baba Tariro begins. 'And your father has requested that you address her not as Mainini, but as Amai, and that you treat her in the same way as a relative.'

We shake hands with our new mother. Her hands are hard and she does not smile much. She is on her guard, as if expecting an accusation. She's right to be suspicious. That same week Rindai summons us all to Kadoma.

'Father has made a decision to marry again and we cannot disagree.' He directs his attention to the women, in particular. 'None of us can look after him and it's best he finds someone to live with. We should all address this woman as *"mhamha"* and treat her with respect.'

Shuvai, a stickler for tradition, coughs and asks, 'But what's her name?'

'MaNyoni.' I help out.

'Where does she come from? Who are her people? Have they been told?'

'Eh, eh, Shuvai,' I say, impatiently. 'Those are details that can be easily found later.'

'But *aiwa vanaBhudhi,*'* Shuvai continues. 'If father wants to marry this woman then it should be a proper marriage, not this pot-beating business. What if anything should happen to her while she is living in our house?'

'And why has she chosen to lock up her property in two rooms and to use mother's kitchen and bedroom?' adds *'menija'* Vimbai. 'You know, these may look like minor issues, but they are matters which can bring a house down. We mustn't take any chances. Not again.'

In his abrupt, democratic way, Rindai lets the argument roll around him, and then sums up, 'Mhamha MaNyoni may not be our ideal step-mother, but we should win her over with kindness and show her the kind of family she is joining.'

But we don't. We never overcome our suspicions.

***

Mhamha MaNyoni, it seems, never cooks. When we visit father (and

---

* '[But] no, my brothers.'

we hardly ever do) the fridge is empty: no meat, margarine, milk, or eggs. No steak, liver, or fish, just a packet of cow's intestines, and maybe a few wrinkled tomatoes or shrivelled sweet potatoes. She wakes up every morning to take all the produce to her stall at the marketplace; in the evenings she retires to the bedroom to count her money. She hardly speaks to us, and we wonder if she feels over-awed by us. When Rindai or I visit father, and we sometimes do, on our way through Gweru on a work assignment, we never stay with them.

We know, instinctively, that father is spending all the money we send him every month on uniforms and school fees for her two sons.

The lodgers dread her. Now they have to pay on the first of each month. The water pump is shut off at nine in the morning to save electricity. All visitors have to be reported. The gates are locked at eight. Conscious that she was a lodger herself, she strives for power over her erstwhile peers.

Once, when Baba Tariro's first son is getting married in Gweru, we all converge on the plot and she says to the children, 'Hello, vazukuru. Come and say hello to *gogo*,' but none of them accept the arms she proffers. Sadly, she hardly knows their names, or who is whose child. We go off to eat hamburgers at a restaurant. Father passes by, straight from the shop, on his way to the wedding, lean and knock-kneed in his suit. I say to my son Takura, 'There, there, Takura. There's your grandfather. Go and say hello.' The boy runs out, stumbles and picks himself up. Father stares momentarily at the little boy at his feet, then sees us crowded and waving at the windows of the restaurant. Suddenly recognising the boy, his only grandson, he stoops to sweep him into his arms.

Father says no to offers of food. Perhaps he thinks it is too ex-pensive and wants to save us some money. I realise now that we should have stopped by at the shop and invited him to join us in the restaurant, to show that he is loved and wanted. Mistakes, mistakes.

At the wedding, we pool together all our money and presents and have them announced as the combined gifts from the Gwanangara family. Sadly, Mhamha MaNyoni does not come with our father. Afterwards we stand together in an accustomed bunch, talking to each other and to friends and relatives.

When we get home Mhamha MaNyoni hasn't prepared any food for us. We'd been eating all day, but we're still outraged.

Maiguru Mazvita, Rindai's girlfriend, was beautiful. She had bright eyes, oily lips and a slim figure that promised to conquer the world. She cooked us a delicious meal of steak, spinach and potatoes. Rindai, she and I ate together at her little table, talking and laughing. Rindai said to me, 'Brace yourself, man. Meet your senior wife.' I said to her, 'Welcome to the club, Madam.' Later on I wrote to her, 'Maiguru M, We're a happy lot and you're most welcome to join us.' And after Rindai had taken her to Gweru to meet the appointed delegation of Vatete Mai Farai, Sekuru Mhasvi and Muzukuru Baba Tariro who had in turn taken her to meet father and mother she wrote back, 'Oh, what open and warm parents you have – what nice people.'

She was a teacher at the local primary school, so I sat at her little table sipping orange juice, marking her pupils' books and listening to the Shadows and the Beatles. On Saturday mornings I accompanied her to the supermarket to help her shop for groceries. She asked me to change into Rindai's jeans and T-shirt so that she could wash and iron my clothes and I said, with little reluctance, 'Well, all right.'

Rindai had virtually moved out of the large, empty research station house to camp with her in her little dwelling. A priest's daughter, she was quiet, thoughtful and polite, but not in a pliant way. Very Manyika, she revealed just enough of herself without seeming to want to know too much about you. She wasn't Rindai's first girlfriend – he had dated and introduced me to two or three other women before but I knew that as soon as he met Mazvita he had found the one he was looking for. They were both twenty-four.

They must have been together for six months when the inevitable happened. She fell pregnant. I saw her medical card on the display cabinet. Pregnancy test – positive, three months. Their fate was sealed. Rindai took it like a man, and immediately accepted responsibility for her. He arranged at once to marry her. We were all surprised by the speed at which things happened, the women especially, and if mother and father were a little disappointed at the haste with

*which their son and first child, in whom they had invested over two
decades of their efforts and labour, was now almost being 'snatched'
from their nest by this young woman, if they ever suspected anything
sinister, they disguised it completely. They unlocked their doors and
opened their arms to her. And, come to think of it, that generation
was less chauvinist, less narrow than ours.*

*The girls, my sisters, were less discreet, initially anyway. Shuvai,
a budding sixteen, openly wept. 'She's too old for him. He's marrying her and he hasn't even worked for the family. She'll reap the
benefits of the education father gave him.' She sulked, and refused
to eat Mazvita's food. I suspect that she had fears of secret potions
being administered to our meals, bit by bit, to soften our brains.*

Mother chided Shuvai, 'Leave my son alone.'

*Father declared to our neighbours, 'I'm happy. Rindai did not
disgrace me by shirking his responsibility, or stealing somebody's
wife.'*

*At his in-laws' house Rindai was an instant hit when, on the night
of the introductions, he joked and laughed with everyone, danced
with his sisters-in-law and, in a typical move against outdated de-
corum, burst into his mother-in-law's kitchen, opened the pots to see
what was cooking and helped himself to a chicken drumstick.*

*'That one,' his in-laws were to forever repeat, in stitches. 'We got
a true* mkwasha *for sure.'*

***

After serving two months in jail for shop-lifting, Kelvin goes to
Kwekwe to seek shelter with Shuvai and her husband, Baba Simba.
Baba Simba calls me to say Kelvin is very ill and I must come at
once. Vimbai and I drive down to find him asleep. He slouches up
to greet us.

He's in very bad shape. His head his shaven. I haven't seen him
for almost eighteen months and feel guilty for it. I never visited him
in prison. I, too, am giving up on him.

'He's got boils all over his back,' Baba Simba explains. Kelvin
lifts his T-shirt to show us the purulent spots. His stomach is hollow,
hair sticks out from his bony chest. Baba Simba says, 'I bathe him
every day, Sekuru, and I tell you, he's wasting away. He's hardly
eating.'

Kelvin goes back to bed. I follow him and sit on the edge of the bed. 'So what do you want to do now?'

He doesn't answer, so I say again, 'Where do you want to go?' He picks at a pimple on his cheek. I am struck by how much he looks like a withered version of me, this brother of mine whose skin once sparkled so much that we called him 'washer-boy'.

'Do you want to come to Harare?' He turns painfully on his side. I shudder at the prospect of another new medical-aid subscription, visits to doctors and endless prescriptions, of taking responsibility and making decisions about sick family members.

'I could go and stay with Sekuru Mhasvi,' he says by and by. 'At least till I'm better.'

'Will he accept you?'

'He looked after me when they let me out of prison.' He says this with maddening calm, and I realise that I am ashamed.

'You mustn't take Sekuru Mhasvi, or any of our relatives, for granted. You must make peace with father. He'll take you back. I know him.'

'With that street woman of his, MaNyoni?'

'That's your problem – calling people names. How do you think Father will take you back if you call Mhamha MaNyoni a street woman?'

'That's the trouble with you. You don't know anything about her, or anyone.'

'Well, I haven't got all day, you know,' I threaten, irritably. 'Look. I'm prepared to drive you to Gweru, to talk to father and that's it.'

'Will Sekuru Mhasvi be there with us? To intercede for me?'

'If you wish,' I say.

He holds a hand to his eyes and nods, almost imperceptibly.

I go out to phone father and Sekuru Mhasvi to warn them that we're on our way. And so, late that afternoon, Baba Simba, Kelvin and I drive to Gweru. We pick up Sekuru Mhasvi and head for the plot. On the way we brief him of our mission. Father receives us calmly. Mhamha MaNyoni conveniently retires to the kitchen without offering us anything to eat.

Sekuru Mhasvi wastes no time on pleasantries: 'Mzukuru Kelvin has come to apologise.'

At night, father's house now looks dreary as ever. The roof creaks, mice scramble in the yawning ceiling of the half-renovated lounge, crickets shrill in the passages, a lodger's baby bawls somewhere in the dark recesses. Mosquitoes feast on our arms. Father wraps his arms around his shoulders and stares at the faint naked light bulb for a good five minutes, coughs.

'One thing I've disliked all my life, Sekuru Mhasvi,' he begins ominously, 'is wasting time. I'm glad you're present to hear me out, Sekuru, you Mkwasha Baba Simba, and you my son Godi. I am seventy years old now and I don't have long to live. I have helped many people in my family. I'm not blowing my own trumpet, but I believe I've worked very hard every year of my life for my children, as any parent should, and it's time I had some rest. Like any human being I have made some mistakes in my life – to the rest of the world the woman sitting out of earshot in the kitchen might be one of my greatest blunders. But I'm not apologising. I don't believe it is proper for a child who has never lifted a finger to help himself or to help *anyone*, to criticise me so bluntly, and to spurn my help.'

'There he goes again!' Kelvin snarls.

'Shut up, Kelvin!' Sekuru Mhasvi orders. 'No one's asked you to speak.'

'But he's always speaking, Sekuru. He *enjoys* the sound of his own voice.'

Kelvin staggers to his feet and wags a finger at father. 'You made me like this! Me, Rindai and mother. All those goblins locked up in your wardrobes, hired to make you money in your lodgers' rooms and your garden are now sucking away our blood and our sanity.'

'Sekuru Kelvin!' Baba Simba pleads.

'Go on,' says father. 'Strike me. Finish me off.'

'You know what you did to us!'

'Get out, get out!' father flares. 'Get out of my house and leave me to die in peace.'

'Who says you are dying?' Sekuru Mhasvi confronts father.

'Do you think I can survive *him* and what he's done to *me* over all these years,' father swears. 'Do you think I'll let him go before me?'

'Are you God to decide who dies before whom?'

'Mark my words. No child of mine will precede me in death. I shall bury no child of mine.'

It's no use.

Kelvin marches out of the house and we follow him. In the kitchen Mhamha MaNyoni says, 'Are you going already, without eating?' No one answers her.

I open the car doors and we climb in. As I reverse down the driveway, father steps aside and is caught in the beam of the headlights, in his blue pyjamas, holding his head in his hands.

We drive in silence to Sekuru Mhasvi's house. Kelvin fetches a blanket he had earlier left there.

'So where are you going, now?' the older man asks him.

'Where else? To the market place and streets where I belong.' Kelvin sets off, with the blanket in his arms, towards the haze of the city lights.

'Take him with you to Harare, Godi,' Sekuru Mhasvi urges. 'At least till he's well.'

It is no use.

I drive after him and hoot. He continues on, his face downcast. I stop. Baba Simba stumbles after him, takes him by the hands and reasons with him.

They come back together to the car.

***

Back in Harare, the young doctor prescribes several medicines for Kelvin's diarrhoea and boils, recommends home-based care and bed-rest and arranges a string of appointments. Kelvin eats little, complains of sores in his mouth, spends most of the time in bed, and hardly speaks to anyone. Sly Gemini that he is, he chooses to co-operate when it is convenient to do so. The only time he moves is to go to the toilet; when he drags himself down the passage, Piwai and Tambu hurry out of his way.

Vongai sings holy songs ... Alleluiah, Alleluiah ... and scrubs the toilet after him. I wonder what she thinks, what she wants to say, or if she has had enough ... But we hardly talk. Can we talk? I wonder if the children are safe from Kelvin's ablutions, his diarrhoea. The maid washes his clothes. I hope she won't leave. I am sorry for Vongai, for everyone, and I realise how years of strife and silence have slowly driven us apart.

Kelvin promptly writes a letter to Sekuru Mhasvi and asks me to post it. Out of curiosity, I unseal the letter and read it:

> Dear Sekuru
> We got here OK and I am seeing a doctor. I am getting plenty of rest but they are not getting me enough fruit or fluids. Also, they are making me wash my own underwear.
> Yours,
> Kelvin

Damn! I tear up the letter. On my way from work I bring him a sack of naartjies and a bottle of fresh orange juice. 'So why didn't you tell me you wanted these?' I say, dumping them on the side of the bed. He hardly eats them.

No one phones or visits. I don't call anyone. I wait stoically for the doctor's next visit.

I am in the office one afternoon when Vongai arrives with Jean, her workmate. They are both serious, but Jean has a suspicious smile on her face.

'Kwakanaka here?' I say. 'Is everything OK?'

'Yes, yes,' says Jean, and adds, after a moment, 'He had a stroke.'

'A stroke? When?'

'Last night.'

'Last night? But I saw him last night. And this morning.'

'No, no. Your sister Vimbai was there and she took him to Gweru hospital.'

'Gweru hospital? But I left him at home in the morning.'

'Your father, not Kelvin,' Vongai explains, bursting into tears.

I stand up very slowly and close the office windows.

***

Later, much later, father would buy a plot with the money he received from the sale of cattle in Chivi plus a loan from his boss. Mother and I read the advertisements carefully, and went out to look at three places. We settled on the plot because it was close to the city; the house was compact and had a separate cottage; there were five acres of arable land with plenty of underground water, pipes, taps and spacious ground to build lodgers' rooms.

We moved out without fanfare from the little four-roomed house in Hoffman Street; a lorry came and we loaded our property onto it and left without ceremony. The people we had lived with in the township for a quarter of a century bitterly complained about our departure, about the way we had left without saying goodbye.

'Dunge left us without a farewell,' they would grumble. 'As if we were jealous of him, or would curse him.'

Now that we had a plot in the city father invited our cousin Bhudhi Tavengwa, his half-brother Chari's son, to take over our dew-in-the-morning home in Gokwe. When Bhudhi Tavengwa moved into it he wrote father a long elaborate letter listing all the things, like cattle, chickens, beds, pots, plates, ploughs, carts and hoes that had been left on the property.

15

Sekuru Mhasvi drives Rindai, Shuvai and me to the mortuary to see father. He is lying on a tray in the blue pyjamas he was wearing when I last saw him two weeks ago. He wears one of his best smiles. I feel a strange relief, seeing that smile, one which gives me astonishing strength. His face seems to be saying, 'It's over for me and you don't have to worry now. Be strong and be sure to bury me right.'

At the shop his boss asks us to compile a list of everything we need for the funeral. When we bring it to him, he strikes out Cokes and Fantas – 'because the bottles might break' – and replaces these with cool-drink powder. Fresh milk is substituted with skimmed milk powder, margarine with jam, and meat is deleted because as Hindus my father's bosses 'are not allowed to purchase or even touch beef'. A casket is too expensive, or perhaps not available; he would have to phone around first.

I say to Sekuru Mhasvi and Rindai, 'Shit! Forty years' service. We don't need this.'

We arrange for the death certificate and the burial order and for the grave to be dug next to mother's. Everyone is willing to help. We hire a bus for the mourners, work out a programme with the priest, and choose a coffin.

'We can't have the service at the church,' the priest declares. 'The body viewing will have to take place at the plot.'

'Why?' Muzukuru Baba Tariro asks.

'He was no longer attending church services. And besides, he was living in sin.'

'Who decides?' I ask, blood rushing to my face.

'The scriptures do.' The priest is barely thirty, one of the fashionable sort more likely to regard priesthood as a good livelihood than a calling.

'But Dunge helped build this church, *mwanangu*,' Vatete Mai Farai protests. 'He paid for bricks, cement, doors, windows, even the pulpit. I was here with him in the fifties and I can vouch for him.'

'I'm sorry. It's the church rules.' The priest insists, stroking his white collar.

'But everyone makes mistakes, Baba,' Shuvai pleads.

'Damn!' Rindai swears.

Sisi Ratidzo arrives, wailing, at the gate, accompanied by a short, squint-eyed man with white hair who introduces himself as Muzukuru Dzorai from Chivi.

And so Dunge Gwanangara's body is viewed at the plot, in the open sun. Rindai looks dignified in his black suit, next to the priest. Our sisters and wives stand guard at the head of the casket; Sisi Ratidzo, Sisi Ratidzo Mhokoshi and Sisi Elizabeth support them. Sekuru Mhasvi waits in attendance, watching the coffin so as to be sure no one drops malevolent objects into it. Tapera mills around on the veranda with his university friends. I don't see Kelvin – he's probably lying on a bed in one of the rooms. He'd even found it difficult to sit up in the car when we drove over. I'd last seen him struggling to sit on a stool trying to eat breakfast with the other men.

When the casket is loaded into the funeral van Mhamha MaNyoni emerges from the mass of women and insists on sitting with Vatete Mai Farai and Sisi Ratidzo in the back of the van. When the messages accompanying the flowers are read out after the grave has been filled she too has provided a medium-sized bouquet:

> My darling husband Dunge
> Just when I thought I had found love and security
> you decided to leave me.
> Go well.
> Your wife MaNyoni

That night after supper, when the gathering has somewhat dwindled, there is a conference in the kitchen to decide on Mhamha

MaNyoni's fate.

'Your man is dead now, Mbuya MaNyoni,' Muzukuru Baba Tariro begins. 'Now that he is gone, nobody can look after you.'

Without raising her head, Mhamha MaNyoni says, 'But I looked after him till he died.'

'Yes, but he was the sole reason for your being here.'

'You can't just throw me out on the streets.'

'If anything should happen to you, there will be nobody to explain to your people what happened.'

'I need time to mourn him, to settle down.'

'But remember you were not married, and he had children.'

'Perhaps we could give you six months?' Sekuru Mhasvi suggests, peaceably, kindly. And then, turning to us, 'This is what your father would have wanted. Did he not ask you to show her respect?'

'No, Sekuru,' says Muzukuru Mai Tariro, firmly. 'Who would look after her? We would be making things difficult for the children. What if she were to die? Her *ngozi* could haunt us.'

'I have nowhere to go,' Mhamha MaNyoni pleads.

'Sekuru Rindai, what do you think?' asks Muzukuru Dzorai.

Rindai coughs, 'Surely she was living somewhere before she came here. I'd give her a month.'

'When your father was alive, he promised to buy me a stand.'

'A stand?' I say. 'What would you need a stand for? You were living here, at this plot, with our father, and we were calling you *mhamha* while all the time you wanted a stand for yourself? Did you want him to build you the house as well? What cheek!'

'And you didn't exactly act like a mother to us,' Tendai buts in. 'Tell me, Mhamha MaNyoni, did you ever once cook for any of us? You were as mean as a rail – *njanji chaiyo* – while using our mother's pots and plates. Do you think we don't know that father was paying your sons' school fees and buying them uniforms with the money we sent him? Did you see how thin he was when he died? Who knows – maybe you drove him to his death.'

'Tendai, no!'

'Let them speak, Sekuru Mhasvi,' Muzukuru Mai Tariro urges. 'It's best to let all the bitterness out.'

'All right then,' said Mhamha MaNyoni, defiantly. 'I'll leave this crumbling, rotten house and its curses and go back where I came from. Did you think I would die here, now that I have no home? I'll leave tomorrow, if that will make you happy. But you'll see.'

'Stop threatening us,' says Vatete Mai Farai.

'Yes, you'll certainly see. I don't have to bother about you, Rindai, because you already have a problem. As for you, Godi, and you, Tendai, and your foul mouths – I won't say much. My name is MaNyoni.'

***

At dawn Sekuru Mhasvi hires a lorry from the police station and the lodgers help him load Mhamha MaNyoni's property onto it and they drive off with her to Mkoba. I think, 'Oh my God, we are being callous,' but I'm not sure.

The new middle class has become ruthless in its own defence.

***

At ten o'clock Muzukuru Dzorai, who has suddenly taken charge of things with Muzukuru Baba Tariro, arranges for all father's clothes – his shirts, trousers, pants, coats, suits, shoes, socks, glasses and even his watch to be taken out onto the lawn for distribution among family members and close friends. The two perform the task with dexterity. Everybody gets something – even our cousins, Dzenga, Jonah and Tavengwa, who are absent. The women are given T-shirts, pyjamas, watches and books. I walk off, like Kelvin, with a suit, two shirts and some underwear. In addition, and not without irony, I secure a warm woollen jersey which Mhamha MaNyoni had knitted for father.

But that is not the end of it. We need to decide what to do with the property and who will live in the house, manage the plot and look after the lodgers, for the time being, anyway. A fierce argument ensues, Gwanangara-style, for three hours. Selling, at this point, is out of the question – the property is a rallying point for the family, the glue of our disparate lives. Three options eventually emerge. One, letting the place through an estate agent – but which agent would take on the property in its ramshackle state? Two, identifying a close relative to act as caretaker – apart from Kelvin, we're all committed to our careers – but which relative would have the time or courage to take over the plot, given its grim history and complex demands? Three, finding a trusted lodger who could be promoted to the position of caretaker and invited to live in the main house – but would we not be creating another Bramson?

Muzukuru Dzorai sits in the kitchen, shelling nuts and listening to us talk. I don't like him at all, pushing his way into our affairs and taking charge. I know his type.

We're so quick to judge and categorise, we're losing our humanity.

'I think I know the person you need,' he eventually announces.

Mbuya Mai Svorai! Sekuru Trueman's wife. Sekuru Trueman is our uncle, our late mother's brother's eldest son. An ex-combatant, he joined the army when he returned after independence. Much of the time, he is away on duty in Mozambique or the DRC and when at home, he lives with his wife and two babies in a one-roomed shack in Marondera.

Mbuya Mai Svorai! How blind we've been! We all agree she will do fine because she and Sekuru Trueman need a place to stay; they have a small, young family and, finally, she is energetic and bright. Rindai sends Tapera to call her from the lawn where she is helping other women to wash up.

***

In the morning, we're preparing to return to our homes. Rindai, Tapera and I are sitting with Mbuya Mai Svorai explaining the books, working out a system for selling produce and collecting rents when Sisi Ratidzo calls me out to the veranda. Kelvin is dressed in the grey suit, red tie and black shoes I gave him and is pacing about with an energy I have not seen recently.

'Muzukuru Dzorai bathed me,' he says. 'I have to go. Will you take me, Mkoma Godi?'

'Where do you want to go?' I ask.

'I made some money selling life insurance policies and the company has never paid me. I need that money real bad. Can you take me to see the agent?'

'I've heard that one before,' I say, before returning to the lounge and the discussion with Mbuya Mai Svorai.

Minutes later Sisi Ratidzo pops her face round the door.

'*Vana bhudhi*, my brothers, come quickly!'

In one of the outer bedrooms Kelvin is lying on a bed shaking. I push through the small crowd at the door. Muzukuru Dzorai loosens his tie and takes off his shoes. Kelvin shudders as if he is about to throw up, then his body falls slack. The children start wailing. Kelvin gives one last gasp and relaxes. Muzukuru Dzorai closes his eyes, folds his hands over his chest and covers him with a blanket. Sisi Elizabeth starts a hymn.

'Call the police,' Muzukuru Dzorai says. 'And call all the mourners back.'

***

He had fallen into a huge pit, the kind that women dig when they're looking for that special ivhu *used to paint the walls of village huts. Dusk had fallen and she couldn't see into the hole. She could hear snakes hissing near the surface and his voice calling, 'Mother! Mother!' She ran into the open field, looking for a fallen branch and shouting, 'Help! Help, anybody!' She found an old fallen stick but when she picked it up, it broke. Then she found a slim* mupfuti *sapling and ran back to the pit.*

'Rindai, wait! Grab this!'

She fished for him with the sapling. His feet dragged in the mud at the bottom of the pit and his cries seemed muffled. The sapling struck his body and he gripped it with both hands, and tried to pull himself up. But he was stronger than she was and as the earth gave way under her boots, she slowly fell forward, into the pit...

In the morning her eyes were red and she had a severe headache.

On another occasion, she dreamt of the church women, all in white and black, singing in the small yard at 33 Hoffman Street. Rindai drove up the path in the Peugeot 404 and squealed to a halt on the lawn near the kitchen, causing the women to scatter all over the yard like frightened hens. Dressed in a grey suit with a white flower at his breast, he staggered out of the car, lanky and knock-kneed. Mazvita, in a white wedding dress and holding a bunch of flowers, followed him out of the car and said, 'Now look, Rindai. See what you have done!'

***

I'm sitting in the hotel lobby, drinking and chatting with fellow participants on the penultimate night of a workshop in Lusaka when it suddenly occurs to me that I should seek out my mother's people before I fly home.

As luck would have it, I find a man driving towards the Copperbelt who offers me a lift. He's a jovial, burly publisher called Sita, and he fetches me promptly at eight in the morning. I feel exuberant and adventurous. I'm out to search for my roots, I'm doing my duty and I'm going to give my mother's people a surprise, albeit a short one. My last visit was when I was four and now all I have is a piece of paper on which Sekuru Trueman scribbled out the name of a hospital and a bus station. We drive into the heart of the country, through jagged cityscapes, marketplaces drenched with the smell of dried fish and human waste, and half-tilled maize fields. Sita explains the Zambia of Chiluba to me: the privatisation, armed robbers and corrupt police. Crates of tomatoes, onions and cabbages line the route. If everyone is selling, and selling the same produce, who is buying and who can make a profit? The only other item appears to be charcoal burnt from firewood garnered from the generous forests – a burnt-out economy. I am cautious not to make too many obvious comparisons. Zimbabwe is fast following this downhill path but I am too steeped in our family problems to notice or care.

We find the hospital easily enough and at the nearby bottle store, my uncle's names ring a few bells. We're directed to a house off the main road and Sita generously drops me off there and proceeds onwards.

The man of the house, a gentle-eyed giant, offers me tea and a prayer. He speaks in English because his Shona is limited and I do not understand ChiBemba.

'Your uncle Peter's second wife is my daughter,' the man explains. 'Your uncle Elias was here minutes ago and should still be on the road trying to catch a lift to Lusaka. I'll send for him.'

A while later, Sekuru Elias appears. My very own uncle, my late mother's third brother, lanky, dark and large-lipped just as he was in the dog-eared photograph mother had treasured. Now he is holding me in his arms and hugging me, 'Ah, Godi! So it was you, my sister Hilda's child, who stopped the combis from picking me up all morning. Ah, Dolly's child, would you have recognised me if you had bumped into me on the road?'

At the small village church, we are joined by Sekuru Elias's wife and one of their daughters. 'That's your Mainini Beaulah,' Sekuru Elias explains. 'She's the one we intended for your father after your mother died, to rekindle your mother Hilda's hearth, but your father said, "No, I will not have a young wife and a string of new children! I will take my own pick." Your father!'

Mainini Beaulah, perhaps eighteen, tender-eyed, lean as a peach tree, with a large crown of jet black hair, proffers a small smile. She is my young mother and I like her, but I can't imagine her managing the large plot or the house and its headaches.

At Sekuru Peter's sprawling compound of dilapidated *dakha* and grass huts, a large crowd of *sekurus* and *maininis* rush to welcome me. Mbuya VaMurozvi, my mother's mother, half blind now, holds me to her breast, kneads my face with her fingers and laughs softly. She is barefoot and I wish, with regret, I had brought her presents – shoes, groceries and perhaps even some old spectacles. Sekuru Peter, my mother's second brother, holds a cackling guinea fowl to my face, dusts his shorts and says, 'Your relish, *muzukuru*.'

Later, as we're eating, Sekuru Peter says, 'So, is everyone well at the plot?' I say, 'Yes, yes.' I had written them long letters following the disasters. It's Bramson they want to hear about, about the house burning down and the size of the flames and the noise of the fire engines; and about father and Kelvin dying within four days of each other and how we had managed one funeral straight after another. I know they already know and want to ask why? why? but I just say, 'Yes, yes.' I don't want to talk about anything painful or difficult.

Sekuru Elias deflects attention away from the ugly stories by saying, 'Your mother Hilda guided you all the way to us, Godifiri. She saw you coming. She watched your every step.'

There is so much to do and say, so little time. I have to try and reconstruct the plan of the compound from thirty-five years ago and pinpoint the position of Sekuru Elias's little old hut. I sing, to everyone's amusement:

Chimba chaSekuru Elias chineman'a![*]

_____
[*] Sekuru Elias's hut has cracks.

Chimba chaSekuru Elias chineman'a wo!

I struggle to remember names, faces and incidents; to throw little stones at the head of unknown graves and pay my respects to the numerous dead. I have to reconcile my childhood belief in my mother's people as smart, well-to-do farmers with current reality, worn down by decades of poverty in a cruel country. Half the family is not here. I recklessly promise to make a proper trip to see them all later, probably in a convoy with the other Gwanangaras. Now I have to return to the hotel to catch my flight home. I delay the announcement of my departure, fearing to dampen the high spirits inspired by my visit, but they set me free without too much argument or regret – me, their expensive relative who is staying in a hotel and might require cornflakes, eggs, bacon, bread, butter and tea in the morning if I were to stay the night.

And so I leave, happy and fulfilled. In the combi, half grateful to be returning to the comfort of the hotel, I whisper into my shirt, 'Thank you, Mother. Thank you, Hilda.'

***

At the church, Rindai signed the register with his usual flourish. Maiguru Mazvita lifted her long train and gave it to her sister, the bridesmaid, then with equal dignity put her pen to paper.

Of the wedding pictures taken of me as I signed the certificate, people would later say, 'You looked too greedy for the camera.'

Father beamed from the elders' benches; our in-laws looked on in customary silence.

Mother blew her nose into a handkerchief and wiped her eyes, not of tears but of fatigue; she had hardly slept for days and her voice was hoarse.

Then we did the bridal steps in accompaniment to music: eight bridesmaids dressed in orange, and eight best men looking like penguins in their best black suits, samba'd up the aisle. Men whistled, women ululated and somebody threw rice as we climbed into the waiting cars.

Vatete Mai Farai presided over the pots of chicken. Muzukuru Mai Tariro expertly took over with fresh packets of long grain rice for the special guests.

We crowded into the small yard of 33 Hoffman Street to eat. Some children stepped hungrily on the beds of spinach; others leaned on the banana trees to hold their plates.

There was no one from Chivi, no one from Donsa, no one from Gokwe. Nobody from Zambia. Sisi Ratidzo would have introduced everyone to everyone and started up a traditional tune and danced, but she was not there. Babamukuru Tachiona would have wept. Sisi Elizabeth would have bantered with everyone.

We had cocooned ourselves from our relatives. Maiguru Mazvita's father, Teacher Zimuto, and Vatete Mai Farai gave the main speeches. The guests asked to be allowed to donate presents. For reasons best known to himself, father stopped them, saying there would be a 'proper' wedding later, at which they could do this. He seemed undecided whether or not this should be 'the' event.

After the speeches we did more steps and danced to records and then the people began to leave. We retired into the house to sleep, the boys in the spare room and the girls in the kitchen. At midnight we heard new-year noises, cars and trains blaring, fire-crackers exploding, people shouting, ushering in a new year.

It was then that we heard bellowing from the spare bedroom where Rindai and his newly wedded wife were bedding down ...

16

Mbuya Mai Svorai is a good *'menija'* at the plot, at first anyway. The enterprising skill certainly runs in her blood. She turns the garden green with spinach, onions, tomatoes, potatoes and winter maize. The fruit trees are watered in the orchard. With her husband Sekuru Trueman's knack for fixing gadgets, she rekindles the house. Light bulbs shine in the once dark corridors, curtains hang on the windows, taps run; flowers flourish along the drab walls. She converts the garage into a breeding space for chicks, replenishes the fowl runs. Hens cackle once more in the yard, there are a few precious crates of eggs for sale every morning, women from the market wait at the gate for her produce. She rules the lodgers with easy authority, cajoling them into paying rent and humouring them into obeying her rules.

Hilda Dolly, the moon huntress, must be smiling, wherever she is. After all, isn't Mai Svorai her blood nephew's wife?

I phone Mbuya Mai Svorai once a week and every month Rindai and I drive down to Gweru to find out how things are. She happily feeds us peanut-butter chicken, shows us the bills and hands over the rent. A person who has mastered the art of persuasion, she has an answer for everything: the problem lodger who is two months behind with her rent, the one who lost a brother just this morning and will pay next week, the plumber who had to do an impromptu job on the toilet, and so forth.

That Christmas, in a spirit of family unity, we converge on the plot, slaughter a goat, buy beer, play music and hold a party and, at Mbuya Mai Svorai's instigation, we lay wreaths at the cemetery.

Sekuru Trueman lets his wife be. He seems content to parade us to his workmates as his vazukuru. Once or twice he hints that we have burdened him with looking after the plot, insinuating that tradition might require him, as a junior *tezvara*, to justify his actions to my mother's brothers later. He allows us the dubious opportunity of circumventing him, and dealing directly with his wife in matters relating to the plot. His marriage to Mbuya Mai Svorai has always been somewhat shaky as often happens with military couples when the man is frequently absent and the burden of the household falls on the woman. Now that he has a roof over his head, a wife, a phone and a thriving garden to go to every weekend, his marriage appears stronger. Or so we think.

Muzukuru Dzorai is a predictably frequent visitor. Pretending to be useful, he helps himself to vegetables and the occasional bag of maize meal. He is about to appropriate a spare wheelbarrow when Rindai tells him off. Muzukuru Dzorai's ultimate goal is to install his son as a gardener, so that he can have better control of our affairs. Mbuya Mai Svorai reports that whenever he stays at the house he claims to have nightmares about handling Kelvin's body as he was dying and demanding a goat or a fowl for presiding over our two funerals 'as required by tradition'. He further claims to have unearthed and destroyed several pots allegedly planted by Mhamha MaNyoni to bring us harm.

Actually, all our erstwhile relatives are suddenly interested in the plot and not short of ideas about how we should look after it.

'Demolish the house and build a new one.'

'Restore the house.'

'Lease the field to a qualified farmer.'

'Sell the plot.'

'Send Sekuru Trueman and his wife away and find a proper caretaker.'

'Promote a lodger to act as a caretaker.'

Nonetheless, although Mbuya Mai Svorai is managing so well, such comments make us feel inadequate. They ferment unnecessary, prolonged and heated debate among us, Dunge Gwanangara's children. Battle lines slowly emerge with the women opting to sell the plot and the men to retain it.

'It will only bring us sad memories,' the women argue. 'Let us get rid of it and share the proceeds.'

'Over my dead body!' Rindai swears. 'We can't be Gwanangaras without a family home. You women can't have your cake and eat it. Rule the men you married, and not your brothers whom you left to manage the plot.'

'Then give the plot to Tapera. He's the youngest of us.'

'No way.'

I wish father had made a will.

Mbuya Mai Svorai takes advantage of the disagreements. She invites her relatives to live in the main house, without paying rent. She agrees to grow beans with the women and uses the rentals to fund her input into the project. When she harvests the beans, she keeps half the produce. Rentals are whittled away to purchase feed for her chickens. The electricity bill increases due to the excessive use of the water pump. She volunteers little from the sale of vegetables. She charges the lodgers for using the phone but still lands us with a huge bill. We lock the phone but she quietly unlocks it and accuses Sekuru Trueman of making long international calls. The phone is eventually cut off.

'The lodgers should pay their rent straight into an account and submit their monthly receipts,' Vongai and Maiguru Mai Nda suggest. 'Mbuya should not be allowed to handle any money.'

When we confront Sekuru Trueman about the way matters are deteriorating, he says, half vengefully, 'How should I know? Ask your Mbuya. You gave her the power, and never consulted me.'

Sometimes he quarrels with his wife; there are rumours that men knock on her window at night when he is away.

We contemplate sending Mbuya Mai Svorai away, and remove all her responsibilities.

Rindai takes over the fields and the supervision of the lodgers. He ploughs, hires two gardeners and pays them from the rent; like the true farmer he is, he turns the field green with maize, sunflowers and paprika. When Shuvai asks to see the accounts, Rindai tells her to mind her husband's affairs.

Tapera and I leave Rindai to the field while we tend to the lodgers and the house. We have the building plastered, windows fitted and, in the lodgers' quarters, we have a meter board installed. Whenever a lodger refuses to pay, or to vacate a room, Tapera and I drive down to Gweru and cause a scene, throwing out the defaulter's property, locking him out or confiscating his belongings. We become notorious for our ruthlessness. We are equally so with Mbuya Mai Svorai and the books of accounts. The tacit understanding is that earnings from the plot will be saved for the benefit of any Gwanangara, male or female, who should fall sick, or should need school fees or to borrow money for any other worthy cause.

***

Good lord,
I regret now,
With belated hindsight,
That in teaching and encouraging you, Tapera,
To be uncompromising with the lodgers
And the accounts
At our mother's plot,
I may have led
To your death.

***

I drive into the school yard in my sparkling new white car. Two prefects, a boy and a girl, meet me at the gate and stand to attention. I give a half salute, grin at them and pull up in the car park.

'Afternoon, Sir,' they chorus, and escort me to the assembly where staff and students are gathered under the trees. The duty master receives me and escorts me to the headmistress. The students look like a flock of sheep in white shirts, black skirts and trousers. The benches creak as the students stand up to welcome me. The headmistress, a small light woman in a black graduate's gown whom I've know for decades, offers me her hand and shows me to my seat.

'Welcome, Mr Gwanangara.'

I adjust my belt and wonder if in my dyed shirt, blue corduroys and khaki jacket, I'm appropriately dressed. I glance at the teachers, mostly young, eager-eyed men and women and I do not see Tapera. In a moment of anxiety, I wipe my brow with the back of my hand.

You have arranged everything; primed me, your brother, to give a talk at your school and here I am, fidgeting with my novels. But where are you, Tapera? We'd agreed to meet after the reading, and go to Gweru together to sort out some matters at the plot.

I begin. I read. Then I talk. I no longer need notes. It's easy as eating bananas. I take a sip of water from the glass and slide into my speech. First memories of 33 Hoffman Street. Grim childhood. Hungry nights. Wet blankets. Mr 'Good Morning!' falling off his bicycle. Gideon walking in his sleep. Stern parents. Books. Helmeted ghosts in the banana trees. Schools choking with the stench of children. Smudged composition books. Dreary poems about an enraged God snuffing out a sinful world. Magazines splattered with blood. Scribbling. Articles half-plagiarised from magazines. Dog-eared photographs. Eager narratives of runaway servants. Ardent tracts about goat-skinned rainmakers. Acres of morning dew. Graveyard apparitions. Scrumptious girls. Scrawny children of war. Thorny harvests. Steps ahead of the self, all the time. Talks about talking. Publishers. Reviews. Interviews. Launches. Bookshops. Trips. Readings...

I talk and talk. I hide my secret yearnings, my immodest ambitions; my cannibalistic nature to self, family and clan. I skirt around the embarrassing strife in my life, the foul breath of unappeased pasts; my residual fear of fate. I happily answer questions and see faces opening up, thawing out, bright-eyed students imbibing, devouring, digesting my words. I hear cheers of recognition from the simple, modest men and women seated around me, dedicated young teachers – I feel a sea of applause. I realise that this perhaps is the only thing that will keep me alive and sane.

Write. Talk. Talk. Write.

But where are you, Tapera? Where are you when I exuberantly have tea with your fellow teachers in the staff room and exchange addresses and autographs that Friday morning? I ask, but no one knows. They are as mystified as I am.

***

You had gone to Gweru to die.

After the talk at your school, I went to your flat and your flatmate said he'd last seen you on Thursday morning. You hadn't gone to

200

work and he'd given you a lecture on 'responsible drinking'. But be-
ing the young man you were I thought you'd gone to see your pretty
girlfriend in Waterfalls– that is, until I received a phone call from
Rindai on Monday morning.

I had just returned from dropping off the children at school and
when I reached home the maid said, breathlessly, tactlessly, 'Have
you heard? Tapera has been found dead at the plot in Gweru!' I went
into the study, sat down and, as calmly as I could, picked up the
phone and said to Rindai, 'Is it true?' and he said yes, that you were
found lying dead, almost warm at six in the morning just outside
the kitchen at the plot. Being the practical person that he is Rindai
tasked me to go at once to your school to get your papers from your
headmistress before I drove to Gweru.

Imagine, my dear Tapera, me driving to your school again on
Monday morning, subdued after my portentous talk, finding the stu-
dents again at assembly, weeping and shaking my hand, and the
headmistress calmly completing your forms and your colleagues
sifting through your desk to give me your belongings.

I drove to Gweru – Vongai was away at a workshop – and when I
arrived, I found that Rindai, accompanied by the police, had taken
your body to Bulawayo for a post-mortem. Sekuru Mhasvi was in
charge at the plot, and he swore that when he arrived, summoned
by Mbuya Mai Svorai, who alone had tried to resuscitate you, your
body was still warm, as if you had just died. There was no wound,
no blood, no sign of struggle, although two lodgers reported having
heard the dogs bark just before sunrise.

***

Imagine, my dear brother, the consternation your death caused. The
post-mortem said you died of heart failure; they cut your chest and
belly open – you who'd been alive and walking barely four days before. Your colleagues arrived just as we were about to lower you into
your new home next to mother, father and Kelvin; your pretty little
girlfriend flung herself onto the mound – Sekuru Mhasvi snatched
her up and she clung to me and sobbed about how I looked so much
like you.

I interrogated the lodgers and quizzed Mbuya Mai Svorai about
how she had handled your body and demanded to know where

Sekuru Trueman was that weekend and why he did not come to the funeral – I even tried to engage an investigating company but there were no firm clues as to how you died. How could I believe the doctors when it might have been angry lodgers, jealous neighbours, avaricious relatives, unappeased spirits, restless ancestors, troublesome *tokoloshes* ...

So how did you die, my dear brother? Why did you not leave us any hints? Why did you die at the plot, outside the kitchen? Did the wretched spirit of Bramson beckon you to your death? Where was the moon huntress when this happened? Where were you at the weekend and who was with you? Why did you go to Gweru alone when we had agreed to travel together? Why was your body warm when it was discovered? Who chased you? What did you see? If you had had a heart problem, why did you never talk about it to anyone? Did you want to be some kind of martyr? Were our sisters right in believing that the plot was jinxed and should be sold off?

17

When we get back to the plot it's dark. I fall headlong into the
lap of Maiguru Mai Charity, my mother's elder sister, and
black out for two seconds. 'See, he's drunk already,' says Vongai.

'No,' says Maiguru Mai Charity, smiling and stroking my head.
'He's just happy to be home, in his mother's bosom.'

'He wants to suckle from his mother's breast,' says Sekuru Elias.
Everyone laughs. I make as if to stand up and Maiguru says, 'Here,
sit on the floor next to me.' We go through the formalities. Everybody
has arrived: Rindai, me, and our wives; Shuvai and Tendai and their
husbands; Vimbai, Sekuru Trueman and Mbuya Mai Svorai, and
all our children. After supper Sekuru Elias announces plans for the
next day.

The previous week Rindai and I had driven to Zambia to fetch
Maiguru and Sekuru Elias for the occasion. We had left them at the
plot to brew beer and make other preparations.

The following afternoon, Sekuru Elias, Maiguru, Rindai, Sekuru
Trueman and I drive to the cemetery. Maiguru scoops a plateful of
earth from the head of mother's grave and chants: 'You, Hilda Dolly
Tsvangira, daughter of Razaro and Maina, your brother Elias and I
have come to take your spirit back to your house, so that you can
be at peace, and look after your children, and their children. We are
taking you back from the forest where you have been roaming while
your children suffered. You will take your rightful place among the
ranks of your kith and kin and shield your children from evil winds.
Bear witness to this, you our great spirit Kodzai and our great aunt

Chipiwa and all our forebears reigning over the mists of time – we have cleansed our sister and retrieved her from the dead.'

Back at the plot a small crowd has already gathered outside, including Sekuru Mhasvi and our city relatives, mostly young people, and a couple of friendly lodgers. Sekuru Elias jubilantly sprays a rich shower of grave soil onto the floors of the rooms and the party begins. The blaring stereo is brought out onto the lawn, Mbuya Mai Svorai starts a tune on a drum and we all join in the refrain:

Mutendi wazorora, muka, mukaiwe
*Muka, muka iwe**

Maiguru Mai Charity plies us with her lethal seven-day brew and her unsalted goat meat. She collects all the bones and stacks them in a corner, to be secretly disposed of later. We dance on the lawn. Our children watch from the veranda, mesmerised, never having seen us so happy before. Used to our fierce Gwanangara altercations, they are perhaps relieved to see us doing something together without argument. Sekuru Trueman laughs his soldier's laugh, and performs his Chimurenga war twist for Muzukuru Innocent, Mbuya Mai Svorai leaps *Jerusarema* style in the firelight, Rindai and I trade giddy steps with out sisters' husbands and Sekuru Mhasvi totters around clinking mugs with the lodgers. Even Vongai and Maiguru Mai Nda start a Pentecostal hymn, clapping their hands together on the veranda. My head is tight with booze, and some swelling, thudding force wants to explode inside my skull. I look to the east, beyond the spot where Tapera was found dead. I see a glow on the horizon and I look for the moon. Finding none, I realise it's dawn! Maiguru Mai Charity holds up a fresh plate of goat meat, and urges, 'Eat, eat, children. You have to finish every morsel.'

Hilda Dolly, the moon huntress, is home.

***

'Mhokoshi, you give my children no rest.'
'I want my weapons back, Father.'
'Shhhhhh. Hush, hush, child. Speak not with a harsh voice. You disturb me where I sleep. You disturb your brothers, sisters, nephews and nieces. It's not I who sent you to the mountains to die like the

---

* You've rested for too long Christian./ Rise arise now.

very animals you hunted. It's not me who made you die unmarried,
without a rat to comfort you in your unmarked grave.'

'They threw away my weapons, Father.'

'Son, your wrath hurts the innocent – children with mucus on
their faces, babes with milk on their noses. You pinch my children
on their tender arms, cut them down mid-breath, hum your hymns
in their heads.'

'They never sought my bones, Father. They called me outcast,
lunatic, fool.'

'But must you then make of them outcasts, lunatics and fools?
Have you no pity? Are you the only porcupine who died alone and
neglected? See, see, the women were cleverly taken care of because
they were not of our kind – Njiki, Maribha and now this Hilda. The
men left it too late. Can't you see, we porcupine men were crossed
out ages ago? Who are you to seek to undo the unknown? Will you
be able to put out the flames if you start the fire? I say sleep, sleep
child and find respite.'

18

Now that we have brought mother back from the grave, what next? We listened to our city relatives who warned us that she could now become a curse – your mother when dead is not your relative but a stranger. Still we did it, we went ahead, we brought her home, but now what shall we do with the waiting hierarchy of departed family members? Will they, too, demand restoration? If it has to be done, who will guide us? Who will know what names to chant, what rituals to perform? The people from Chivi were not even present when we brought mother back. Hadn't father said, 'Leave the dead alone. The more you worry about them the more you get entangled with them.'

***

But Hilda, the moon huntress, must be happy. Didn't her own sister chant the words and scoop the soil from the head of her grave, and feed us her brew and her unsalted goat meat and chant, 'Eat, eat children.'

***

The stranger at the Oasis Hotel draws elaborate geometrical diagrams of the plot with its lawn, garage and fowl run. Then he points with his red pen, 'Here, it happened. Right here, outside the kitchen. That's where he was found.'

I say bluntly, 'How do you know all this? What else do you know? Why are you telling me? Who sent you to talk to me? Why should I trust you?'

Undeterred, the man refills his glass and jabs at his diagram. 'It's something in the house. Here. I can tell you what happened inside the house.'

I ease my stool away from him while peering down at the diagram. 'So what do you think we should do?'

'Come to my flat and we'll talk.'

'Do you want money?'

'I don't take money.'

'Are you a fortune teller?'

'Not really.'

'Do you belong to a church?'

'Not really.'

'How do I know you didn't read or hear about us?'

The man scribbles a name, address and phone number on a wet till-slip. 'Take this.'

I consider telling Rindai and the women about it. Vongai, of course, won't hear of it, wedded as she now is to her church. Rindai has not been well lately and such news might strain or over-excite him. I remember our trip to Gutu. Memories of the family half-naked, bathed by strangers in unknown streams and the aftermath.

The man polishes his glass, lights a cigarette and stands to go. 'You never know what might help you,' he says. 'See you.'

***

I'm driving past a restaurant at night when a woman hails me for a lift. I've heard about such ladies trapping you into the hands of car-jackers but I stop for her anyway.

'Howz?' she says, and I say, *'Mushe. Kanjani?'*

I drive five kilometres without saying a word, till she says, 'Why are you so quiet? For a man who has almost everything, I'd say you're too uptight.'

I glance sideways at her and then back to the road.

'You're a hunter,' she says. 'Just like one of your grandfathers. He hunted for meat but you hunt for money and what goes with it.'

'How do you know?'

'I just know. Didn't he die hunting in the mountains? Nobody found his weapons or his bones. He transferred his skills to you, don't you see?'

'You're bluffing.'

'I could tell you more, about what your family has been through. You've sought help from dozens of people in dozens of places.'

'Go on.'

'You're fighting with your wife. You're almost separated. She goes to a new Pentecostal church and detests these traditional rituals that involve you and all your family. She's turning your children against you. Didn't you have a fierce argument with one of your daughters recently, the one who dropped out of school with her mother's encouragement?'

I slow down and stop at the side of the road, the engine running.

'What else do you know?' I gasp.

'Think of the genes that run in your family; the similarities and differences over generations. The repetition of lives. Think.'

I think of hunters, artists and seers. Of flower-gatherers and plant-breeders. Of pontificators and peacemakers. Of believers and sceptics. Of the outspoken and the candid. Of saints and cuckolds. Of tears and laughter. Of madness unending.

Good God in the heavens, how clear the tapestry of our lives now seems! How related it all appears in its disparateness. How the repetitions, nuances and contrasts fall into place.

I drop the lady off at her cottage.

'I know an old woman who can help you,' she says and gives me an address.

***

Vimbai, Shuvai and Tendai have been talking earnestly about the need for us to seek out our blood relatives. We phone and visit Bhudhi Tarirai more frequently. We go to Vatete VaQueen's funeral. We attend Muzukuru Alex's graduation party. We present ourselves at the wedding of Sekuru Mhasvi's step-daughter. We reciprocate Sisi Elizabeth's visits. We come out of our lofty cocoon and discover the joy of involving ourselves in other people's lives. We attend the funeral of Fadzai Gwanangara, our blood cousin, in Chivi. While there, we bump into Sisi Ratidzo. She takes my hand, laughs, eats with me from the same plate, and introduces me to everybody explaining how we are related. She says, enigmatically, 'Bhudhi Godi, I'm done with *midzimu*. I now go to church. We should all go to church. Now that our fathers are dead there should be no Tachiona or Dunge. We are all Gwanangaras.'

I wish I could believe her.

On the way back we give Sisi Ratidzo a lift and stop by Maiguru Mai Dzenga to pay our respects to the graves of Bhudhi Dzenga and Cousin Jonah, both dead in the last two years. Maiguru Mai Ratidzo prepares us brown rice with chicken, smiles her reticent smile and invites us to come again with our children. 'I'm the only grand-mother they have now,' she adds with a note of regret. I know the next time I see her will probably be at her funeral.

Oh, the tragedy of relatives. Meeting only at weddings and funer-als; laughing, exchanging addresses and pretending that everything is all right.

Afterwards when we're alone Maiguru Mai Nda says, 'Tete Ratidzo and Maiguru Mai Dzenga are not as bad as they seem. In fact, none of the Chivi people seem half as bad as we were made to think they were. Perhaps we should make a fresh start.'

Do I believe this is possible?

* * *

We, Dunge's children, quarrel a lot about the plot. Eventually, when the disputes become too heavy, we kick out Mbuya Mai Svorai. Oh, the callousness of it all! First Mai Kurai, then Mhamha MaNyoni and now Mbuya Mai Svorai. In her place, we hire two young gar-deners. There's a lot to be done. Windows. Toilets. Ceilings. A new roof. A new coat of paint. An overhauled water pump. Sprinklers for the field. New water-storage tanks. The women think we're pouring money down the drain because we'll never keep pace with the re-quirements. They say father would turn in his grave to see the house in such a dilapidated state. They think we should sell the property at once and share the proceeds. Sell and run to avoid the shame. Rindai and I are solidly against the idea. To begin with, no buyer would look twice at the place now. We suspect our sisters are influenced by Bramson's ghost and apprehensive of whatever spirit it was that ate Tapera. Vimbai thinks we should demolish the house and build a new one. Rindai and I laugh off the idea, pointing out that we have mortgages and children's university fees, and in inflationary times too. If Tapera were alive, I'm sure he'd side with us and the vote would be even. As it is the women are in the majority, but we hold our own.

We think the plot could be revived. We could make enough to start a Gwanangara fund to provide family loans for emergencies or 'self-help' projects. What kind of Gwanangaras would we be without the plot to call our own? What would our parents say if we sold off the family land, the fruit of their life-time's endeavours? I think our sisters are flatly refusing to see beyond their noses. And, look, I'm not a chauvinist but I'm not sure what the inheritance laws have to say on the matter. However, in the absence of a will, and, as the eldest surviving sibling, Rindai would surely have the last word.

***

We quarrel a lot about the plot but we do not quarrel with each other. In fact, we're bonding as we never did as children. We talk about ourselves and each other. We admit that we were callous towards Kelvin's 'wife', Mai Kurai, and Mhamha MaNyoni and Mbuya Mai Svorai. We agree our parents were not always right in the way they raised us. We acknowledge that no parent gets it right all the time. We concede that we were snobbish towards our rural family.

But you should see us when we meet, and listen to our family lingo. We hug each other closely, laugh, reminisce. We invite each other and our children for lunch or dinner parties, and like the moon huntress we are quick to set up camp when there is a family problem, to bail each other out. You should get a taste of the resilience of the Gwanangaras. Nothing bonds surviving siblings more than the knowledge that at any moment one of them might be taken from this world. We continue with our jobs, our degrees, our projects; send our children overseas. We are determined that if any one of us should fall sick, we will be rational about it and seek help in the hospitals and from the medical profession. We are done with herbs.

***

Sekuru Elias visits regularly from Zambia. He thinks he might want to return and resettle with his family in Zimbabwe but we think that at sixty he is too old and matters are not settled here. We do our best to discourage him. Still, you should see him at Sanganai Inn in his cowboy hat and farmer shoes, dancing to Oliver Mutukudzi and chatting up the waitresses. Whenever he visits, he takes back suitcases full of second-hands for himself and our other uncles and our aunts. He complains that now that we've persuaded him and Maiguru Mai Charity to perform a ritual for our late mother, we don't write or visit them any more. He seems to think we don't need them. We promise to keep in touch.

Promises. Promises.

***

Last week I dreamt of myself, barefoot, trying to cross a shallow stream choking with greenish human filth. My friends said it meant success – money. What crap!

I don't dream much, but my most recurrent ones are of helicopters circling over our dew-in-the-morning village, long after the war. Green and brown, brown and green. Once I dreamt of father swimming strongly downstream in a clear blue river. His body looked young and athletic. I didn't see his face but I knew it was him. He walked out of the river, the water dripping from his shorts. I tried to follow him but he vanished into the shadows without turning or speaking to me. The following night I had a strange dream of the heads of de-horned cattle floating in a river. My friends said, 'Your ancestors are trying to tell you something.'

Oh, the confusion of unfinished business.

Once, only once, I dreamt of mother smiling, her face healed and beautiful. I spoke to her but she didn't answer. I never dream of Tapera or Kelvin or Bramson. I wonder where they are and what they are doing.

I don't believe much in dreams. To be honest, I don't know what I believe in any more. Science, bones or Bibles? All I know is my family should not have suffered so much; somebody should have stopped Bramson burning down my mother's house; and that arrogant young priest should have allowed my father's body to be viewed in the church which he built. How much must one suffer in order to believe? Like good old Job in the Bible? Someone should have respected my father.

***

I have just received a phone call from Maiguru Mai Nda in Kadoma.

It was about Rindai. He hasn't been too well lately. Her voice was shaky. After a lifetime of worry, one imagines oneself learning to take all kinds of news with stamina. I'll probably drive over tomorrow and see him. God, I'm tired. But I'll go. God, I'm tired.

I'll finish this story first; then I'll go.

19

*O*n *a plain, half-lit stage Godfrey Gwanangara, somewhat distraught and dishevelled, with greying hair, paces about, drinking from a bottle of beer, holding up his falling jeans and desperately looking for a belt. He clutches books under his arms; one or two of them tumble in a flurry like chickens onto the floor and when he stoops to pick them up the whole lot come crashing down. Enter, from the left side, Tradition, a bent, wizened old man dressed in goat-skins, cupping snuff in his left hand.*

TRADITION: Hello, *muzukuru.*

GODI: *(startled, hitching up his trousers)* Er, Er, hello.

TRADITION: Remember me?

GODI: *(gathering up his books and straining his eyes in the half-light)* Er, er, yes, I think so …

TRADITION: I'm your great-great-grandfather. Here, take this bark string to fasten up your trousers. Then kneel and take a pinch of my snuff and I'll teach you your totem and the ways of our people. *(He proffers him a length of woven bark cord and holds out his cupped hand. Godi sniffs unpleasantly at the air and hesitates, backing away from the old man.)*

GODI: Who are you?

TRADITION: Your blood, your genes, your history. Your very soul, your benefactor and protector.

GODI: *(begrudgingly)* But you are long dead and you are only human. You are not God.

TRADITION: I'm your link to *Mwari*, to God.

GODI: If you care so much, why did you let my family suffer as they did?

Tradition coughs painfully and wipes his misty eyes. He once more proffers the cord and the snuff but Godi again looks away. Hurt, Tradition drops the cord at his feet, takes a pinch of snuff, and brushes his hands clean. Godi walks away. Tradition totters after him.

TRADITION: *(mournfully)* Don't worry. You'll soon know me. You've always known me. You'll always know me. I don't change. Things never change. It's never easy, even for *Mwari*. You can't run away from your past. *(exits)*

Enter Patriarchy with a well-to-do belly and shiny cheeks. He is wearing a grey robe and riding on the backs of two sweating women and whipping their sides with a stick.

PATRIARCHY: (to Godi) See, son. Men always know best. They run the world.

GODI: How do you know?

PATRIARCHY: Don't question your elders, son. Weren't your father, uncles and brothers always right?

GODI: How do you know? How do you know my grandmother Njiki was not right, or my mother Hilda? Didn't Vongai breathe sense into our household? Didn't she always tell Rindai, 'Take your pills, for God's sake!' And all those matriarchs of history – Nehanda, Nefertiti, Nzinga, Ghandi …? What have you got to say about them?

PATRIARCHY: Fool, fool child to submit to the whims of women. Where has that got you? Haven't your sisters urged you to sell your father's home?

GODI: *(chasing the Patriarch off the women's backs and off the stage)* Leave my sisters out of this! Maybe they were right, after all. I don't want anything to do with you. You're an old reactionary.

Enter Fatalism, a fat old woman in a black cloak and veil.

GODI: And who might you be, Ma'am?

FATALISM: My name is Fatalism.

GODI: What do you want with me?

FATALISM: To tell you that you cannot change your future, no matter how hard you try.

GODI: So what use are you to me, if you can't help me change things?

FATALISM: To tell you that whatever has happened in your family was determined long before you were born. That all the births, deaths and tragedies were predestined before time began.

GODI: *(hitching up his jeans)* So was losing my belt today pre-determined?

FATALISM: Fool child, mocking the truth and the wisdom of the ancestors!

GODI: Mock or not, what difference would it make? Are you God?

FATALISM: Not really. But I can tell you about yourself.

GODI: Get behind me, *Mhamha*. I've been told before. I don't care. Who says I'd want to know, anyway? What difference would it make? Look. My siblings and I invested power in events, in you and your sister Fate. We were intimidated by our mother's fears and emotions, became willing victims to a terrible self-fulfilling prophecy. Now it's too late. We can only pick up the pieces and brave on.

FATALISM: Then I shall leave you to wallow in your blissful ignorance.

Exit Fatalism. Enter Shame, hermaphrodite, neither man nor woman, wrapped up in a thin brown cloak, head bowed in deep embarrassment.

SHAME: *(almost inaudibly)* If I were you, I'd fix the plot and rescue your siblings from humiliation. Think of your glorious childhood, the esteem in which people held you in that small town. Now this. Your family is in tatters. I would not set foot in that town until I'd fixed things up. What is the public saying? What do you think of yourselves? Aren't you ashamed?

GODI: Oh, not another one! Do you think I live for the public, for our image? I used to, but no longer. Let me tell you something. If my siblings and I had not suffered from so much shame, hypocrisy and superstition, we could have wrested back control of events. Out with you, Shame!

SHAME: *(leaving the stage)* Very well then.

Enter Modernity, a stunning woman in her mid-thirties with natural dreadlocks, large ear-rings, blue jeans and a fashionably oversized T-shirt.

MODERNITY: Hi! I'm Daphne. I hear you lost your belt? Shame. Here, you can borrow mine. Your waist can't be much bigger than mine. Unisex, you know. Want a cigarette? So what are you up to? Are you going to buy me a drink? I've just moved to this suburb, renting a cottage. Just divorced, you know. I have two kids in primary school, aged eight and six. Been alone four years now. Long time, hey? But I learnt to survive, to be on my own. Oh no, my husband is not dead. Not AIDS, no. Not an accident, either. Not one of those catastrophes casting foul breath on the roads, haunting the nation. Look, if you drive drunk or take a faulty vehicle out on the highway, you're bound to have an accident. Plain and simple. No jinx, no nothing. My ex-husband and I were happy together. I worked as a tax consultant and he as a marketing executive. We had a large house; I had my car and he had his. We were equals – he paid the mortgage and I bought the groceries. When we were overseas he even washed dishes, baby-sat and changed nappies. Imagine! His pub mates talked him out of it when we returned home. He never bothered about my bank account. We loved and respected each other. I went to a Christian fellowship church and he went to the pub. We allowed each other space. Space – that's the secret, you know. Our people don't give each other space. Most of them have never heard of the word. Then when his father died he started going to Murewa every weekend to see his mother. For some time that was OK with me. I never liked her much and she couldn't stand me. Who says we should love our mothers-in-law? She thought I was too much of my own person, too educated, and may be she was right. She was the proud, traditional type that clings onto their sons even when they're married. When the old man died she refused to have his clothes shared out among his folks. People said she had creatures in her home – wild cats, goblins and crocodile teeth – and dust falling off the old man's suits. Poor woman! You know how a village can destroy you simply by labelling you a witch. Not that I ever believed in that shit – goblins, brewing beer and consulting n'angas and so forth. But there is no smoke without fire. When I discovered my husband was taking another woman to see his mother, I was devastated. She was older than me, had three kids of her own and was pregnant by him. She pretended to like the countryside so as to be in good books with his mother. She and my mother-in-law plotted my downfall. Slowly, he began to starve me and the children. My dream died. I confronted him and he admitted his crimes. His aim was to have two wives, me and the other woman. The polygamous instinct dies hard. Even in Europe and America. I wouldn't hear of it. Me, Modernity! I moved out and filed for divorce. We sold the house last month and shared the proceeds. And here I am. I'm not dead, am I? No, I'm better off without him. Life goes on. Who knows what tomorrow will bring?

Godi: Talk about Modernity! My dear lady, there is no formula for relationships or for life. Or even for beliefs. There is nothing called a modern relationship, or a traditional one for that matter. My grandfather, my great-great-great-grandfather, we share the same genes. It took me a lifetime to realise that human nature hardly changes, only its material form does. There'll always be love, greed, jealousy, hatred, friendship and misery. And this applies to everyone – black, white, yellow, brown. Perhaps our grandparents were better off. Everyone knew his or her place in society. Nobody ever said, 'I don't know what to do with myself.' They had systems and stuck to them, while we flounder with our misconceptions of the past, present and future. They had goblins and crocodile teeth stocked in their granaries with which to assault their spouses, we have guns, and legal papers in our safes; durawalls, razor-wire, electric fences and Rottweilers to shield us from our neighbours. Who is better? Superstition has merely changed its format, its imagery. Even the priests spreading incense are superstitious. What better way to enact the partaking of human flesh and blood than the Eucharist? Now we believe in gadgets, in feeding our blood pressures, diabetes and cancers with refined foods and other poisons, while having alternative lives acted out for us on television. The movie is one big superstition, don't you think? Our relationships, our marriages, are a mess. One person out of two is divorced or separated. But then, who says marriage is the ideal? Who says we need relationships any more? Sorry, Madam, I talk too much. I'm just caught in this middle-class trap. I suppose all blacks who grow up poor, then find themselves with money can't resolve that problem, the false assumptions that wealth equals progress, equals respect. Ha! It's right back to square one.

MODERNITY: *Mhaiwe!* How you can talk. Where do you find all these ideas? If you were a teacher your students would chase you out of the classroom with broomsticks, for sure. But I like you. You're not like those well-shaved men who talk about cars, football, their perks and their salaries all night. I have to go now. If you give me your cell number, maybe I'll buy you a drink and we can talk some more. Bye now. See you later. Have a nice day!

Exit Modernity.

Enter Education, a young lady professor in an academic gown, holding a huge encyclopedia.

EDUCATION: Don't ask me who I am. You know me. You've known me for over twenty years. I'm Education. Think of how I've nurtured you. Think of what I've done to bring health, knowledge, understanding and progress to your people, to Africa. Look at those books you are carrying. They've made you who you are. But why did you, Godfrey Gwanangara, and the rest of your very well-educated family, need to subject yourselves to so much superstition?

GODI: *(adjusting his new belt and peering ruefully into his now empty beer bottle)* Excuse me Prof, but what is superstition?

Education: According to my dictionary, it is the belief that particular events happen in a way that cannot be explained by reason or science.

GODI: Fine, but don't give me dictionary explanations. They cannot always explain things accurately – in fact they offer a very limited view of reality. Think of the strange things that have happened in your own family – accidents, illnesses, deaths, coincidences, bizarre events devoid of explanation. Come on, every black family has them, even whites, Chinese and Indians too! Can you account for them? From time immemorial, your very science has been subverted to inflict pain and misery on the weak and the powerless. Reason and science only describe a figment of reality. Facts, equations and formulae are boring. They belittle the power of the human spirit, the potential of the human mind. Imagine, for instance, the probability of other life forms in the universe, of time travellers and time warps. Are these not possible in an African context? Can my great-great-grandfather not communicate with me from a hundred and fifty years ago? Or at least reincarnate himself in me? Do you not believe in life after death?

EDUCATION: It's the essence of most religions.

GODI: Let's not talk about religions. That's too contentious. We'll step on the delicate toes of some people. Let's talk about the average human spirit. Where do you think it goes after death?

EDUCATION: It dissolves with the flesh, I suppose.

GODI: What nonsense! What school did you go to, I wonder, Madam Prof? Did they feed you porridge and beans every day? How then would you explain ghosts, visitations and spirits, whether avenging or benevolent? How would you begin to explain the common concept of heaven and hell?

EDUCATION: Beware of blasphemy, Mr Gwanangara!

GODI: Come on, Prof. Heaven and hell may be a state of mind but they can manifest themselves in other ways.

Education: Can you explain what you mean?

GODI: Let me put it this way. I come from a long tradition. Some of my forbears were benevolent, others malicious. Some were pleasantly ordinary, others were jealous and vengeful, like all humans. Like gods even. Some retired with their deeds to the grave; the more fickle and determined returned to haunt us, their third and fourth generations. Just as in the Old Testament. I'm educated like you. I'm not very keen on hunting for these spirits. To be honest I would banish them from my life and live clean if I could. But I am their product – a highly complex one at that – and I can't just ignore their existence.

EDUCATION: Explain, Mr Gwanangara, explain!

Enter Medicine, a young male doctor with a neat tie, a white overcoat and a stethoscope.

MEDICINE: You don't listen. I told your brother Rindai to take his pills and stop drinking. Had he done so, we could easily have controlled his epilepsy. As for your younger brother, the one with schizophrenia – you worsened his condition by taking him to all those wretched *n'angas*. You got him worked up, thinking he was a spirit medium. As for your mother, if you had brought her to us early enough we could have operated and removed the cancer cells. What you seem to forget is that we all have choices. To assume that life is controlled by fate, by the ancestors, or by God is a choice that we make. And every choice will have its consequences.

GODI: *(half cynically)* OK. OK. But what about my young brother Tapera?

MEDICINE: He had a heart problem, didn't he?

GODI: But why should he have to die in Gweru, suddenly, at the plot? Why should every one have to die at the plot? Another weird coincidence, I suppose.

MEDICINE: Look, heart attacks are often due to stress. Was he not stressed after your mother's funeral? You can believe what you like, but there is always a rational cause if you stop to think about it. We treat each problem as a straightforward medical case. Look at what stress did to you. Look how quickly you recovered with rest and medication.

GODI: You doctors think you know everything.

MEDICINE: *(taken aback)* What do you mean?

GODI: There are some cases which medicine can't cure.

MEDICINE: Aren't you being superstitious, Mr Gwanangara?

GODI: No, I'm just being honest.

MEDICINE AND EDUCATION: *(together, Education thumping a fist on her encyclopedia)* Explain, Mr Gwanangara! Explain!

S HIMMER CHINODYA was born in Gweru, Zimbabwe in 1957, the second child in a large, happy family. He attended Mambo Primary, Goromonzi High and St Augustine Mission schools and was fortunate to enjoy both a rural and an urban childhood. He studied for an English Honours Degree and Graduate Certificate in Education at the University of Zimbabwe, and after a spell teaching and working in curriculum development, he attended the Iowa's Writer's Workshop (USA) where he earned an MFA in Creative Writing.

His first novel, the idyllic *Dew in the Morning,* a vivid evocation of his childhood in Gokwe, was written when he was eighteen and published later in 1982. This was followed by *Farai's Girls* (1984), *Child of War* (under the pen name Ben Chirasha, 1986), *Harvest of Thorns* (1989), *Can we talk and other stories* (1998), *Tale of Tamari* (2004), *Chairman of Fools* (2005), *Strife* (2006), *Tindo's Quest* (2011) and *Chioniso and other Stories* (2012). His work has appeared in many journals and anthologies, including *Staffrider* (1990), *A Voyage Around (1990), Nimrod* (1996), *Malahat Review* (1997), *Migrating Words and Worlds* (1999), *Images of the*

West (2000), *Tenderfoots* (2001), *Writing Still* (2004), *Writing Now* (2005), *Laughing Now* (2007), *The Warwick Review* (December 2009), *Cheese Cutters and Gymslips* (2009), *Africa Ablaze I (2013)* and *Heart of Africa! (2014)*. He has also written children's books, educational texts, training manuals and radio and film productions, including the script for the award-winning feature film, *Everyone's Child* (1996). He has won many awards for his work, including the ZBPA and NAMA awards, the Commonwealth Writer's Prize (Africa Region, 1990) for *Harvest of Thorns,* a Caine Prize shortlist for *Can we Talk* and the prestigious NOMA Award for Publishing in Africa for *Strife* (2007). He has travelled worldwide reading from and discussing his works and taking part in writing workshops and seminars. Among his several fellowships abroad was the chair of Distinguished Dana Professor of Creative Writing and African Literature, which he held at St Lawrence University in upstate New York from 1995 to 1997. His translated works include *Harvest of Thorns* and *Strife*, which have been published in German. *Dew in the Morning* and *Harvest of Thorns* have been serialized on radio and he directed and produced a play, with music, dance and readings, of *Harvest* at HIFA, Harare in 2013.

Glossary

aiwa – no

ambuya – grandmother/mother-in law/brother-in-law's wife. Also common term of respect for a mature woman.

umzukulu – grandson/granddaughter

babamunini – husband's young brother

bira – traditional beer party held to honour ancestors

burakwacha – literally: black watcher i.e. black policeman/guard

chakata – sweet soft fruit with pips

chibhoyi – Africanness/blackness

chiiko? – what is it?

chipako – a small carved container for storing snuff/tobacco

chitirobho – a leather rope for harnessing oxen

dare – place where elders meet to talk

dhandahead – dunce, dunderhead

derere – okra

dhandahead(s) – slang term for 'slow learner' at school

doro rechikaranga – beer for the ancestors

futi, futi – and, and

gogo – affectionate term for 'grandmother'

he, hede! – an expression used when laughing or expressing incredulity

hes blaz – hi brother

humwes – communal work parties accompanied by drinks/food/alcohol

ingozi – avenging spirits

iwe – you

jharadha – long partitioned block for housing lodgers/workers

Krismas – Christmas or short-hand for a gift or an annual bonus

kukara – greed, usually for food

kwakanaka here? – is everything all right?

madora – mopani worms (edible)

madzimai esungano – women who worship in special churchgroups *maininis* – mother's young sisters or mother's brothers' daughters

maita – thank you

majoni – policemen, as they were known in the 50s, 60s and 70s

makadii – how are you?

mamhepo – bad spirits

mapadza– hoes

mariposa – plastic shoes worn long ago; old fashioned attire

maroro – sweet soft edible fruit which turns yellow when ripe

mashuku –- loquat fruit

mashura – strange happening, usually foretelling disaster

mazhanje (umhobohobo) – another name for loquat fruit

mbanje – marijuana

mbaura – metal bucket with holes, used for fires in winter

mbuya – grandmother/mother's brother's wife

mbwire-mbwire – traditional powder made from ground roasted maize grains mixed with salt

menija – manager

Mhai! Mhai! Mhaiwe! – Mother! Mother! Oh mother!

Mhai ndofa! – Mother, I'm dead.

mhamha – mother

mhamha nababa – mother and father

mhiripiri – red/green spice/powder

midzimu – ancestral spirits

misi – a young woman who works in the Reformed Church

mhondoro dzinomwa – great spirits drink

mroora – daughter-in-law

muchakata (umkhuna) – tree bearing chakata fruit (see chakata)

mudhara – old man

muhacha – the other name for muchakata

mukoma – brother

mukwasha – son in law married to speaker's daughter/sister

muneri – priest

munyai – the 'go-between' in marriage consultations

mupfuti (itshabela) – a tree whose wood is good for firewood

mupositori/mupositori – member(s) of the Apostolic church

muramu – wife's sister to a man or husband's brother to a woman

mushe kanjani? – fine thanks and how are you?

mutomba (ihabahaba) – tree bearing *mutomba* fruits
mutakura wenyemba – maize grains baked with wild beans
mutakura wenzungu – maize grains baked with groundnuts
muunga – thorn tree
muzukuru – grandson/granddaughter/nephew/niece
mwana – child
mwana wamai vangu – my mother's child
mwanangu – my child
Mwari – God
n'anga – traditional healer/herbalist
Ngara – name of a Shona totemic group
ngororombe – type of Karanga dance
nhedzi – a wild mushroom
nhodo – game played by children
ngozi – avenging spirit
nyimo – round nuts
nyora – incisions made on skin for healing or for decorations
nyovhi – type of wild vegetable
ona – see
rupiza – porridge made out of a type of peas
sekuru – uncle, term of respect for older man
shangara – a type of Shona dance
shuku – loquat fruit (single)
tada tovi – sadza with peanut-butter relish
tokoloshe – a sprite or a mischievous goblin. *Tokoloshes* are called
    upon by malevolent people to cause trouble for others.
tsvimbo – knobkerries or walking sticks
vanabhudhi – brothers
vanamuneri – white priests
vanasekuru – uncles/grandfathers
varoora – daughters-in-law
zambia – printed cloth, popular in Zambia, worn by women in Africa
zvauriwe – and because its you
zvipiko imi! – what!

Revision Questions

Chapter 1

1. Comment on the opening of the novel.
2. Discuss the presentation of the moon huntress in this chapter.
3. Explore the husband-wife relationship delineated in the chapter.
4. Examine Chinodya's use of symbolism and imagery to present the theme of the novel.

Chapter 2

1. Discuss the presence of disease in this chapter.
2. Compare and contrast the relationship between Rindai and his mother and that between he and his father.
3. Examine the neighbours' attitude towards Rindai's purchase of a car.

Chapter 3

1. Is there any significance in the appearance of the totemic animal, the porcupine, at the centre of Kapadza's yard?
2. Explore the place of alcohol in the scheme of Rindai's life.
3. Discuss the meeting between Godfrey and Mai Fanwell. How does this meeting define Godfrey's understanding of life?
4. 'Oh, the follies of superstition!' Comment on this statement.
5. Discuss the development of the relationship between Gwanangara and Njiki.

Chapter 4

1. Comment on Chinodya's use of authorial voice.
2. Kelvin believes that 'education is not everything.' Do you agree with this standpoint according to what you have read so far in the novel?
3. 'Dutch-reformed, English wasted, Indian starched father!' Is this a fair description of Dunge Gwanangara or does it suggest a

latent hostility?

4. Discuss the mood of this chapter.

5. It is often said that *every son falls in love with his mother and is jealous of his father*. Do you think this might be a valid argument, which could help us to understand Godfrey's relationship with his parents?

Chapter 5

1. Describe your reaction to Kelvin's actions in the chapter.

2. How would you rate the *bira* as an attempt to cure the ills plaguing the family? Give reasons to validate your answer whether positive or negative.

3. Compare and contrast the two brothers, Dunge and Tachiona Gwanangara in this chapter.

4. What roles are ascribed to the women in this chapter and how do these roles impact on the movement of the plot?

Chapter 6

1. Discuss the attitudes shown towards Dunge's dreams by a) his mother and b) the menfolk at the *dare*. What do the reactions reveal about the characters?

2. Rindai's suicide attempt hits Dunge very badly. React to the presentation of Dunge by Rindai's bed in the hospital scene in this chapter. What do we learn about him that we might not have known before?

3. Analyse Njiki's character as presented in this part of the story.

Chapter 7

1. 'Your true relative is the neighbour who lends you a hand when your beard catches fire'. Comment on his statement by *muzukuru* Baba Tariro.

2. 'Prescriptions need to be managed with care. Medicine is not like sugar to take just when you feel like it.' Discuss the significance of this statement in the story.

3. Explain the significance of, and comment on, Mbuya Matongo's cleansing ceremony in this chapter.

4. In your opinion, why do the Gwanangaras not go to their uncle Tachiona's funeral? Was it a rational decision, or were they led by their emotions or their memories? Explain your answer.

Chapter 8

1. Explain Godfrey Gwanangara's guilt over their failure to attend *babamukuru's* funeral.
2. Discuss the symbolism of the slaughter of Blantyre.
3. Comment on the following statement: *'Midzimu yepi yaDunge? Midzimu yepi yechiKristu?'*
4. Explore the interplay between Christianity and African traditional beliefs.
5. Discuss the significance of Kelvin's discarding of Zevezeve's traditional paraphernalia, *chipako*, his walking staff and white cloth in this chapter.

Chapter 9

1. Analyse the validity of Godfrey's statement that 'I can see and with sharp regret, that this (psychiatric unit) is where we should have brought him (Kelvin) in the first place and not dabbled with *n'angas*.' Does the verb 'dabble' really indicate what the family were doing, or does it say more about Godfrey's current thinking? Explain your answer.
2. In your opinion, where does Dunge Gwanangara disappear to in the chapter? Give reasons for your answer.

Chapter 10

1. 'Oh, how strife can destroy rationality.' Comment on this statement.
2. In what ways may Dunge Gwanangara be regarded as the author of the problems that visit his family? Might the same be said of the mother?
3. *'Hamubatsire imi!'* How relevant is this as a description of Dunge Gwanangara?
4. Is there any justification for Kelvin and Rindai's falling out with their father?

5. Do you think the author presents a story that is biased in favour of his mother? Give reasons for your answer.

Chapter 11

1. 'Mbuya Matope, if the illness should leave my son but has to inhabit another person, then let that be me, not any of my children.' Comment on this statement explaining how it illuminates the character of Hilda Tsvangira.
2. Explore Chinodya's use of language and imagery in this chapter.

Chapter 12

3. Explain Godfrey's anger on page 152.
4. Discuss Tachiona's letter to Dunge. In what ways does it illuminate the relationship between the two brothers?
5. In your opinion, why does Bramson commit suicide in the Dunge household?

Chapter 14

1. What does Kelvin's letter to Sekuru Mhasvi reveal about his character and state of mind?
2. There are a number of letters written by different characters in this novel. Analyse them and explore how they contribute to theme and plot development.

Chapter 15

1. 'We cocooned ourselves from our relatives.' In your opinion, how suitable is this as a solution to the Gwanangara problem?

Chapter 16

1. In what ways can the novel, *Strife*, be described in Godfrey's words as a 'dreary poem about an enraged God snuffing out a sinful world?' How realistic is this statement? Why do you think Godrey used this adjective? What adjective might you use?
2. What is the significance of Godfrey's characterising his nature as cannibalistic to self, family and clan? Do you think he is a very reasonable or very emotional person, or both? Give examples to

explain your answer.

3. Are there any explanations for Godfrey's guilty conscience concerning the death of Tapera in this chapter?

4. Critics of the novel point to its melodramatic tendencies. Do you think they have a point? Why?

Chapter 18

1. 'I think of hunters, artists and seers. Of flower-gatherers and plant breeders. Of pontificators and peacemakers. Of believers and sceptics. Of the outspoken and the candid. Of saints and cuckolds. Of tears and laughter. Of madness unending.' Explore the quoted statement showing the ways by which it summarises the novel, *Strife*.

2. Comment on the significance of the following statement by Ratidzo: 'Bhudhi Godi I'm done with *midzimu*. I now go to church.'

Chapter 19

1. Summarise each of the arguments presented by TRADITION, PATRIARCHY. FATALISM, SHAME, MODERNITY and MEDICINE. If you had to choose only one of these systems of knowledge or belief, which would you choose and why?

2. Fiction is an important way of exploring different realities, different truths and the nature of memory. Reading a book changes our perceptions of the world. How has reading *Strife* altered your perception of the world, if at all?